"I NEED YOUR HELP WITH SOMETHING THAT'S NOT PRECISELY LEGAL."

For too long after she spoke, Callum simply looked at her. At the shape of her mouth, the color of her eyes. He never forgot a face, and he remembered her eyes as brown. But today they had a mind to be hazel.

She lifted her brows, waiting for his reply. But there was only one sort he could give, no matter how beautiful she looked when she smiled.

"I am sorry to decline, my lady. My position as an Officer of the Police makes it impossible for me to take part in anything, as you put it, *not precisely legal.*"

"Yes, I understand that. But this is one of those rare instances when legality and rightness aren't the same at all."

Rare indeed. Though not nonexistent. As soon as he finished this interview, he'd be off to Newgate because of another such case.

That decided it. "All right. Tell me everything."

Other titles by Theresa Romain

LADY ROGUE

THERESA ROMAIN

ZEBRA BOOKS
KENSINGTON PUBLISHING CORP.

http://www.kensingtonbooks.com

ZEBRA BOOKS are published by

Kensington Publishing Corp.
119 West 40th Street
New York, NY 10018

All Kensington titles, imprints, and distributed lines are available at special quantity discounts for bulk purchases for sales promotion, premiums, fund-raising, educational, or institutional use.

Special book excerpts or customized printings can also be created to fit specific needs. For details, write or phone the office of the Kensington Sales Manager: Attn.: Sales Department. Kensington Publishing Corp., 119 West 40th Street, New York, NY 10018. Phone: 1-800-221-2647.

Zebra and the Z logo Reg. U.S. Pat. & TM Off.

First Printing: May 2018
ISBN-13: 978-1-4201-4543-4
ISBN-10: 1-4201-4543-6

eISBN-13: 978-1-4201-4544-1
eISBN-10: 1-4201-4544-4

10 9 8 7 6 5 4 3 2 1

Printed in the United States of America

Chapter One

May 1818
London

Perhaps Isabel shouldn't have asked the butler to show Officer Jenks into the drawing room. That was, after all, the room in which the Bow Street Runner had first met Isabel eighteen months before, as her husband's gun-shot corpse lay upstairs.

The association was not ideal.

But where else could they meet? The morning room was dreary in late afternoon, and Isabel had never liked the oil painting of Bacchus and his maenads that hung on the wall. So smug, those naked nymphs, with wine pouring over them dark as blood. In all Isabel's months of widow-hood, why had she never taken the irritating thing down?

Because this still felt like Andrew's house, and because the painting was one of his precious acquisitions; that was why. The late Andrew Morrow, art dealer and *bon vivant*, had possessed particular ideas about which paintings ought to be displayed, and where, and how.

The more Isabel had learned about those paintings since his death, the less she'd wanted anything to do with them.

Thus her summons of Officer Jenks.

The last of the Tuesday morning callers, who really trailed in throughout the afternoon, had departed a short while before. They'd left behind whispers of floral perfume, faint indentations on the seats of the upholstered fauteuils, and here and there a crumb on the carpet.

Isabel had not lost the habit of seeing a room through Andrew's critical eye; she wondered if she ever would. With a quick glance at the drawing-room door—still closed—she darted from her seat and picked up all the crumbs on the carpet. There, now it was a plush, perfect expanse of woven flowers again. Crossing to the window, she undid the latch and tossed the crumbs out. Let the remains of Lady Teasdale's cakes nourish a few blackbirds.

For a moment, she allowed the late spring breeze to tickle her cheeks, then regretfully latched the window again. She had just returned to her chair when Selby tapped at the door to the drawing room, then opened it to announce the arrival of the officer. As soon as Jenks entered the room, the butler departed, leaving Isabel alone with her visitor.

"Officer Jenks." Isabel rose to her feet.

"Lady Isabel Morrow." The Runner bowed.

They faced each other in silence, as though they'd never met before. As though Officer Callum Jenks hadn't investigated a death in this home, and as though he and Isabel hadn't later had an affair. Or ought one to call a single encounter an affair? Perhaps not. Especially if it happened at Vauxhall Gardens, where such wild intimacies were commonplace.

They were not so for Isabel—not before that time, and never since. But she'd had an excellent reason for wishing to escape on that day.

She tugged her thoughts back to the present. "I hope you did not have to wait long before Selby came to fetch you."

"You know I did not. I'm seven minutes after the requested time."

He was so disconcerting, all bluntness when a polite demurral would be more the thing. "That is true," Isabel replied. "Perhaps you ought to apologize to me."

"Would you enjoy that?" His dark eyes held humor that never quite traveled to his lips for a smile.

"Ladies always enjoy a bit of prostration. Would it make you feel worse to apologize? If not, you might as well."

He swept her a ridiculously deep bow. "My apologies, Lady Isabel. I was detained at a mock auction."

"A mock—what?"

"A common enough cheat, though they're usually held in the evening. Daylight's no friend to the cheap items put up for sale, bid up by shills at the expense of honest buyers."

"And what did you have to do?"

"Stuff the auctioneers into hackney coaches and send them before the magistrate." He spoke the words as blandly as another man might observe that water was, of course, wet.

"In that case, I must wonder at your arrival only seven minutes late. But please, never mind the time, Officer Jenks." She sank back into her seat. "Shall I ring for tea?"

Did one give tea to an officer of the law? Etiquette training never included such situations. Probably the proper etiquette was not to be involved with an officer of the law at all.

"Lady Isabel." He drew a chair from the opposite end of the room to sit directly facing her. "I'd like to know why you summoned me."

He looked large and rough in the delicate antique chair, with its white-painted wood and decorative carving. Like Isabel, he was neither tall nor short. But where Isabel dressed carefully in the latest fashions, Callum Jenks was everything frank and stark.

Today he wore a plain dark coat and waistcoat; buff breeches and boots nearly black; a cravat simply tied. A gentleman, or a tradesman? One could not tell. Beside him, Isabel felt thoroughly impractical. She wore a demure half-mourning gown of gray muslin spotted in black, with long sleeves and a small ruffle about the wrists. Her dark brown hair was dressed in a style straight from a lady's magazine. The overall effect was elegant and decorative, although not comfortable in the least.

She fought the urge to squirm on her seat. The fact was, the reason she had summoned him was far more uncomfortable even than her gown. She would have to introduce the subject carefully.

"I asked you here," she said, "because it is more private than calling on you at the Bow Street court. You see, I want to hire you for a case in a personal capacity."

He regarded her for a long moment. Then his gaze wandered upward, as if piercing through the ceiling to the chamber in which he'd begun his previous investigation.

"This particular case does not involve death in any way," Isabel added.

"That is generally to be preferred." When he looked at her again, she could not help but smile. Jenks had a way of holding his mouth when he finished speaking—as if he had more to say, but had halted himself on the brink of an injudicious statement. Once, only once, Isabel had got him to admit exactly what was on his mind.

"I had better show you the letters first," she decided, standing. Jenks rose to his feet at once, mannerly as any marquess.

There were not many places to hide something in the spring-sunny drawing room, which boasted high ceilings, tall windows, and a scatter of Andrew's beloved elegant furniture over a large antique carpet. A chair here, a small table there for games; a harp no one ever played and a pianoforte Isabel sometimes did.

To the pianoforte she crossed. From atop its lid, she removed a branched candelabra, a few artfully arranged novels, and a tidy pile of sheet music. Pushing the instrument's lid up, she retrieved a packet that had been gummed to the underside of the lid.

"Allow me, Lady Isabel." Silently, Jenks had come to stand beside her. He lifted the heavy lid from her hand, then lowered it carefully into place again. With great precision, he replaced the items atop it.

"You are observant," Isabel said. "If those are an inch from their original positions, I will eat every one of those tapers in the candelabra."

With a forefinger, he shoved the stack of novels over six inches, then darted his eyes sideways at Isabel.

"Obvious flummery," she said. "No candle-eating."

"Pity. I'd have liked to see such a trick." Facing her, he did that not-a-smile thing again with his lips. "Am I to see those papers?"

"Please. Yes." She handed them over, then stood beside him as he scrutinized the packet on all sides before working a fingertip under the wax seal. He smelled of starch and coal smoke, the scents of clean clothing and the London air.

She watched as he reviewed the papers in the packet. They were few and not long, yet he looked over them for minutes that seemed endless.

"What do you think of the letters?" she pressed. "I was tearing my hair out before I'd spent half as much time reading them."

He turned over a page, then held it up to the windowlight and squinted at the paper. "You have hair enough left to pass in society. I wouldn't worry."

"But about the letters?"

"Those, you can worry about if you wish to." He returned the letter to the small stack, then shuffled through them. "So. Your husband, and then you, were repeatedly contacted by a man named Butler who required payment for services rendered."

"It was unexpected. I thought it was blackmail at first. Though for what"—her voice caught—"I couldn't say." *How could Butler have known? How could anyone know what a couple did—or didn't do—behind the door of a bed-chamber?*

"Couldn't you?" His tone was flat.

"No. I couldn't say," she replied firmly, "and rightly so, because it was not blackmail at all. I believe the letters are exactly what they seem. This man worked for my husband, and with Morrow's sudden death, he wasn't paid for all his work."

"Why not simply pay him, then?"

"I did." As if Lady Isabel Morrow would ever fail to do what was expected. "The payment wasn't the problem. It was the work that concerned me."

"I gather from the letters' vague wording that the employment was of dubious legality."

"It was, and it wasn't. That is, there wasn't anything wrong with the work itself, but with what Morrow did with it."

Jenks stared at her, waiting out her silence. Though he was so inscrutable, she had the feeling he was displeased with her answer. His jawline was hard and stubborn; his hair and eyes battled to be the darker brown.

"If you wouldn't glare at me," Isabel said, "I could explain better."

One of his brows arched. "This is the only face I have. I apologize if you don't like it."

"I didn't say that." Lovely. Her cheeks were warm. "Look, let us sit down." As they resumed their seats, she went on. "You know that Andrew—Mr. Morrow—dealt in art. Collecting it on the Continent, selling it at high prices to aristocrats and the newly wealthy."

"Yes. I recall from my previous investigation."

The one involving Andrew's death, he meant. She took a

deep breath, her stays tight about her ribs. "The problem is that Morrow didn't always give his clients the art they paid for. He gave them nearly identical art created by Butler."

Jenks understood at once. "So they were in the business of forgeries."

"Yes." Strange that Andrew's trespasses felt like Isabel's own, even a year and a half after he'd left her a widow. "I did not know it at the time. Remarkably naïve of me, I suppose."

"Not necessarily. Fraud isn't the sort of thing a man brags about to his wife."

Sometimes Jenks's terseness was comforting.

"So," he added, "the late Mr. Morrow cheated his clients. And this man Butler was party to it?"

"I am certain of the first part. Not of Butler's role. But his letters raised questions, and I couldn't rest until I found the answers. Figuratively, that is." Although she hadn't rested well for quite some time. It was rather hard on one's conscience to realize how many lies one had lived with.

"These letters are months old," said Jenks. "Since you've arranged matters with Butler and found the answers you sought, you have no need of my assistance."

"But I do." She lifted her chin. "I am the one fully acquainted with the details of the case, so I am the best judge of what I need."

"I've never thought you couldn't judge what you needed, Lady Isabel." He held her gaze for a beat too long. Her lips parted; slowly, her whole body flooded with heat. She remembered a warm evening the previous May, a hidden grotto in Vauxhall Gardens. His hands on her breasts, his lips on her throat, and a driving, hot pleasure that left them both breathless.

His kisses had been delectable. Slow and sweet, hard and pushing. She could not quite believe now, in this sedate room, what they had done together.

She looked down at her hands, which were knotted in her lap. Tightly folded hands; proper widow hands.

The Lady Isabel Morrow the world knew was courteous. Calm. Gracious. She didn't take up more space than she absolutely had to. Only Jenks had seen her otherwise: in the fragile moments right after Andrew's death; then months later, in the blissful abandon of that night at Vauxhall.

She had missed being that honest. That unguarded. But it had been only an aberration in her carefully ordered life.

Before she could reply, a footman entered the drawing room with the tea things. Though Isabel had not rung for tea, Selby would never overlook a courtesy. On the heels of the servant trotted a beagle that wound busily around everything from tea table to chair legs before sniffing Jenks's boots.

"You have acquired a watchdog," Jenks observed as the tray was set down.

"This is Brinley," said Isabel, "and he is no kind of a watchdog. He barks at everything but likes everyone. So he is as likely to wake the house for an inhabitant as for an intruder, and as apt to fawn over an errand boy as he is over me."

Proving the truth of her words, Brinley tipped his head back and gave a squeaky, drawn-out *halloo*. He was a sturdy little beagle with a dark brown body and ever-wagging tail. His long chestnut ears were constantly pricked, giving him a curious air.

Jenks scratched at the dog's head, earning himself Brinley's lolling tongue and a tail that beat his boot as rhythmically as a drum.

Once the tea things were arranged, the servant bowed. Andrew had always liked the household to be formal, down to the employment of liveried footmen for every little task. "I apologize for the intrusion of the dog, my lady," said the man. "I'll take him out now."

"Thank you, Douglas," she said. "See him brought to Miss Wallace."

As the footman seized the beagle by his leather collar,

Brinley regarded Isabel with mournful accusation. *You're sending me away? Me, the finest watchdog in England?*

"Silly pup." Isabel plucked up a biscuit from the tray of delicacies and tossed it toward the dog, who caught it from the air with a snap of his jaws. Then, submitting to being tugged from the drawing room, he let out another *arooo* by way of farewell.

Jenks followed them through the doorway with his eyes. When the door closed, he turned back to Isabel. "Nice little fellow."

"He is, yes. He was the runt from a litter of my brother's hunting dogs. Lord Martindale offered him to me rather than having him drowned."

"A fortunate little fellow too, then."

"Fortunate I," replied Isabel. "There were days after Morrow's death when Brinley was almost the only companion I had. So many people don't know what to say to a widow, and so they write vague letters full of platitudes and keep their distance." Even now, she had far fewer callers than before Andrew's death.

Perhaps the distance had been for the best, though. Isabel had been shocked to be widowed, but not truly sorry. One couldn't allow even a hint of such disloyalty to get about.

Which brought her back to the reason she'd sent for Jenks today. "Please forgive the interruption, Officer. You asked, I recall, why I summoned you if I had already found answers. You see . . . I need your help with something that's not precisely legal. But it's right, all the same."

For too long after she spoke, Callum simply looked at her. At the shape of her mouth, the color of her eyes. He never forgot a face, and he remembered her eyes as brown. But today they had a mind to be hazel.

She lifted her brows, waiting for his reply. But there was

only one sort he could give, no matter how beautiful she looked when she smiled.

"I am sorry to decline, my lady. My position as an Officer of the Police makes it impossible for me to take part in anything, as you put it, *not precisely legal*."

"Yes, I understand that. But this is one of those rare instances when legality and rightness aren't the same at all."

Rare indeed. Though not nonexistent. As soon as he finished this interview, he'd be off to Newgate because of another such case.

That decided it. "All right. Tell me everything."

"If I do, you have to either help me or forget any of this ever happened." She was a little too thin, with dark hair and the sort of paleness wealthy women cultivated with parasols. Far from appearing frail in her slenderness, though, she sat straight as a column of stone in her gray gown.

"I can't promise that," he said.

"Then I'll have to find someone else. I am sorry to have wasted your time—and pulled you away from the intrigue of a mock auction." She started to rise.

He held out a staying hand. "Lady Isabel, wait. Please. Are you in some trouble?"

"No. At least, I don't think so." She sat back again, then smoothed back her already-smooth hair. "I would like not to be. But really, this whole matter is for Lucy's sake."

"And who is Lucy?"

With her thumb, Lady Isabel twisted the wedding band she still wore. "Lucy is the Miss Wallace I mentioned. My husband's ward until his death; my ward now. Morrow had little family, so he left her to me, along with this house and all his belongings."

"He deeded you a person?" Callum had never met the man in life, but he'd formed an opinion of the late Andrew Morrow all the same. It didn't bear speaking of.

"He did, though I should have wanted her to stay with me even if he hadn't. She came to live with us about a year before Morrow died. She's a sort of sister to me. Or a daughter? A bit too young for the first, too old to be the second. Perhaps I'm like an aunt."

With a smile, she shook back the little ruffles about her wrists. "Do pardon me. I ought to have poured out the tea already. Do you take sugar?" She reached for the teapot.

"Never mind the tea. Tell me about your ward."

"Oh. All right." Abandoning the teapot, she considered. "Where to begin? I believe Andrew was a second cousin of hers, though the real reason she was given over to his guardianship was, of course, his money. Which was once my money, and now is again."

She spoke calmly, choosing her words with care. What would she say if she slipped the bonds of politeness and spoke her mind? Callum only hoped he'd be there if it happened.

"And Miss Wallace," he replied, "is involved in a potentially illegal yet morally right behavior in what way?"

"In no way, and so it should remain. Lucy is just eighteen, and she made her come-out in society this year. I should like her to make a good marriage. If she is associated with any scandal, though . . ."

"I understand. Scandal does not often go hand in hand with an advantageous match," Callum said dryly.

"You see my dilemma, then. This whole matter has all got to remain a secret, even from Lucy. I'll pay you for your help." She dangled the words before him like diamond earrings. "Please, Officer. I know Bow Street Runners—"

"Officers of the Police."

"—Officers of the Police, right. I know they often take independent commissions. And I would much rather work with someone I know."

She was correct about this. Many officers made the bulk of their income through private consulting, though they received a small salary from the police force as well.

But Callum had never taken a case only for money. He wanted to see justice done, always.

He had wanted to call on Lady Isabel, too. He had wanted to see her again, and never mind the reason.

The deep pools of her eyes pulled at him, returning suppressed memories to the forefront of his mind. Of burning lamps like stars fallen to earth, bright against an ink-black sky; of smooth skin, bared and stroked and pleasured.

Not that any of that was relevant right now.

Ultimately, it was the word *work* that he permitted himself to consider. He couldn't help her for sentimental reasons. He couldn't take part in anything immoral. But if it *was* moral, and it *was* merely a job, then perhaps it would be acceptable.

"All right," he said. "I will consider your case. Tell me everything, especially the moral bits and the illegal bits."

"Thank you." She let her eyes fall closed, a long blink like a sigh of relief. "Shortly before his death, my husband sold a Botticelli painting to the Duke of Ardmore."

"A Botticelli painted by Botticelli? Or a Botticelli by Butler?"

"The key question, and you asked it with remarkable facility. I am afraid, Officer Jenks, that it was the latter. And now the duke plans to trade it to Angelus to cover his gambling debts."

"Angelus?" Callum's brows lifted. "Not the usual sort of company for a duke to keep."

He had not expected to hear the name of a notorious lord of the criminal underworld spoken in this elegant parlor. Yet was there a family in high society without a taste for gambling or horse-racing? Courtesans or pugilism? As powerful as Lord Liverpool was in Parliament and the Duke of Ardmore was in London society, Angelus was everywhere else. Lady Isabel might have learned of the crime lord's existence at a younger age than Callum had.

"If the exchange takes place," she said, "and Angelus finds out he's been given a worthless fake painting, then he'll go after the duke for restitution. And the duke will trace the substitution to my late husband, and Morrow's reputation will be . . ."

When she trailed off, Callum said, "Known accurately."

People generally hated it when he completed sentences for them.

"Yes," Lady Isabel agreed, catching him by surprise. "It would be accurate. But his choices were not Lucy's, and they would be the death of her prospects."

The marriage market of society was more competitive than the Epsom Derby, if one credited the satirical prints loathed yet coveted by the ton. A bit of scandal wasn't always a bad thing, but it had to be connected to a large fortune and blood as blue as a jay's wing. The ward of an art dealer was unlikely to possess either.

"You've a particular scheme in mind to protect your ward, don't you?" he asked.

"I do, yes. I have not been able to borrow the painting from Ardmore, despite explaining my request with the most sentimental of reasons. So I can think of only one alternative." She laced her fingers together, leaning forward to fix him with the full force of earnest hazel eyes. "Before the duke can surrender the painting to Angelus, I need you to help me steal it."

Chapter Two

Newgate Prison was not a pleasant substitute for Lady Isabel's sumptuous home in Lombard Street. Nor was the incarcerated Sir Frederic Chapple as delightful a companion as Andrew Morrow's beautiful widow.

But as an Officer of the Police, Callum's first duty was to prison and prisoner, not to noblewoman. Or defrauded duke. Or Botticelli.

"I can't help you," he had explained to Lady Isabel before taking leave of her. "I must uphold the law. I cannot intrude into a duke's household and steal one of his possessions."

"But to switch it for one of greater value!"

"Lady Isabel. My career would be at an end."

She'd looked so disappointed that he'd added, "You don't need me to work with you. You can sort out the problem yourself. Only think, what would an investigator do next?"

She'd thought about this. "Collect clues. That is, information. If we're going to switch the painting, we need to know where it is and how it is framed and mounted."

We. He'd liked the sound of it on her lips.

"Don't be so hasty with your use of the word 'we,'" he'd made himself say. "But yes. Those are excellent steps to take." He'd stood, preparing to depart. "And I'll forget I heard anything about them or about your plan."

"What plan?" She'd blinked innocent eyes at him, then smiled. "Thank you for your time, Officer Jenks."

With that same polite farewell had their association ended eighteen months before, when the investigation of Andrew Morrow's death had been abruptly shut. The case had troubled Callum from his first sight of the body. A bullet entered a man's head in particular ways depending on who held the gun and who pulled the trigger. This bullet . . . he couldn't tell without an autopsy. Had Morrow's death been suicide? Had another person pulled the trigger, then placed the pistol in the hand of a murder victim?

Though Callum had raised these questions, there had been no inquest. Lady Isabel's influential relatives had arranged the silence of a coroner here, a magistrate there. The scandal of potential self-destruction had been averted, the unlikely possibility of murder quashed entirely. Andrew Morrow was buried in hallowed earth, with a stone over his head calling him a beloved husband.

Callum did not believe Morrow had been anything of the sort, any more than he believed Lady Isabel was party to the subversion of justice. But once a case was closed, no one consulted Bow Street anymore.

Even so, Callum had never stopped wondering about the truth.

After bidding her ladyship farewell, not without a twinge of regret, he'd turned his steps toward Newgate Prison. It was not a long walk from the crisp wealth of Lombard Street—less than a mile if one followed the bustling length of Cheapside.

Here was shop after shop selling cloth—dressmakers and haberdashers; milliners and dry-goods stores—all with windows full of neatly arranged products. Callum's hat was unfashionable and his clothes plain, but the same stubbornness that kept him from hiring a hackney also kept him from eyeing the high-crowned hats of felted beaver and the boots that shone glossy. If he didn't need something, he didn't buy it. Or hire it. Or eat it. Life was made up of only his work, and saving his coin.

For what he was saving, he hadn't decided yet. But he knew there would be *something*, someday, that he'd want. Maybe something he'd want even more than he wanted to see justice done daily. And if he had frittered away his savings on shiny boots, he would have no chance to jump at an opportunity.

Even so, he wondered about the shiny boots. The high-crowned hat. Or a many-caped greatcoat. If he looked more like the wealthy gentlemen with whom Lady Isabel associated in society, would she regard him differently? Would she call him something other, maybe, than *Officer Jenks*—that continual reminder that he was in her presence only by virtue of his employment?

Callum's mind ran constantly with questions of all types, and these were the fruitless sort. It was almost a relief to reach the forbidding stone block that was Newgate Prison.

He was familiar to the guards, who motioned him through without requiring him to be escorted. Likely they knew why he was here. He ought to stay away, but he couldn't seem to.

Because Callum never, *never* stopped wondering about the truth. And tomorrow, Sir Frederic Chapple—barrister, baronet, and accused mastermind of a daring robbery from the Royal Mint—would stand trial in the Old Bailey.

By God, it was good to know *Freddie*, as the baronet asked everyone to call him, would finally see justice served upon him.

Within the prison's stout walls, cells were stacked in story upon story. They flanked a central space, open from floor to the ceiling high above. The noise was like a wall in itself: prisoners' voices calling and pleading and cursing, every syllable rebounding off the endless angles and planes of stone. Light spilled in from somewhere above, too much to hide the signs of dirt and neglect, but not enough to feel like true daylight.

The air was heavy and humid despite its coolness, and by the time Callum reached the right corridor, clammy perspiration was creeping beneath his neckcloth. He pressed at it impatiently, knowing the baronet would notice any wilt in the starched cloth. Sir Frederic was attuned to appearances and impressions. He was a master of them.

Sir Frederic had lived for months in Newgate awaiting trial, but this wasn't the punishment it ought to have been. His cell was in the state area of the prison, with more comfortable lodgings. Jailers could be bribed to bring in just about everything, and as a result, the dirt and filth and lice stopped at the entrance of Sir Frederic's space. His cell was a brick vault like all the others, with a window at the far end and a barred front. But instead of a bare floor, his was covered by a woven carpet, thin underfoot but pleasant to the eye. A privacy screen painted all over with flowers folded across a corner, and clothing in fine fabrics hung from hooks just visible above the top. The cell's corner shelf held an assortment of bottles—doubtless full of expensive wines, knowing Sir Frederic's tastes. The usual cot was made plush with fine linens and a thick coverlet.

Sir Frederic was lounging on it at the moment, his feet in Chinese slippers and a book in his hands. When Callum's shadow fell over the book, he snapped it shut.

"Officer Jenks! I thought I'd be seeing you today. You're later than I expected."

A point for the baronet. Callum frowned. "I had other business to attend to, Sir Frederic. You weren't a priority."

"Ha! Oh, nonsense. I know how you are about this case."

Damn the man; another point for him.

Sir Frederic sat up with a heave of his massive form. He had been a man of indulgent habits before his arrest, and prison had not changed him. "I must apologize for not offering you a chair, Officer, but I haven't one."

"That's why you're apologizing to me. For not offering me a chair." Callum glared at him through the cell bars, declining to take off his broad-brimmed hat. This was not a social call.

"Yes, well, I *am* your host. I know we've had our differences in the past, but—"

"You're no one's host. You're a prisoner." Callum rocked back on his heels, almost tempted to smile. "Which is why I came to visit you today. If you didn't see me until we were in court tomorrow, you might be too flustered to give honest testimony."

A point for Callum? Maybe.

"Thoughtful of you, but you could have spared yourself the trouble. We won't be in court tomorrow."

"We . . . what?" Another point for the baronet. Even if he was lying, he'd got Callum's jaw to drop open.

"The fourth conspirator was found dead this afternoon—of drink, poor fellow, and right outside the prison walls. I heard of it from one of the guards." Sir Frederic adopted a pious expression. "They couldn't identify the body. Naturally, I felt it my duty to help, so I asked them to describe the man. I recognized his description at once."

"The day before your trial was to begin, you just happened to encounter new evidence in your case. How convenient." This should have been a point for Callum, but the baronet seemed to have changed the rules.

"Fortuitous timing." With a supporting hand against the cell wall, the older man shoved himself to his feet. He crossed the cell to the corner shelf and took up a bottle, squinting at it. "Madeira? I think so, yes. A Madeira would be lovely." He turned a mild look upon Callum. "I would offer you some, but as you informed me, I'm not your host."

He took up a glass, tutting at it not being the proper shape for this sort of spirits, then poured out a generous measure of the fortified wine.

Taking a sip, he held it in his mouth, then swallowed it

with a smack of fleshy lips. "Not as good as what I left behind in Northumberland—"

"You mean, the Madeira in the barrel that held the stolen gold?"

"—but it's better than what you're used to, I'll warrant. And it's good enough to celebrate getting out of prison. Which should be any hour now. My counsel is making the necessary arguments and arrangements."

Callum gritted his teeth. So many points to Sir Frederic. All of them, really. The baronet, wealthy and amoral, did not play the game fairly, and Callum could never match his stakes.

They had first met the previous year, in the course of Callum's investigation of a notorious robbery from the Royal Mint. Six trunks of then-unreleased gold sovereigns had been stolen by a quartet of thieves, and four guards killed.

One of the guards had been Harold Jenks, Callum's eldest brother.

Callum had seen his brother buried. Had swallowed enough grief to choke him. And then, determined as a hound after a fox, he had taken up the order from King's Bench to locate the coins wherever in England they might be. A substantial reward had been offered.

Callum hadn't given a damn about the reward, or about the stolen gold. He'd wanted to find the men who had killed Harry and the other guards. But it had made sense that the criminals would be with the gold, and gold was easier to trace than rumor.

In the end, a bit of both had led Callum to the Northumberland estate of Sir Frederic Chapple. A baronet new to the title, Sir Frederic possessed far more wealth than one might expect from his barrister's background.

With the unwanted but not entirely useless help of Lord Hugo Starling, son of the Duke of Willingham, and the resourceful Miss Georgette Frost, Callum had sorted out clues enough to determine that the four thieves, who called themselves the John Smiths, had betrayed each other. After taking the gold to Derbyshire, three of the thieves had split from the fourth, each removing a trunk. The fourth had been captured in Derbyshire. One of the remaining three had been killed by his accomplices, who took the gold north. There it had been found on Sir Frederic's land—some melted down in a blacksmith's shop, much of the rest hidden in a great barrel of Madeira.

A farmworker of Sir Frederic's was unmistakably guilty. He was arrested, tried, and sent to Australia. Callum, of all people, had argued for him to be transported rather than executed. Too many people had already died for the gold.

It was clear that Sir Frederic had been involved in the robbery—either as one of the four thieves, or as a mastermind. When confronted, Sir Frederic had nearly blown out his own brains. But he'd been convinced to calm himself, to take up the mantle of responsibility. To atone by seeing justice done.

The past eleven months—spent in a Northumberland jail, then in Newgate—seemed to have changed his mind.

The Old Bailey was notoriously slow at hearing cases, and the high profile of all matters related to the royal-reward-turned-national-treasure-hunt had slowed the wheels of justice yet further. Testimony was rehearsed and picked apart and rehearsed again. Witnesses were summoned, questioned, protected. No one could afford a mistake.

But Sir Frederic could afford anything. Even a body to take the blame from his own shoulders.

The bones of Harry Jenks rolled over in their grave, cold and despairing.

"Why now?" Callum asked. "Why not months ago, Sir Frederic?"

Translation: *I know you're lying, and you know I know.*

But why didn't you lie like this last June and save yourself time in prison?

"I felt . . . morally culpable," said the baronet, and for the first time Callum caught a flash of genuine feeling in Sir Frederic's eyes. But then he tipped back his glass, draining the spirits, and the moment was gone. With a clack of glass on stone, he set down the empty vessel. "Yet the John Smiths knew no one was supposed to be hurt. Certainly not to die. And really, who's to say I meant the John Smiths to carry out any crime at all? Perhaps it was only an experiment in thought."

"*You're* to say you meant them to carry out a crime. You said yourself you had organized it."

"What proof have you?" The baronet looked genuinely puzzled.

"The ears of others who were there. Including the son of a duke."

"Lord Hugo Starling, you mean?" Again, Sir Frederic tutted. Callum had the urge to shake the bars of the cell until they rattled, then do the same to the baronet's teeth. "He's not available at present. Up in the north of England somewhere—or is it Scotland? Somewhere like that. He has a cottage. Quite a pleasant home, I'm told, and—"

"I. Do. Not. Care. About his cottage," Callum ground out.

He was certain Sir Frederic had been one of the four thieves. But Sir Frederic had never admitted as much, and it couldn't be proven. The stolen gold had been returned to the Royal Mint. Lord Hugo had claimed the reward for the gold found up north, building himself a fine reputation as a tonnish physician.

And Callum had pressed the Bow Street magistrate for further investigation. He didn't want notoriety or fame; he wanted justice for his brother. The brother ten years his senior, who had taught him how to play cards and hold his liquor and how to read willingness on a woman's face.

Callum's whole youth had been bound up in adulation of Harry.

"He was engaged to be married," Callum told Sir Frederic. "My brother Harry, who was shot to death at the Mint. I don't suppose you knew that about him. They all had lives, those four guards. All of them, people who loved them and relied on them."

"A terrible tragedy. I've told you time and again, I never intended for anyone to be hurt. Of course, I bear the blame for encouraging those young ruffians in their scheme. I just told you as much."

He spoke fondly of the thieves, as if he weren't one of them. As if they were all impulsive children rather than men in their thirties and beyond. Sir Frederic had run a ragged school for homeless boys in London once, and just as Callum never forgot a face, the genial Freddie never forgot if one of his pupils had a gift for a certain petty crime. As a barrister, he was above suspicion himself. As a baronet, more so. Even with the evidence of gold coins found in his own wine cellar; even when the poor could be executed for taking but a few pounds' worth of goods.

"You're a damned liar." Callum's voice was blank. Utterly calm. He was stating naught but fact.

"Come now, Officer." Sir Frederic took a step toward him, his silk slippers blood red against the carpet on his cell's floor. "You can't expect an innocent man to go through the ordeal of a trial when the whole matter's easily squared away."

"An innocent man? By your own admission, you're far from innocent."

"You look dreadful." Another step, closer to the bars. "You really should have a drink, Officer. If you can find anyone to host you."

Harry would have. Harry had. On his brother's final birthday, Callum had taken him to pub after pub, until the

usually quiet Harry was laughing, leading a drinking song
from atop a table.

Callum ripped the hat from his head and crushed the
brim in his hands, just to hold himself steady. "You're not
going to slip away from your trial. I'll see you stand in court
yet, to account for the harm you've done."

"No. You won't." Sir Frederic smiled, all geniality. "I'll
be off to Northumberland. And you'll be off to whatever
you do. Annoying the good people of London."

"Capturing the bad ones," Callum muttered.

There was so much more to say, but there were no words
for it right now.

With narrowed eyes, he took a step back, then another.
Watching Sir Frederic as he reversed his steps, as if keeping
the baronet in sight meant that the man couldn't be freed
from his cell.

As soon as the cell had folded flat into the row of others
and Callum could no longer see any bit of it, he turned on
his heel and ran. Flat-out ran, pounding past cell after cell,
ignoring the din and the hoots of surprised prisoners and
even the halloo of the guard who had let him pass in.

He whipped by them all, tore through the entrance to the
prison, sprinted through the streets. South, then he caught
the corner of busy Fleet Street and followed it until it
became the Strand. Darting through traffic all the while,
winding through carriages and pedestrians. Leaping from
pavement to street and back, wherever he saw an opening.
Running, running, until his lungs burned and reminded him
he lived and drew breath; until his boots were heavy on his
feet and reminded him that he moved atop the earth one step
at a time.

For Harry, he ran, cutting right onto Drury Lane and
heaving through the last bit of the familiar path to the
magistrate's court on Bow Street. This was the brain and
conscience of Covent Garden and beyond, as the officers

based here solved cases and apprehended criminals wherever their warrants took them.

Callum flung open the door of the stone building, scanning the familiar lines of the high-ceilinged courtroom: railing, desks, seats. His fellow officers, lounging or questioning witnesses. Petty criminals, yowling their protests. And at the top of the room, the magistrate's bench. The cramped office lurked behind it, its door open. Callum blundered past everyone else on watery, tired legs.

"Fox!" he called. "Fox," he said again, then bent double to catch his breath.

By the time he straightened, the chief magistrate had come from behind the desk to face him. This was Augustus Fox, stout and deliberate, with graying hair and mournful black brows and the sort of voice that brooked no disagreement. He was a little taller than Callum, but just now his head was bowed.

"Jenks." His sonorous voice was muted. "You've heard then, haven't you?"

"I just . . . came from Newgate." There was not quite enough air in the room. "Sir Frederic's trial . . . he told me . . ."

"It's off, and for good. I'm sorry." The magistrate put a heavy hand on Callum's shoulder. "He has powerful friends, and we haven't enough evidence. We can't hold him any longer."

"But this dead man he claims was part of the robbery from the Royal Mint . . ."

"An excuse that allows everyone to save face. He walks away innocent; we have someone on whom to pin the guilt."

Callum shook off the magistrate's hand. "You know it's all a lie."

"I can't know anything without evidence. And neither can you." Fox straightened, catching Callum's eye with one of bright blue. "Jenks. I'm sorry. We've got to let this one go."

And how was he to do that? Was he simply to stop caring

that his brother had been killed? That someone culpable was going free?

"Move on to a new case," Fox was saying. "See justice done where you can." The magistrate regarded him closely, then tried out a smile. "Our friend Janey's been accused again of thieving. Maybe you could have a talk with her. Sit down for a few minutes, catch your breath."

"Right," said Callum. "Right. Of course."

He waited until Fox had turned away again before striding from the court. No, he wouldn't talk to Janey, a cutpurse and informer who was brought in at least once a week. No, he wouldn't sit while Sir Frederic went free. No, he could not stand it.

Yet he was weary in body and spirit. He stopped to lean against the familiar rough stone of the building, shutting his eyes. He was weary of the wealthy, who paid to hide the truth. Weary of being forced to drop cases with unanswered questions, unresolved deaths. He was weary of seeing the hand of justice stayed, of seeing the poor punished and the rich walk free.

Furious, he kicked at the stone wall, adding a scuff to the toe of his already-battered boot.

Damn, damn. Damn them all. And damn him too, for having his hands shackled as if he were a criminal. For being unable to help. To do what was right, and make it stick.

The sky was drifting to a darker blue, but sunset was hours away. The days of early summer seemed endless sometimes.

But . . . since there *were* a few hours of daylight left, the fashionable inhabitants of London would still be home. They were more likely to return home from their revelries after sunrise than to leave before sunset.

Which meant that he had time to return to Lombard Street, if his tired feet had a few more miles in them. Sir Frederic wasn't the only one who'd bent the law away from justice. Lady Isabel Morrow's relatives—and her late husband—had bought so-called justice too.

Now Lady Isabel wanted to correct a trespass against the truth. To step outside the law not for gain, but because of integrity. After seeing Sir Frederic, that weighed more with Callum than it had earlier in the day.

Along with everything else he'd just cursed, he would curse the law too. Only once, for the chance to see a wrong righted. No matter how small.

In Harry Jenks's grave, the bones settled into a troubled sleep.

Chapter Three

Isabel had not expected Callum Jenks ever to return to her drawing room. Yet here he was that same day, as afternoon began to fade to evening.

"I'll help you, Lady Isabel." Far more rumpled than he'd been earlier, and with grim lines bracketing his mouth, he was practically growling. "But we'll do this my way."

"What changed your mind?" The question slipped out—but at the dark look on his face, Isabel held up a hand. "Never mind. It doesn't matter. You've said you'd help me, and I intend to hold you to that."

"And you'll do as I say?"

His tone was harsh. "Someone has made you angry," she commented.

"Yes," he said. "It wasn't you, though."

"I'm glad for it. And I agree that I'll do as you say if it seems right to me. If it doesn't, I'll tell you."

His eyes narrowed. She narrowed hers back.

Then he sighed, tension bleeding from face and shoulders at once. "Of course, my lady. That is reasonable."

Years of training kept Isabel's posture straight, but within, she too relaxed. If she'd spoken so frankly to Andrew . . . well, they wouldn't have been speaking of *help* in the first place. Help was something about which one had a choice. Duty, its compulsory cousin, was far more familiar to Isabel.

"Thank you," she replied. "For returning, and for helping. Though you told me to act as an investigator, I was not certain of what to do next."

"And now?"

"Now, I will show you the painting that has caused so much trouble."

"Lead on then, my lady."

If only it were that simple. "I will take you to see it, but it's not as though it's simply hung on a wall somewhere."

"That would be unwise," Jenks granted. "Considering it's meant to belong to the Duke of Ardmore."

"For a short time longer."

Ugh. She hated visiting the paintings. *It's for Lucy*, she told herself. *It's for Lucy. To help Lucy.*

Dear Lucy, who had spent the day painting here and drawing there, reading in between. As much as Andrew Morrow had loved trading in art, Lucy enjoyed creating it. In doing so, she was often solitary, passing days on end with no company save for Isabel and the servants and Brinley.

Lucy swore she did not mind the quiet days, but Isabel knew they were her own fault. She was the younger woman's chaperone, her entrée into society. Upon Isabel rested the responsibility for Lucy's success this Season. If she wasn't getting invitations to the most tonnish affairs, because she'd been away from the center of society for too long . . .

Never mind. Never mind that now. She rang for Selby.

When the butler entered the drawing room, he was followed by Brinley. Selby pretended not to notice as the beagle tracked a winding path around the carpet, tail wagging wildly. *Snuff snuff snuff* went the little black nose, leading Brinley to the leather boots of Officer Jenks. The dog tipped back his head with a yip and a yowl, then returned to his determined sniffing around the visitor's boots.

Jenks folded his hands behind his back, ramrod-dignified as a soldier, but his expression as he regarded the dog was . . . sweet? Yes, it *was* rather sweet, with a crimp at the corner of his mouth and the tension about his eyes all melted away.

Isabel pretended not to notice. She was as good at that as her butler. "Selby," she said, "I require a lantern."

"Very good, my lady." There was no surprise in his expression. Not that a good butler would ever betray an emotion, but Isabel suspected he knew the reason for her request. Since Andrew's death, the hidden room had become the worst-kept secret in the house, apart from the affair between the upper housemaid and Douglas, the footman.

"I should like a flint and tinder, too," she added. "And a set of tapers, and several spills."

"Yes, my lady." The butler bowed and exited. Almost imperceptibly, he snapped his fingers. Brinley's head jerked up—and yes, he howled again. At least he obeyed the butler, heeling and following him from the drawing room.

Jenks resettled his feet. "I've been walking all over the city today. Seems your dog enjoys the scents of London."

"He has taken a liking to you, Officer Jenks."

"Lucky me." The officer's dark eyes met Isabel's. The directness of his gaze awoke a flutter in her belly. Silly of her. But she'd become unaccustomed to being looked at by men.

Jenks turned toward the window. "It's not as dark as all that yet. Why the lanterns and candles? Are we going exploring to find this painting of yours?"

"*Exploring* is too pleasant a way of putting it. And please, do not call this painting mine. It never was or should have been."

He acknowledged this with a nod as Selby returned to the drawing room, dog-less and with requested items in hand. Rather than bringing one lantern, he carried two.

"Your ladyship is not alone this time," he said. "I presumed to bring an extra."

"Thank you, Selby." Both lanterns were lit already, and Isabel took their handles. Jenks accepted the tinderbox, spills, and tapers, tucking them into various of his pockets.

As the butler left, Jenks said, "Whatever you have in mind, you've planned for it with plenty of supplies."

Isabel clenched her fingers around the flat metal of the lantern handles. "One has to get shut up in the dark only once before one never wants it to happen again."

"An anecdote you'd like to relate?"

"There's little more to it than that." The punched-tin lanterns threw light in dots and squares, dimly visible on the still-sunlit carpet. Isabel handed one to Jenks. "If you'll follow me, Officer?"

They proceeded to a bedchamber that both of them had entered before, though neither for quite some time. When Officer Jenks had previously been in Andrew's bedchamber, there had been a corpse on the floor. Quite a bit of blood, too. For Isabel, it had been a day so strange and startling as to seem unreal, and the passage of time had hardly changed that impression. Only the new Axminster carpet—a replacement for the one soiled by the contents of her husband's head—made the room look different from the way it had looked during the late Mr. Morrow's life.

"I recognize this room," Jenks said as Isabel crossed to the far wall and set down the lantern at her feet. "You've stopped using it as your bedchamber?"

Isabel's hand halted, an inch from the wall. "I beg your pardon?" She turned her head, peering at him over her shoulder.

"The space isn't being used anymore." With a flick of his hand, he indicated the cold hearth. The bare-topped desk with writing implements tidied away. The air of mustiness that not even the most conscientious maid could banish. "I understand why, Lady Isabel."

He intended to be kind. Or courteous, perhaps.

"You mistake the matter, Officer. It was never my bedchamber, or ours. Only his. So no, it is not being used anymore."

She turned back to the wall, not caring if she sounded terse. It wasn't uncommon for wealthy couples to separate at night as they so often did during the day. Most of them likely did so for different reasons than the Morrows had, but that was none of Jenks's affair.

She pressed up and down along the lines in the dark oak paneling. The spot she sought was somewhere around here—maybe up higher on this seam?

"I never knew there was a secret space," she said, still searching with her hands. "Until shortly after Morrow and I returned from Sicily, where we lived during the war. I came in here once for writing paper from his desk, and I saw a panel of the wall open."

Jenks's voice came from just behind her. "How unexpected."

"It was. This is meant to be the outer wall of the house, you see. I'd no notion it was anything but wood and brick."

Flame sparkles from his lantern danced over the wooden wall—and *there*, the light illuminated a crack hidden by the pattern of the wood.

"Ah! Here's the spot." With the heel of her hand, she pressed at it. A click and creak, and a doorway-sized piece of the wall swung open. Behind it was a cubby of a space, with a narrow staircase parallel to the bedchamber wall.

"Impressive discovery," Jenks said.

"'Impressed' is not the word for how I felt when I saw this. I'd rather have found rats in the walls." She had to laugh. "That didn't stop me from going inside. Curiosity has led to a great deal of discontent in the world."

"It has. But so has doubt."

"I was fated to feel one or the other about this space."
Even now, with the lantern's handle clutched in both her
hands, she hesitated to step in. That first time she'd gone
into the space, the panel had shut behind her. It had been a
long wait in fathomless darkness, pressing for a latch at
every bit of the wall she could reach until her fingertips
were raw. When at last a light bobbed into view far above,
and Andrew appeared, she had flung herself at him with a
relief that had embarrassed them both.

"There, there." He had patted her on the back. "Funny
old bolt-hole, isn't this? I was just looking at some family
papers."

She had accepted this and had not been eager to investigate again. But sometime after Andrew's death, when she'd
read Butler's letters and noted a reference to paintings stored
in "the hidden space," she had wondered. And she'd looked.
And she'd found evidence she wished she had never seen.

That night, she'd gone to Vauxhall in search of distraction. And oh, how she had found it, in the form of Callum
Jenks.

That had been nearly a year ago. She wondered now how
she'd had the boldness for any of that: the search, the intimacy. Taking what she wished.

She wondered if she'd ever be bold enough to do something similar again.

"I assume," Jenks said, "that we are to climb those stairs.
Would you prefer I go first, or that I follow you?"

"You go first," Isabel decided. "You will be able to hold
up your lantern higher than I."

So he did, carrying his lantern with an outstretched
arm. To squeeze up the narrow stairs, he had to turn sideways, shoulders against the wall. The staircase was a
stacked tower tight as a spiral, but rude and rough with

corners and switchbacks. Isabel trod behind him, skirts
brushing dust from the walls.

"Your husband can't have had an easy time fitting into
this passageway," Jenks grunted as ragged wood caught on
his jacket.

"It was worth the trouble to him."

After that they climbed in silence—one story up, then
two. Wooden treads creaked underfoot; the air smelled of
dust and dank. The lantern light was weak and strange,
flinging dots of light everywhere, but never enough.

At the attic level, at last, a door faced them. Dim light
leaked from around it.

Isabel sighed. *Here we go.* She handed Jenks a key for
the lock. "Open it, please, Officer."

When he did, they stepped into a narrow room. A glass
skylight admitted fading afternoon light. Isabel stood under
it and stared up at the sky, as if her eyes could drink in the
sun they'd missed during the dark climb up the hidden
stairs, storing it for the climb back down.

Then she set her lantern on the floor, watching as Jenks
scanned the room with the same focus he'd given earlier to
Butler's letters.

The hidden room ran the full width of the house. Dozens
of framed artworks lined the space, leaning against the inner
wall. The pieces were covered with cloths, but their gilt and
wood frames peeked out at floor level. Facing the collection
of covered paintings was a small sofa from which one might
sit and view. The space was tight and full of the scents of
dust and old wood, and the temperature hovered between
warm and hot.

"It's clever, isn't it?" Isabel knew she sounded wry.
"There are no windows to reveal the room's existence to
anyone from the street or mews. Why, the servants slept in
attic quarters and never knew it was here."

"And what is it, besides a place the servants do not know of?"

"They know of it now. Though not what's kept up here. This is the home for the paintings Morrow wanted for himself. Officially, he sold these. In truth, they have all been copied, and these are the originals."

"Our friend Butler has been busy."

Jenks lifted a cloth covering and peered beneath. Paintings leaned in a stack against the wall: face after face, form after form. He flipped through them with slow, careful movements, minding their fragility. Isabel knew what he saw: jewel-bright paints and gold leaf; fleshy nude figures done in warm tints that breathed of life. Romantic modern portraits of young women under stormy skies, their eyes rolled to heaven and their hair in disarray.

"Did Mr. Morrow collect nothing but pictures of women?" he asked.

There was the question Isabel wished she had known to ask before her wedding day. Not that she'd known then about the secret room, or the forgeries, or any of it.

"He traded in many sorts of artwork," she finally said. "These paintings are the ones in which he had a private interest."

That skirted too closely to the truth, and for a moment she thought Jenks would press her for details. But no, he got that halted-on-the-edge-of-speech look on his face, then turned back to the paintings.

A particularly large one faced the wall. Pushing it away a few inches, he squinted—then let out a low whistle. "I've seen this one. At the Pall Mall Picture Gallery."

"You haven't seen the genuine one until now."

Gently, Jenks released the artwork and let it settle against the wall again. "I never suspected. Butler's a talented fellow as well as a busy one."

"He is. The forgery still passes for the genuine piece, and

collectors and artists far more expert in painting than you have not noticed." Isabel hesitated. "That raises an additional problem. It's not only Morrow's reputation at stake, and mine, and Miss Wallace's. It's the reputation of anyone who bought or validated one of Butler's paintings, thinking it a genuine antique. A great many people will be humiliated if the truth comes out."

"The behavior of other people," he said, "is not your doing, Lady Isabel. Nor are their choices yours."

"Thank you, Officer. I do realize that. And yet . . ." She rubbed at her forearms, her long sleeves scratchy in the heat of the room. "The choices of others still have the power to hurt me. Or Miss Wallace. And if I don't take steps to protect us, I cannot be certain anyone else will."

"Hmm." He was the most unreadable man possible. She couldn't tell if he was being further convinced to help her, or if one more sentence would send him striding indignantly from the house. "You didn't know your husband dealt in forgeries. What did you think was the source of his income?"

"Me." She gave a humorless laugh. "Maybe I should be relieved that he had other sources of income, even though fraudulent? He appeared wealthy and acted wealthy, and my father assumed he truly was. A man can get far with confidence and charm, if he is willing to lie by omission."

"So your family thought it a good marriage?" He was again flipping through the paintings, yet she had the feeling his attention was focused on her words.

"Is that relevant to forming a plan to switch the paintings?"

He lifted a painting of a nude Venus, frowned at it, then replaced it. "One never knows. An investigator should collect as much information as possible."

Ha. "Is that so?"

"I would never mislead you about the role of an investigator." When he turned to her, his eyes were frank—yet humor touched the corner of his mouth.

A knot she'd not realized was tugging at her shoulders began to unravel. "It's not as if any of it's a secret at this distance in time. My father was pragmatic. He cared that my elder brother, the heir, married well and had children. I am much my brother's junior, and my own marriage was of little interest to our father. As long as my husband moved well in society and had a plump purse, he was satisfied."

"'Was,' you say. Your father is no longer living?"

"My father is living, but he is not well. My mother died at my birth. Lord Martindale, my brother, carries out the duties of the marquessate." A sort of Regency in their own family.

Not that Isabel's father, the Marquess of Greenfield, was mad like the unfortunate king. He was simply absent, his mind having slipped away in bits over the years. Probably that had already begun when he'd first met Andrew ten years before. Neither Greenfield nor Isabel had asked the questions they ought to have. They had both been too trusting.

"I see." With that simple reply, he set aside the subject. "So, which of these paintings ought to belong to the Duke of Ardmore?"

Right. The reason they were up in this secret little chamber. "It is this one." She eased free a painting from one of the stacks, then held it out, making of herself an easel. The painting was not overly large, perhaps two feet wide and three feet high.

Jenks studied it as if he were reading a page, eyes traveling from top left to right, then down a bit, again, again. There was no sign of desire in his features as he scanned the picture, as there would have been in Andrew's. Thank heaven; Isabel let out a throttled breath.

She peered over the top of the painting to see what Jenks saw, though she knew its image by heart. Three young women stood in a ring, clad only in gossamer draperies.

One had her back to the artist—the viewer?—displaying buttocks of impressive roundness. The women's arms were linked, raised, intertwined, as if they were in mid-step of a complex dance. Their hair was long and unbound, yet held back from the face in tiny knots and braids and frizzes.

To Isabel, their faces were far more arresting than their graceful nakedness: features sharply outlined, gazes averted from each other. The one whose face showed best had a bit of a downward twist to her lips. For all their intricate dance, these lovely centuries-old women were each alone and unhappy.

Or maybe she read her own feelings into their faces. These women were like all those in the paintings Andrew had kept: bare breasted, bare of hair at their women's parts. Their forms were painted with depth, the flesh pale as marble. Almost lifelike, yet determinedly unreal.

"I can't imagine taking a private interest in this sort of thing," Jenks said. "But what do I know? I'm a humble Officer of the Police."

"Something about the way you say that doesn't sound humble at all." At his shrug, Isabel set down the painting and turned its face to the wall. "This is a study of a piece of a much larger painting. The Italians call it *La Primavera*, the coming of spring."

"Are the three women spring, somehow?"

"They are not. They are minor goddesses, the three Graces. There was no chance of taking the enormous finished painting out of Italy, but Morrow was determined to purchase this study. He thought it had been painted first, before the *Primavera* painting as a whole." She drew the covering sheets back over the stacked-deep artwork.

"Why would the artist have done this part more than once? Besides financial benefit."

Isabel cleared her throat before she turned back to Jenks.

"It is the piece, I would guess, in which gentlemen would have been most likely to evince a private interest."

"God save us from gentlemen," muttered Jenks. "All right. So you have this painting, and the Duke of Ardmore has the other."

Isabel nodded. "And I mean to see them switched. It's possible, I know, that the fake would go unrecognized by Angelus. But if he were to spot it . . ."

"A possibility voided by your clever scheme," Jenks replied. "If the duke hands over a genuine painting to Angelus, unwanted questions would never arise."

"That was my reasoning as well." Was the lantern guttering? She hoped not. Though they had another lantern, plus tapers and spills, queasy memories of being locked away made her shiver. "So, you see what we have to work with. Shall we return to a part of the house that's not horribly hot and hidden behind a false wall?"

"In a moment." The room was not large, and when he took a step toward her, he seemed very close. "I've said I'll help you, and I will. But I must warn you that I won't ignore any evidence I find." The clear brown of his gaze, the firm set of his jaw, were all determination.

She tipped her head, not understanding. "Evidence of what?"

"Evidence related to your late husband's death."

"Can there be any at this point in time?"

"I don't know. But if there is, then I won't ignore it. And I might even seek it out."

She held his gaze for a moment, then looked around the hidden space. Here was evidence of a sort, and she hadn't blundered upon it until six months after Andrew had died. "That is fair enough. You've my blessing, Officer Jenks."

"There is a possibility," he added, "that we'll learn undesirable facts about the circumstances of your husband's death."

"What could be more undesirable than the death itself?"

He raised his eyebrows.

She sighed. "I don't suppose I want you to answer that. You must have twenty different responses at the tip of your tongue."

"No more than half a dozen."

Isabel crouched to pick up the lantern she'd set by the door. She felt calmer as soon as it was in her hands, the handle warm, the little flame winking in the deep blue light of early evening.

"The investigation was closed," she said slowly. "Should it not have been?"

"What do you think?"

She bit back a denial, considering her words with care. Jenks, more than any other person Isabel had met, was unbothered by silence. He simply waited for her reply, watching her with endless patience.

No, she didn't know whether the investigation ought to have been closed or not. Had Martindale been less determined to shield Isabel, she suspected Andrew would have been called a suicide. Buried in unconsecrated ground, his assets frozen for a year. Which would have meant shame and poverty—even if temporary—for Isabel.

Instead, the death was tactfully determined to be death by misadventure. Morrow must have been cleaning his firearm, poor man. Looking into the barrel to see whether he'd got out every speck of soot.

The law had been followed. But no, if Isabel were honest, justice hadn't been done—yet that wasn't for Andrew's sake. It was a kindness to her. Or maybe it was just the easiest way for her family to put a period to a marriage that had never been much of a success.

"I think," Isabel said, "that you must follow your judgment in this matter. And so we have a bargain. You shall bring the investigative skill and the nose for inconvenient fact. What shall I offer our partnership?"

For the first time today, he truly smiled. The expression

hinted at danger, his eyes sharp and feral. "You," he said, "are the inside woman. We will need you to enter the duke's house and find the painting. We need its exact location if we're to switch it for the genuine article." His smile faded. "Can you do that? Have you a reason to call on Ardmore?"

"I can fabricate one." She handed him her lantern and took up the second. "Under the guise of manners, Officer Jenks, many battles have been fought. I shall enter the enemy's camp tomorrow. And"—she added sweetly—"I shall do it over tea and cakes."

Chapter Four

As Isabel had hinted to Jenks, a woman trained in the manners of high society possessed a formidable arsenal of weapons. There was the knife cut of a snub, the club of a set-down. The slow poison of a veiled insult. The scattershot volley of gossip.

Men underestimated these weapons, yet women used them daily to shape society. Let the gentlemen have their Parliament; the ladies held sway in the ballroom.

Or in the drawing room of a ducal home. The afternoon following the venture into the hidden room, Isabel and Lucy paid a call on the Duchess of Ardmore during her at-home hours. They were now sharing tea as Lucy eyed a plate of seed cake.

The call was pleasant, all conversational weapons tucked away for the moment. While Isabel considered the duke her foe in the matter of the Botticelli painting, she rather liked the company of his wife and daughter.

It was not the duchess but her daughter who dominated the room. "You've not met Titan yet?" Lady Selina Godwin, a pretty brunette who loved company and conversation, lifted a fluffy gray cat from the floor to the sofa. "I fairly dote upon her! My brother, George, brought her home for me last week."

"She is beautiful," Isabel agreed. In truth, the half-grown cat looked confused, as if she still couldn't believe this life of ease was now hers. Lady Selina had placed her on an embroidered pillow, and when the duke's daughter petted the cat's head, a purr like a baby rattle sounded through the room.

Besides Isabel and Lucy, the duchess and her only daughter had welcomed Lady Teasdale, an older woman with a sharp sense of humor and beautifully dressed silver hair, and Mrs. Gadolin, a young woman who had recently married far above her station and bore much the same fuddled-by-fortune look as the cat.

Isabel had hoped for a larger crowd, but in her impatience to find the false Botticelli, she and Lucy had called on the early side of fashion. Now she would have to be careful not to draw notice for unusual behavior. As she sipped her tea, her eyes darted around the room. No fake *Primavera* on that wall . . . that wall . . . that wall. She would have to make an excuse to leave the room before the polite quarter-hour's visit was up, so she could search more of the house.

"May I pet her too?" Lucy asked. She'd been all but silent so far on this call, but the company of an animal had the effect of easing her awkwardness.

At Lady Selina's cheerful agreement, Lucy slipped from her chair and crouched on the floor before the sofa. She crooned to the cat, who blinked eyes gone sleepy from petting and sloth.

Isabel had a dual motive for this call. Besides locating the study of *La Primavera*, she wanted Lucy to befriend the Godwins. Isabel had grown up with George, the elder sibling, who was twenty-eight as she was. Lady Selina, at age twenty-one, had spent time enough in society to become thoroughly comfortable with it, and she would be a fine friend for Lucy. Likely she'd wed this year. Rumor placed the heir to the Liverdale marquessate—a pleasant man in his late thirties—as a frequent caller in Lady Selina's drawing room. It would be a good match, the fulfillment of the two powerful families' long-held wish to unite. One wondered, in fact, why the heir had not yet proposed.

Perhaps, Isabel realized, the Duke of Ardmore needed his gambling debts to be forgiven before Liverdale would consent to the match. Or perhaps Isabel was seeing conspiracy everywhere.

She wished for the unflappable presence of Callum Jenks. Though he'd fit into this iced cake of a drawing room about as well as a fallen tree, he would know what was likely and what was ridiculous.

"You must get a pet of your own, Miss Wallace," said the duchess in her languid voice. Perpetually half-dazed with laudanum due to an illness no physician had ever been able to diagnose, she was sleepily courteous as she reclined on a silk-covered chaise longue. "Every young lady of fashion must have a cat."

"I shall get one directly!" promised young Mrs. Gadolin. "My darling Gadolin will know the perfect place to get the best sort of cat."

"The best sort of cat, in my belief," commented Lady Teasdale, "is the sort that stays out in the mews and keeps the mice from eating up the hay. A good big dog, now, that's the sort of pet that can make itself useful."

Isabel jumped in to this conversational opening. "Like a watchdog, you mean? Your Grace, I believe you keep several here."

When the duchess only said, "Mmmm?" Lady Selina replied, "Yes, much to everyone's dismay but my father's! They ought to live in the country; they would make excellent hunting dogs. Instead, they prowl about the house at night and put fear into the servants. Every time my father rings for his poor valet at night," she laughed, "Thursby must take off his shoes and sneak about, lest one of the dogs should wake and spring for him."

"It is so funny," said the duchess vaguely. "We laugh and laugh."

"How many dogs have you?" Lucy asked, still petting the little cat.

"Only two, though they're large and loud enough to seem like a whole pack." Lady Selina chuckled. "Dreadful dears. Right now they're shut up in my father's study. He enjoys their company as he answers his correspondence, I suppose."

A good hint. The two dogs would have to be accounted for when the time came to swap the false painting for the true.

Now, how could she slip away to look for the painting without drawing notice, especially from Lucy?

Dear Lucy. Eighteen years of age, she was pretty as a painting herself, with wide blue eyes and hair that curled in soft ringlets. Smooth-skinned and slender, she could have posed for all the fashion drawings in Ackermann's Repository.

And yet. So far this Season, she "hadn't taken," as mamas were wont to describe girls who simply hadn't drawn much male attention. It wasn't as though she were shy, or difficult. She was friendly and extremely agreeable. So much so that Isabel sometimes found herself holding back on offering an opinion, so she could determine what Lucy wanted. Lucy was a difficult girl to fool, though. It seemed like a game to her: "Oh, whatever you'd like," she'd say, her eyes extra-wide.

Men wanted biddable wives, in Isabel's experience. But maybe not that biddable? Or maybe Lucy was just a little . . . not enough. Not quite rich enough, not quite spirited enough.

There was one exception, and that was when Lucy was around animals. She could croon to and play with an animal for hours. Perhaps this little Titan would be the bridge between Lucy and a friend with two legs instead of four. Lady Selina seemed most pleased by the attention given her pet.

For a moment. Then, once Mrs. Gadolin had decided she

would put her darling husband on the hunt for two large and bad-tempered dogs, Lady Selina turned her gaze toward Isabel.

"It's been well over a year since you were widowed, has it not?" Lady Selina cast a curious glance over Isabel's gown. It was another in gray, this one edged in a narrow band of lavender silk ribbon and trimmed with black bugles. "You still wear your ring, and you remain in half-mourning?"

Isabel made some noncommittal noise. Let Lady Selina think her excessively sentimental. She thought of her pale clothing and the ring on her finger much like the faded winter plumage of a bright bird. It kept anyone from noticing her, so she could go about her life unbothered.

It wasn't always the sort of plumage she preferred, though. She regarded Lady Teasdale's scarlet gown and turban with covetous eyes.

"You will forgive me for asking," said Lady Selina with the confidence of one who was forgiven everything. "You see, I have matchmaking on my mind, hoping for a happy announcement soon myself." Her smile was all dimples and mischief. "Have you not thought of looking for a husband for yourself along with one for Miss Wallace?"

"Hmm. Miss Wallace." Lady Teasdale looked thoughtful. She had a son of marriageable age, Isabel recalled—though she was perhaps more interested in seeing him wed than he was himself.

Lucy looked up, smiled vaguely, and returned her attention to the cat.

"Miss Wallace must have romance enough for us both," Isabel prodded her gently. "I've no interest in wedding again."

She had been only eighteen when she'd married Andrew, who was twenty years her elder. He'd valued Isabel as an asset—pretty, aristocratic, pleasant—just as he had the artwork in which he'd traded. She was to help him add to his collection by being a living supplement to it.

As a widow, she ought to be free to act as she wished. Yet she was still living for others, wasn't she? Cleaning up the evidence of Andrew's wrongdoing. Guiding Lucy to make sure the girl had a good life.

The stubborn, handsome face of Callum Jenks flashed into her mind. Reminding her she wasn't alone in her scheme—for now.

"You ought to consider it nonetheless, Lady Isabel," Lady Selina said. "And this time, you could choose whomever you wish."

"A marriage for love, you mean?" Lady Teasdale's eyes were merry. "You're telling fairy tales, my girl. Marrying for love is a luxury women can ill afford."

Lady Selina looked doubtful. As she lifted her teacup, sunlight winked in a jeweled ring she wore. Likely she wasn't accustomed to being told there was something she couldn't afford.

"I shall tell my darling Gadolin . . ." His young wife ground to a halt. "What ought I to tell him?"

"That marrying for love is a dream few of us see become reality," said Lady Teasdale dryly.

"Tell him that he ought to get you a cat," suggested Lucy. "If you want one."

"Hear, hear," added Lady Selina. "Tell him to get you a cat. My brother can tell you where. He's probably blundering about somewhere in the house."

For the next few minutes, the women talked of everything and nothing. This sort of conversation felt like a warm bath, comforting in its easy familiarity. Gentle, watchful flattery that folded the other person's attention back upon herself and allowed Isabel to observe, to learn.

And to drop back, so that she could seize a moment to excuse herself. A murmured *beg pardon*, an embarrassed dip of the gaze, and everyone would assume Lady Isabel Morrow had to use the necessary before she paid her next call. She made her way around the edge of the drawing room, then ducked out through the gilded door.

Every part of the Duke of Ardmore's town house was rich and gilt-spattered, and this corridor was no exception. Elaborate plaster medallions painted in gold; silk hangings on the walls; gold-framed portraits and paintings every few feet. Quietly as her slippers could carry her, Isabel tiptoed in the direction opposite the entry hall. She knew Butler's Botticelli wasn't hung there, nor had it been in the dining room the last time she dined here. She must hope it wasn't in the study, where duke and dogs were closed away, but if she had to make some excuse to look in there, she would.

Sliding her hand along the wall, she listened—but the silence was so complete, it seemed like a weight in her ears. One could not hear the London streets from this part of the house, and the soft carpets underfoot stole even the sound of her own footfalls. She peered into another room—a music room, it appeared, smelling of cut flowers and lemon polish—then poked down a new corridor. The Duke of Ardmore had a large collection of art, and every which way Isabel turned, there seemed to be another work. The man had hung paintings frame to frame in some places, clustering them so thickly in the stairwell that the pattern of the wall-hanging was all but hidden.

She cast a glance toward the door that she guessed led to the duke's study, then regarded the stairwell thoughtfully. Maybe the troublesome painting was on the second story, hung amidst the family's quarters.

She must hurry. A few more minutes, and the callers would be leaving. Already they must be wondering at the state of poor Lady Isabel's insides, to be gone so long in the necessary. Quick-footing it, she hurried up the stairs, rounding the curve—right into a person.

"Steady there, miss—oh, Isabel! Hullo there."

"George!" Isabel recovered her balance, then gave her

old acquaintance a smile that was quite genuine. "How do you do?"

"Oh, fine, fine." Though he returned her smile, he looked nothing of the sort. At only twenty-eight, he wore his years heavily. Reddened eyes, a softness about the middle from too much drink. Because he was practically nocturnal, his skin was fish-belly pale.

Despite all this, George had a kind, if selfish, heart. He was, after all, the one who had first alerted Isabel to the sale— or trade, really—of his father's painting to Angelus, eager to share what he thought to be ripping news. His father's gambling troubles were a matter of continual amusement to him.

"Were you fetching something for my sister?" he asked. "Can I help you find it?"

Right. She'd just plowed into him on the stairs to the second story. "Oh—no, it's not that." Why not be honest? It would be easier than remembering a pack of lies. "I was hoping to get a look at your father's Botticelli. A study from *La Primavera*—do you know the one?"

"With the dancing naked ladies?" George laughed. "I should think so."

"It's lovely!" Isabel protested. "I grew fond of Botticelli when Morrow and I lived in Sicily. I just wanted a look at it."

"Ah. You've got some memories tied up in the old thing, haven't you?"

Isabel smiled, permitting George this incorrect assumption.

"Ardmore keeps it in his study these days," George replied. "He did have it upstairs for a while, but he likes having it close at hand now. Making his good-byes, maybe, before he sends it off to Angelus—next week, I think."

They had only a few days, then, to make the switch. "I shouldn't want to bother him in his study," Isabel demurred.

Dutifully, George insisted that it would be no trouble at all, and back down the stairs they went to the one door

Isabel hadn't opened. George rapped at it, and a furious round of barking ensued.

"Come in," called the duke, barely audible over the dogs' clamor.

George opened the door partway. "Father. Brought a visitor for your dancing naked ladies." Then he shoved Isabel in with more enthusiasm than politeness.

"Gog! Magog! Sit," said the duke. The two large dogs—both hunters of a sort much larger than Brinley—set their haunches on the floor and looked at Isabel with what could only be described as a pout on their jowls. "Quiet, boys."

"Your Grace." Isabel dropped a curtsy, then extended a hand for the dogs to sniff. They stretched out curious heads, then growled, hackles rising even as they remained planted on the floor.

"Sorry about that," said the duke. "They don't much like anyone but me."

"It's true," grumbled George. "I can't tell you how much calf's liver I've fed the dreadful beasts since Father bought them—"

"You fed them *what*?" interrupted the duke.

"—and they still won't obey a single command I give."

Isabel laughed, as she was meant to, though her heart was pattering more quickly than usual. There was the painting, half-hidden behind the standing duke—and then there was the duke himself.

She ought to be comfortable around an old acquaintance like the Duke of Ardmore, yet she never felt so. Oh, his smile was everything friendly, his voice mild, his manners assiduous. But his blue eyes were so watchful. Much like Jenks's, she supposed, yet the effect was entirely different. Jenks seemed merely to be observing; Ardmore was judging.

But Isabel could win a politeness battle with anyone in society. "As your son said, Your Grace, I hoped for a look at your Botticelli. I have loved it since the day my late husband acquired it."

All right, that bit was a lie. But the mention of a dead spouse was always good for a sympathetic response, and the duke, standing at his large mahogany desk, welcomed Isabel to step around behind it. "It is lovely work, Lady Isabel. I don't wonder you became fond of it."

The study was small, cluttered now with three people and two dogs and a desk larger than the table in Isabel's breakfast room. The Butler-celli hung centered behind the desk, between two narrow windows draped in elegant swags of silk velvet.

"It is just as I remembered it," Isabel said for the sake of saying something, as she forced herself to memorize every detail here. Two windows; that would be the fourth and fifth back from the street. The first story, so a bit of a climb from the ground floor if they entered through the window. The frame was elaborate and unmistakable. They would have to take time to swap the real painting into the same frame. It would be possible since Butler's forgeries were exactly sized.

"Lovely." She drew a deep breath that she hoped sounded enraptured, then stepped toward one of the windows for a look at its latch. "Do you mind, may I look at your view? I am thinking of moving houses."

"Of course," said Ardmore in his mellifluous voice. "You must wish to move away from the sad associations of your current home."

"Indeed," agreed Isabel distantly, studying the metalwork that locked the sashes. "Such sad associations." She was no expert, but the latch looked like the one on her drawing room window. She could practice with that one, maybe, sorting out how to force it from the outside.

Her mind whirled with observations. Thank heaven she had a bit of pencil and a pocketbook in her reticule, though of course she'd left that behind in the drawing room.

Be a good investigator, she told herself. *Be a good partner for Jenks*. She must remember all of this, so he would smile again in that interestingly wicked way when she told him what she'd learned.

"Are you really thinking of moving houses?" George's voice came from behind her, surprised. Gog and Magog growled, and George addressed them with a word he ought not to have said in the presence of a lady.

Isabel turned back to face him. "Yes, I really am."

This impulsive falsehood was the first time she'd considered the idea. Until now she'd been bound up in the notion of being Andrew's widow, of not wanting to rattle the bones of all the skeletons he'd left behind for her. But she liked the notion, now that she thought it over. Yes. She liked it very much.

"I would prefer something smaller, I think," she said. "A little jewel of a town house. Or maybe one at the edge of London, with a bit of garden behind it for flowers and a bench to take one's leisure." If one tried sitting outdoors behind the Lombard Street house, one would only get a lungful of foggy coal smoke and pungent dung from the stables. For variety, maybe the sharp scent of lye on washing day.

"It sounds a most attractive prospect," said the duke mildly. "I've the name of a good house agent, if you wish some help in your hunt for a new property."

Isabel accepted the name, printed on a bit of foolscap, then curtsied her good-bye. The dogs hated that even more than they'd hated her entrance, erupting into a flurry of barking.

"Rotten dogs," George said as he shut the study door behind them. "The only command they know is 'sit,' but at least they obey it well. Sometimes. Oh! Hullo, there's my sister."

"*There* you are, Lady Isabel! I wondered where you'd got to." Lady Selina turned from waving her callers down the stairs to shoot the new arrivals a grin. "Now I see, you ran into my reprobate brother."

"It's always good to see an old friend," said Isabel. A bland reply, but eighty percent of her mind was full of measurements and plots. "And I got to meet the famous dogs."

Lucy stood in the doorway, holding her reticule in one hand and Isabel's in the other. "Were they very—oh! Lord Northbrook." Lucy managed somehow to curtsy to George and shrink back at the same time.

"They were indeed *very*," sighed George. "They are always *very*. Ah, well. If you'll excuse me, ladies?" With a nod, he thundered down the stairs—onward to wherever he'd been heading before Isabel smacked into him.

Lucy stepped forward again and handed Isabel her reticule. "Thank you for your hospitality, Lady Selina. And for the loan of your cat."

"The loan of a cat?" Isabel's brows lifted in some alarm.

Lady Selina laughed. "Only while Miss Wallace is here, never fear. I know you have a dog of your own, and poor Titan is all but overset when she encounters Gog and Magog. But Miss Wallace, you must come back and visit Titan anytime, and me as well."

With that friendly farewell, Isabel and Lucy descended the stairs and clambered into the carriage that had been waiting.

As the carriage lurched into motion, Isabel itched to write down her observations, but a question had to be posed first. "Lucy, dear, I noticed that you were shy of George— that is, Lord Northbrook. Is there some reason for your shyness? Has he . . ." Isabel searched for the right word. George would never disrespect a lady, but he could be, as he had said of the dogs, *very*.

"Oh, no! His lordship has been everything amiable." Lucy's eyes went wide. "I hope I didn't embarrass you. Only I did not expect to see a gentleman there, and I fear I curtsied rather badly."

"You need not startle around him. Oh—unless you were

thinking of him as a potential match? Because I really wouldn't advise it."

"I would never look so high," insisted Lucy, a jut to her jaw.

"It's not that," said Isabel. Although Lucy was probably right; when George wed, it would be to a woman of as lofty a pedigree as his own. "He is not a bad man, but his habits are not what I would wish for in a husband for you."

Lucy looked embarrassed, so Isabel turned the subject on impulse. "The duke's loud dogs gave me an idea. I wonder if dogs can be trained to be silent? We've assumed we have to live with Brinley's barking, but perhaps not."

Lucy frowned, thinking. "Brinley is such a good little dog, but he *does* bark at everything. I could try to train him out of it. What do you think, would meat be good as a training treat?"

Isabel recalled George's complaint about Gog and Magog being immune to bribes of liver. "Perhaps cakes," she suggested. "They are my favorites. Why not a dog's as well?"

She was rather proud of her suggestion. Lucy loved Brinley, and she could take on the helpful task of sorting out what quieted a stubbornly loud dog. Not that there would be time to train Gog and Magog, of course. But if Isabel could get them to consume a drugged cake . . .

As the carriage pulled up before the Lombard Street house, Isabel marveled at how quickly her life had changed. For a few months after Andrew's death, she'd simply been a colorless widow. Then, faced with a secret, she had taken a lover and gained a secret of her own. Over the past year, she must have been changing without realizing it—for now her house didn't fit her correctly, the ring on her finger seemed too binding, and she was plotting how to break into a duke's home and drug his beloved dogs.

Andrew had guided her so firmly during his life. In a

way, he had also determined what she'd made of herself since his death.

Finally, she was becoming something she rather enjoyed.

Once the footman had helped Lucy down, he held out a hand for Isabel. She reached out—then changed her mind. "No, thank you, Douglas. I shan't come in just yet." Calling to her coachman, she asked him to take her to Bow Street.

The carriage door closed with a satisfying clunk. Through the window, Isabel saw Lucy's pale face, surprised, in the doorway of the house. But then the carriage rolled away, and she tugged the pencil and pocketbook of paper from her reticule and began to scribble notes.

When she finished, just as the carriage pulled up before the court building, she tucked her items away again. After a brief hesitation, she tugged off her ring and tucked it into her reticule too.

Not because she was going to see Callum Jenks. Just because it didn't feel as if it belonged on her finger anymore.

Chapter Five

"I've cleared my case load, Fox," Callum told the magistrate. "You said if I had time, I could pursue further inquiry into the Chapple case."

"Jenks. No."

"I recall it perfectly, sir. You said that once I—"

"I shouldn't have made the offer." Speaking below the ever-present clamor in the courtroom, Augustus Fox eased his bulk into the seat behind his bench. "Nothing more about that business with Sir Frederic Chapple. It's not possible."

"It *is* possible," Callum said. "I just need your blessing to—"

"Jenks. No," Fox said again. "You know I'd give a different answer if I could. But as matters stand, we're lucky Chapple didn't ask for an apology."

"An *apology*?" Callum spat out the word. "For letting him return to his soft life without any consequences?"

"He did spend nearly a year in prison," Fox said mildly, searching through the case notes before him. "Ah, is Janey appearing before me again today? Good to see a familiar face. Hmm, a shopkeeper has accused her of picking his pocket. Must've been off her game."

"Let her off with a warning," Callum said. Janey was one of the officers' best informants in the area. The occasional stolen purse was worth the trade.

"I'll fine her this time, I think. We've been seeing her too often of late. If she truly did pick a pocket, she'll have the means to pay it."

Fox looked up, taking in the crowd before the railing that separated the bench from the rest of the courtroom. The room was not large, and it seemed full of arms and legs and indignant gestures, drab clothing, and the occasional bright feathered bonnet. It smelled of wet wool and recent rain. "Are you *certain* you cleared your case load?"

"That's why half these people are here," Callum said. "Petty thieves, the man who's been smashing shop windows along James Street, and another fool holding a mock auction."

He tried one more time. "You know it's not right, sir. The baronet might have spent a time in prison, but my brother is *dead*. It's unjust for Sir Frederic to blame his dead conspirators for his own crime."

Fox's heavy brows knit over his large blade of a nose. "I've never argued that it was. But we haven't the evidence or means to open the case again. You know that."

He rubbed a hand over his eyes, sighing. "On a similar note, I'm quite certain Angelus has fixed the games in that gambling hell in Great Earl Street. But getting proof of anything related to him, especially in Seven Dials . . ." With a harrumph, he jammed the curled, powdered wig onto his head and took up his gavel.

Angelus again. The man was everywhere, but he couldn't be pinned down. Rather like the wind, or the yellow fog that crept over the pavement on a quiet London night.

Callum gave the magistrate a curt nod, accepting his dismissal. Fox was a voice for justice, but he was only one man, and there were those with voices much louder and more powerful. Voices not for justice, but for secrecy and gain, and Sir Frederic had blended them in a harmony that lifted him free. Likely he had already left London, if he'd truly been released from Newgate yesterday as he'd expected.

But Callum was an Officer of the Police, and there were always more cases. An endless stream of victims and criminals. They all needed attention. Some needed help. Some got under his skin; some caught him about the heart.

Turning away from Fox, Callum shoved through the hinged gate in the railing—only to be bookended at once by a pair of lanky redheads.

"How do you do, storm cloud?" said his fellow officer, Charles Benton. "Didn't get the answer you wanted from old Foxy, eh? Still on about that Royal Rewards case?"

"Leave him be." His twin sister, Cassandra, pulled a face at Charles. "He was fond of his brother. Though if elder Jenks was anything like you, Charles, I cannot understand why."

Callum shook his head. Always bickering, always together, the Bentons looked as similar as if they'd stepped out of *Twelfth Night*. Yes, Callum knew his Shakespeare right enough, and there was little difference to speak of between the twin brother and sister. Both were tall and wiry with a strong jaw, though Cass's chin was softened by a cleft and her features by a wide smile.

"It's fine," Callum lied. "Doesn't bother me in the slightest. The Royal Rewards case was a year ago. I'm content just to keep busy."

"You're a fair liar, but I can always tell." Cass tweaked his nose. "Your nostrils flare when you're lying, as if your own words stink."

Callum clapped a hand over his nose and tried to glare at her, but it was impossible to stay out of temper around Cass. She was always sunny, thriving on the energy of the court and never forgetting a detail of a case. It was a shame she couldn't become an officer. She'd likely have been the best on Fox's team, not even excepting Callum himself.

"Hullo, hullo." Charles elbowed him. "If you want to

keep busy, Jenks, there's a prime piece to occupy you. Looks like a nob. What do you s'pose she's doing here?"

"Janey probably stole her purse," grumbled Cass.

Dropping his hand to his side, Callum looked in the direction his fellow officer indicated. And he was grateful for all his practice keeping a stone face, for if Charles and Cass knew how his heart thudded at the sight of Lady Isabel Morrow slipping around the edge of the courtroom, they'd have teased him mercilessly.

Instead, he managed blandly, "I'm acquainted with the lady. She has engaged me for—"

"A few sweaty nights?" Charles laughed.

Callum rolled his eyes. "Never mind. It was going to be a fascinating tale, and now I won't tell you."

"Charles, you are such a ruiner!" His sister batted him on the arm. "Jenks, who is she?"

Grudgingly, he revealed Isabel's name. Cass, with her alarming memory, recalled the Morrow case at once.

"That poor woman," she breathed. "To see her husband accidentally shot, just like that. And now she's in some sort of trouble again?"

"Definitely not," Callum said firmly. "A person can solicit help without being in trouble."

He waved off his friends, then shoved his way through the clamorous crowd toward Lady Isabel. Today she was in gray again, with a funny sort of black bonnet over her hair. Unmistakably a lady, yet in her sober garb she drew no notice from the impatient sorts around her. It might as well have been a disguise.

"My lady," he said when he reached her side. The way she smiled up at him did nothing to slow the thump of his heart. "I didn't expect to see you here. Do you need assistance?" *Did you come to see me?*

"I have news," she replied. "About our artistic venture. I'd no idea the courtroom would be so crowded, though. Should I tell you here, or is there a quieter location?"

Callum glanced at the large timepiece on the wall, though the drift of shadows would have given a more accurate notion of the hour. Midafternoon, drawing on three o'clock, and Fox had still to hear the latest cases.

Callum *could* stay to help, nudging miscreants along. He *could* take evidence from people waiting; collect fines from those whose judgments had already been passed down.

Or he could slip off with Lady Isabel Morrow and let Charles Benton carry the load for once.

"Come with me," he decided. "I know just the place."

"It doesn't look private, but no one will listen to anything we say here," Callum told Lady Isabel. "If we went back to my rooms, my landlady would be sure to listen at the door."

"Wouldn't it be scandalous for me to go to your rooms?" She looked around at the public room, brows lifted, taking it all in.

"Not to us. Not if we were only talking. Which is what we'll do here. Unless you want to eat too." He clamped his mouth shut so he wouldn't continue uttering silly little sentences.

The Boar's Head on Hart Street was named for the tavern favored by Shakespeare's Falstaff, which was the sort of indulgence theatrical folk loved. Though actors were rare birds who flocked together in their own favored haunts, the Boar's Head was pinned halfway between the theaters in Covent Garden and Drury Lane. Thus, it collected stray actors and their patrons, as well as the everyday working folk of the surrounding streets, and no one looked twice at an odd new face. As it was but a quick jog from Bow Street, Callum had eaten many a meal here, met with many an informant.

It was solidly respectable, but that was about the only compliment he could give it. He saw the public room as Lady Isabel must: dark and cool and a little dingy, its days of fashion left behind a century before. If one were to create a room opposite that of her home's drawing room, it would look much like the one in which they stood.

"I have never been in a place like this," observed Lady Isabel.

Callum held his tongue against more silly little sentences—these ones questions. *Are you afraid? Is it too plain? Do you feel as if you're visiting a menagerie?* More than once, he'd encountered a wealthy person who treated him as if he were a different species entirely.

"Hmm," was all he said.

"Your evergreen response." She looked as if she was trying not to smile, then only shrugged. "Until today, I had never been in the Bow Street magistrate's court either. It's time I went to more places. Do you want something to eat while we are here, or only to talk?"

And that was that. It was a place, and the people were people, and if she hadn't still been oh-so-Lady Isabel Morrow-ish in her half-mourning gown with her blue-blooded pedigree, he would have been sorely tempted to gather her in his arms and plant a smacking great kiss on her lips.

Instead, he crossed to the bar, where he ordered and paid for two pints of porter. "And one for yourself," he told the barman.

The grizzled man caught the coins with thanks. "Sally will bring 'em right over."

A trio of rough-looking men sat at the table in the corner that Callum preferred. Striding over, he leveled a glare at them. "Gentlemen, it's time for you to go."

For a few seconds, their gazes held his. Then with grumbles and curses, they got up from their seats. Edging around the table, they touched their caps to Lady Isabel and scowled at Callum.

"You have a supernatural ability, Officer." Lady Isabel

sounded surprised. "I've not seen a glare have that withering effect since I was presented to the Queen in 1808."

Callum was tempted to leave her with the impression that he possessed a stare more powerful than a weapon, but conscience forced him to admit the truth. "One of those men was my brother Jamie. He and the other two work at my parents' grocery. I was being literal when I told them it was time to go. It's far too early for the dinner hour."

"Another brother," she mused, and he realized she must have put together his name with that of the dead guard from the Royal Rewards case the year before.

"That's all of us remaining," he said shortly. "Jamie. Me. And one sister too. Here, have a seat."

He put two fingers to his mouth and whistled, the custom here for summoning the barmaid. The sound hung above the low patter of speech. When the dreamy young barmaid drifted over, pints of porter in hand, Callum deferred to Lady Isabel.

"I'll have whatever the gentleman recommends," she said. So he ordered a loaf of bread and a pot of jam.

When the barmaid left, taking away the tankards left behind by the three previous customers, Lady Isabel asked, "Does Angelus ever come here? Would you know him by sight?"

Callum wiped at a sticky spot on the table. "Maybe. He's good with disguise. One doesn't usually find out about him until after he leaves. I've never heard of him coming here, though. Why?"

Her mouth pressed into a hard line. "I almost think I'd offer to settle Ardmore's debts myself, if I met Angelus. It's not as though I'm short on paintings."

"You're finding criminal behavior more difficult than you'd assumed?"

Her lips curved. "Doesn't that speak well of my character?"

"My lady, I've always thought well of it." Too much. He cleared his throat, turned the subject. "You wanted to tell me something, you said. You have information about the *Primavera*?"

"The Butler-celli, I've started calling it in my mind. Yes. I paid a call earlier this afternoon, and I hope you'll be pleased by what I found." Laying her reticule atop the table, she drew out a pocketbook. A gold ring clacked out onto the tabletop with it, a sound that somehow carried through the loud public room. Everyone recognized the sound of precious metal.

Callum slapped a hand down on the ring, catching it before it rolled off the table. Slowly, carelessly, he looked around the room—and anytime a curious gaze caught his, he held it until it fell away.

Returning his gaze to the table, he lifted his hand gingerly. "Your wedding ring?" Yes, it was; her ring finger was bare. "Why did you remove it?"

She snagged the band, then stuffed it back into the reticule. "It was time."

This was all she had a chance to say before the barmaid glided back with a crusty loaf of warm brown bread on a platter, plus a pot of jam. Callum flipped her the payment in coins, and she caught them and dropped them into her apron pocket before wandering off.

"This is the second time I've been given tea today," Lady Isabel observed. "Doesn't that jam look good?"

The pot had likely served many others, had many knives in it. But it *did* look good. It was a tempting plummy color, with whole currants in it, and it smelled darkly tart and pleasant.

But. "There's no tea here. Do you want to order some?"

She waved a hand. "No, no. Tea is not only a drink. It is a ritual. People feed each other when they want to be together."

"Do you . . . want to be with me?" He swallowed heavily. Mustn't let his eagerness creep into his voice.

She looked at him with some surprise. "Of course I do. I have to tell you about the Duke of Ardmore's house."

"Of course," he agreed, and drowned his disappointment with a swallow of porter. It was bitter and strong.

When he set down his tankard, she opened the little book of paper and showed him the notes she'd written down. Precise and detailed, in a clear and flowing hand. "You've a good eye," he said. He noted the position of the painting. The number of windows. The type of latch—

"I tried to draw it," she explained, "but it was difficult. It's the same as the latches on my drawing room windows, so the next time you're at my house, you can work with them."

"Will I be at your house again?"

"I certainly hope so."

He raised a brow, holding her gaze. Her cheeks suffused with color.

"Why, Lady Isabel." That was all he needed to say for the blush to deepen. Then manners dictated that he pull back. "I'd be honored."

She shook her head, smiling. "Rascal."

It was pleasant, joking together. And he realized, with a flash of lightning clarity, that he *liked* Lady Isabel Morrow. His attraction to her aside, his determination to see justice done aside—he liked being with her.

He didn't like being with many people. He'd liked his brother Harry, of course. Cass and Charles, in small doses. His other fellow officers and Fox were agreeable to work with.

His remaining family? That was more complicated. He wished he liked being with them, but being in their company involved so many strings and weights and obligations that it was easier to keep a courteous distance.

But Lady Isabel, yes. He liked her. Very much.

In a physical sense, he knew her with deepest intimacy. Yet there were so many things about her, great and small, that he did not know. The air between them seemed composed of questions.

"What is your favorite food?" he blurted.

She flipped forward a page in the little book. "Why? Do you want to order it?"

"I only wondered. It might be relevant to the case," he mumbled, not missing the humor in her eyes.

"Let me think." After cutting a slice of the dark bread, she spread black-currant jam over it from crust to crust. "If it could have a bearing on our attempt to retrieve the Butlercelli, I must give you an accurate answer."

He snorted.

Her expression turned faraway. "I have it." Without seeming to realize it, she handed the perfectly jammed bread to him. "When I was six years old, my father took my brother and me to the seaside. My brother was eighteen then, and he was remarkably patient with me. One day, we spent hours collecting oysters and clams and little shrimps and winkles in a big pot of salt water, and we boiled them over a driftwood fire and ate them so hot we burned our fingers. I was footsore and sun-browned the next day, but oh, it was worth it. I've not had anything so delicious since."

Then she blinked, laughing. "That's a much longer answer than you were expecting, I'll warrant."

"No, no." He could have listened to her speak for hours, telling him whatever she wanted him to know. "But it was different from what I expected."

"You thought it would be all lobster patties and spun sugar, did you?"

Yes. "It wouldn't be wise of me to assume."

"Yet people do all the same. And at this distance in time . . . well. It's probably only a trick of memory, or I'm recalling the adventure of it. Either way, I don't suppose one can get freshly boiled sea creatures here." She sat up and added brightly, "So. What's your favorite food?"

He regarded the sliced bread with jam, still held uneaten in his hand. "This is good."

"You are teasing me," she said. "Fine, so be it. I shall become all business again."

He took an enormous bite of the bread, savoring the sweetness of the jam. "Go ahead, then," he said through a deliberately full mouth. It was not the best thing he'd ever eaten, but it was the only thing he'd eaten that she had given him. Which made it at least twenty-five percent more delicious.

Oblivious to his mooning thoughts, she drew the little book back toward her. "Let's see. You saw the bits about the windows and the latches. I should like to leave no trace that we've been there. I don't want the duke to know his painting was switched, or even that anyone was there at all."

Callum finished his bite. "Which means the two dogs must be dealt with." He leaned closer to her, squinting at the page. "What is this next note—'cake for dogs'? I can't be reading that right."

"You are. It is not a brilliant idea, but it's the best I've had so far. Lucy—my ward, you remember—is going to try coaxing Brinley with cakes to be quiet. If it works, we could do the same with Ardmore's dogs. Only those will be dosed with laudanum."

"I retract my earlier comment that you are stymied by the criminal mind. Clearly you understand it well."

As he'd hoped, she laughed. "But I am also a proper lady, Officer Jenks, and if I need to collect more information, I can pay another proper call with Lucy. Lady Selina dubbed Lucy the sweetest girl in the world, so we would be welcomed."

Callum chewed thoughtfully at the final bite of bread. "I'm missing something. Just how large is Lady Selina's acquaintance?"

"You're not missing a thing. 'The sweetest girl in the world' is understood to mean a young woman of tolerably pleasant manners. 'The prettiest girl in the world' is a young woman of middling to great attractiveness. Often a girl is the prettiest *and* the sweetest, which means she might sit out only a few dances at a ball due to the lack of gentlemen."

Every group had its own codes. The lilting rhyme-slang of the Cockneys, the rough cant of thieves in the East End. It only made sense that the ton would have a secret language too. "Thank you for translating. Now, are you going to join me in food or drink?"

She took a sip of her porter. When she set down the tankard, she looked into it with some caution. "Isn't it bitter?" She took another swallow. "I think I like it, though." Another swallow. "Maybe. I'm not sure." Another, then she set aside her tankard with a thoughtful look. "No, I prefer tea."

Callum hid a smile behind his own pint. "You must come for tea at my lodging sometime. It'll be perfectly respectable, because my landlady will be eavesdropping, and it is good tea. I always get it from my parents' shop."

"The grocery, is that right? Where your brother Jamie works?"

"The very one."

She looked puzzled. "Only imagine, seeing one's brother often enough to drink tea from a family shop and boot him from his seat in a pub. I hardly ever see my brother."

"Not all brothers are created equal. Harry, my eldest brother, was as fine a man as you'll ever meet. Jamie and I have never got on as well."

"Too different?"

Callum chuckled. "I suspect we're too similar, my lady."

"Oh, heavens. You needn't use the honorifics all the time. Really, you know more about me than anyone else, so you might as well call me Isabel."

Knowing about wasn't the same as *knowing*, but if he had his way, he'd turn the first into the second. "Thank you. Isabel it is." He tasted the name on his lips, sweet and ringing. "And my Christian name is Callum, if you wish to use it."

"I know." She gave her pint a quarter-turn, then turned it back. "I overheard someone mention it during your investigation of Morrow's death. It was an unusual name, so I remembered it."

His name was only two syllables, yet the fact that she'd known it and remembered it felt like a grand gift. It was warm, to be remembered. A pleasant sort of warmth, like a sip of brandy when one came inside from winter weather. It warmed one from the inside, from the pit of the belly to the tingling fingertips.

This was again the sort of moment when a man of gentle birth might take a woman's chin in hand and kiss her. But he was a plain man of plain stock, so he only made a joke. "It's clearer than ever, you've a natural sleuthing ability. I'm fortunate that you turned your talents to the side of justice, if not precisely to the law."

This made her laugh, and they clinked their tankards together with mock ceremony. "So." He kept a straight face, though inside that steady warmth still buoyed him. "I must return to Bow Street. May I get you a hackney first—Isabel?"

She looked surprised by the new familiarity; then she smiled. "No, my carriage is waiting outside the court. If I may walk back with you, I'll meet it there."

"You left your carriage on Bow Street? Where anyone might recognize it?" Callum stood, then held out a hand to help her from her seat.

"You sound dismayed. Will it not be safe?"

"It's safe enough. But if any of your acquaintance sees it, they'll suspect you of some scandalous crime. Why else would you be at the Bow Street magistrate's court?"

"Nonsense. I could not create a scandal if I tried." But she looked much struck by the idea.

As they left the Boar's Head, her hand on his arm, he remained aware of the gulf between them. Not one of distance, but of birth and fortune. If not for one chance after another, they would never have met at all.

And yet. She had narrowed the gulf by inviting him to use her name. By drinking porter with him in a pub. By trusting him with embarrassing truths about her marriage.

By taking off her wedding ring?

He wasn't sure how narrow the gulf could become between a grocer's son and a marquess's daughter. But given time and opportunity, he was damned well going to find out.

Chapter Six

Isabel slipped around the edge of the house, drawing a plain brown cloak more tightly about her body. Beneath the cloak, she wore the gown her upper housemaid donned for her half-days off: secondhand and cheap, a dark blue printed fabric that showed neither dirt nor wear. Her hair was covered by a straw bonnet studded with shiny beads, another find from her housemaid's quarters. Bless Polly; she'd been willing enough to sell these to Isabel for "someone who needed them." Likely she already had her eye on something else in a secondhand shop that would impress Douglas, the footman.

Coming from the servants' entrance, Isabel would be invisible to anyone passing on Lombard Street who might recognize Lady Isabel Morrow stepping out of the front door while dressed in expensive gray.

Success! She'd joined the people walking on the pavement without drawing a second glance. Turning her steps eastward, she set off toward the West India Docks. The sky was blue, with sooty fingertips of smoke drifting from chimneys here and there. The sun shone mildly, and the air carried the not-unpleasant smell of horses. She was free on this pretty spring day, and she was taking a step toward righting a wrong. As she walked, she hummed a little tune.

Before she'd walked past three houses, a hand seized her shoulder. "Lady Isabel."

Her heart tripped and hammered. Should she run? No, better to brazen it out. She shook off the touch and whipped around, an excuse already on her lips.

It dissolved at once. "Oh! Callum Jenks." The sight of him brought instant calm. After having tea, or porter, with him the day before, she hadn't expected to see him again so soon. "What brings you here?"

"I'm disguised as a servant and off on a mysterious errand." He frowned, his eyes a shadow beneath his low-brimmed hat. "Wait. My mistake. That's what you're doing."

"So I am." Isabel stood on her tiptoes to whisper in his ear. "I'm going to call upon Butler. He lives near the West India Docks."

She was rather proud of herself for arranging this errand. Callum did not seem to share this emotion. The hand that had taken hold of her was now clenched in a fist at his side. "That's most unwise."

"No, it *is* wise. He needs to know of our plan about the paintings, so he doesn't later betray the truth. I wrote to him, and he agreed to meet me this afternoon."

Callum drew her aside, tugging her down a step into the railed-off area before the Pettibones' house. "You are calling on him? Not he on you?"

"I didn't want to raise questions. I thought it wiser not to be seen having a new caller, and Butler is rather conspicuous." This was putting the matter mildly. No one who saw Butler would forget having met him.

"I've been a recent caller at your house."

"Yes, but you are not conspicuous. You make a point of it."

From top to toe, he dressed plainly and forgettably. His form and face, though most attractive, were not of the sort that drew the eye of strangers. They were the sort that one's eye settled on more and more often as one got to know him, until it was difficult to imagine how one had not at once admired his appearance.

Isabel flushed, her own thoughts bolder than she'd expected.

"Even so." The line of his mouth was hard. "You weren't going to tell me about this? It's not safe for you to go alone."

"I have a pistol." Its weight was heavy in the pocket of her gown. It was the same pistol that had killed Andrew. The realization made her shudder.

"Can you use it?" Callum's fingers caught one of her forearms.

"Yes." How interesting. The knuckles of his hand were white, though his grip was gentle. "You are concerned about my well-being? There are hours before sunset, and Butler told me daylight was a safe time to call."

"Easy for him to promise."

Isabel laid a hand over the one Callum had placed on her arm—then lifted it off. "Let me by, please. I need to move along now."

As she climbed back up to the pavement, he was right behind her. "You're not going without me."

"All right." She waited for him.

When he stood at her side, he looked at her with curiosity. "No argument? You won't try to slip away?"

"You are thinking of me as one of your criminal informants," she chided. "I'm your partner, remember? Truly, I'd rather go with you. But I didn't want to ask. I know time is short, and mine is an extra job for you atop your real employment."

They set off eastward again, weaving between servants carrying baskets and passing by carriages and wagons with jingling harnesses and well-groomed horses. After some silence, Callum said, "Every job I take is a real one. Including yours."

Isabel darted a sideways glance at him. He was studying

her as he walked. How did he do that, without tripping over everything in front of him? He must have the sharp sight of a bird.

"We are already taking enough risks, Isabel. Please don't put yourself in any danger."

"Why, Callum, you truly do care about my safety," she teased.

"Hazard of the profession."

"I'd have expected your profession to have the opposite effect. To make you jaded."

He looked rather grumpy at this, so she did not press him. A smile played on her lips; a tune wanted to be hummed again. She had been a little afraid to walk to the docks alone, but she'd chastised herself for this fear, reminding herself how many new places she'd gone this week. This would be but one more, and she had taken pains not to look like a target for any thieves that might roam around.

But with Callum walking beside her, she wasn't afraid at all. Who would know the streets of London better than a Bow Street Runner—beg pardon, Officer of the Police?

Lombard Street renamed itself Fenchurch and swept its way north, so they took a jog southward onto Rood to continue their direct path to the docks. "Thank you for coming with me," Isabel said.

"I happened to be in the neighborhood," he grunted.

"You were in the—no, impossible. Bow Street is not an easy distance from my house."

"Nor are the docks, yet here we are walking to them."

"Because they are our destination."

"Maybe you were mine."

In what way did he mean that? The words were quiet, powerful. Each one was like a marble dropping to the floor: it resounded, then rolled about within Isabel, stirring up confusion and wonder.

He drew her arm into his grasp, fingers covering hers. Neither of them were wearing gloves, and the unaccustomed bareness of hand on hand was a sweet shock to Isabel's tingling nerves.

Yet he sounded distracted. When she looked up at him, questioning, she realized he was scanning their surroundings. Top to bottom, left to right, again and again.

Isabel peered. Squinted. All she saw were the familiar tidy rows of stacked-up town houses. "What are you looking for?"

"Anything that's not as it should be." He touched the brim of his hat. "Beg your pardon. It's a habit of mine, but it's not good company."

"No, it's fine. I want to see how you act when you're investigating something. What you would do if I weren't here with you."

"Besides have my hands to myself? Which I don't plan to do this time."

"I didn't ask that of you." Holding fast to someone else—it was nice. As if he was looking out for her as well as the rest of London.

Her feet peeked from below the hem of the skirt with each step, shod in boots of fine kid. "Oh! I thought I'd planned so well, but I didn't borrow shoes. Now my disguise is incomplete."

"Don't worry about it," he said dryly. "You're walking with me. No one would assume your boots to be anything but battered as mine."

"Brinley loves them just as they are," she replied. "May we talk, or will conversation be too distracting as you look around?"

"No more than simply being with you is distracting."

"I . . ." Hmm. She wasn't sure how to answer that. It sounded as if it ought to have been a compliment, but his tone was so matter-of-fact that it could have meant anything from glumness to irritation.

"What is on your mind?" he asked.

His strides were long, eating the pavement in great

stretches. She scurried a little to stay at his side, keeping their arms linked. "Were you near my house because of a case?"

"I'm sure I could think of a case to bring up."

"That is not quite an answer." She thought. "Yes, it is. You weren't there because of a case. Why, then?" She moistened her lips; her throat and mouth felt dry.

"In truth," he said, neatly dodging a governess with a pushchair, "it *was* because of a case. Yours. I have been thinking about when to time the switch of the paintings. Two nights hence, there will still be very little moon. I suggest we switch the paintings that night."

"So soon?"

"Yes. The moon is waxing, and too much light at night will be our enemy."

"That makes sense. And I know we must act soon to catch the painting before it leaves the duke's household." All the better, then, that she was drawing Butler into the scheme today.

As they crossed the shadow of the familiar old spire of St. Margaret Pattens, Callum drew her to a stop. "Let's get a hackney rather than walk onward."

"I don't want to be conspicuous."

"I understand that. But conspicuous is better than hurt or dead, and we'll be crossing the edges of Spitalfields and Whitechapel. The major streets are all right, but it takes only a few seconds for someone to dart from an alley and— hmm." He pressed his lips together.

"Do I want you to finish that sentence?"

"Probably not. And the smell of the tanneries alone will have you staggering on your feet."

She agreed, and Callum hailed the first hackney he saw. It was pulled by a shaggy black horse with two white stockings and a comfortably round belly. Like the horse, the hack was worn but well-kept, with the crest of its former owner a faded shape beneath the black paint on the carriage door.

The jarvey touched his cap to them, but when he heard the destination, he whistled and demanded payment in advance.

Callum hesitated.

Isabel understood at once: he hadn't the money. "I have a purse. Hold a moment."

Drawing her hands free, she found the purse of coin she had pinned within the pocket of her gown. She had to wrestle with the pin a bit to get it free. By the time she pulled out the required fare, it probably looked as if she'd had a tiny fistfight with herself.

They took their seats within, the only passengers in the small carriage. The squabs were slick with wear, and the interior bore the scents of pipe tobacco and old hay.

"I should have paid for the hackney," Callum muttered as he settled onto the rear-facing seat.

"Merely because you're a man? Please do not think that I have such an expectation." Isabel smiled. "How rude that would be of me to put you to any cost. This is my errand, upon which you were kind enough to join me."

He said nothing, but she felt his scrutiny beneath the brim of his hat. It was an annoying hat, allowing him to look at whatever he wanted without his eyes being visible.

As the hackney drove them eastward, traffic increased in volume and decreased in size. Rather than glossy private carriages, here were carts pulled by donkeys or men. Children darted about, their parents nowhere to be seen. Pie sellers and broadsheet sellers and publicans all called out their wares, creating a clamor over which the ring of horseshoes on cobbles was almost inaudible.

"You must think me naïve," she said.

"Because of this errand?" At her nod, he said, "Not at all. I think you well-intentioned. That is not the same as naïve."

She wasn't quite certain what street they were on now. Her eyes roved the lines of the structures fronting the pavement, the eddies of people and wheeled traffic. "I should have known the city would change wildly as I traveled across it. This street is too busy, maybe, to be perfect."

"What if it is?" he asked. Never was there any sort of condemnation in his voice. She'd once felt he was interviewing her. Now she wondered if he was simply curious. All the time, always, about everything.

"If the surface is imperfect in Mayfair, it must be fixed or one will be judged."

"Being judged isn't a bad thing. It's how some people go free."

"Spoken like one who spends a great deal of time in a magistrate's court." Now it was her turn to look at him aslant. "It's how some are found guilty, too."

"Which are you, Lady Isabel?"

As the hackney jounced and bounced them over every uneven cobble in the street, she considered. Her house, too large. Her clothing, still gray. The invitations she hadn't received during her mourning, and the friends who had stayed, and those who would never speak to her again. "I think I'm finding my way to freedom. And I think I would like myself more if I were braver."

"Who would not wish to be braver? Yet in the matter of the Duke of Ardmore's painting, you are brave enough to do the right thing for the sake of someone other than yourself. There are many who are not so brave."

"I don't want to compare myself to the lowest. I compare myself to what I think I ought to be."

"And that is?"

As she had in the public house the day before, she considered her answer. Really thought about it, until she hit upon the truth—and smiled. "A woman who wears red when she wants to, or the blue of a summer sky. Who chooses her own menu. Who eats when she wishes, and not when the clock says it's proper. And who makes the sort of friends who gladden her heart, not those who can help her meet some goal set by someone else."

What a life that would be. Just speaking the words lifted her spirits.

"Ah. You think you ought to be braver for yourself, then."

A bump bounced her from her seat, cracked her teeth together. She rubbed at her jaw. "It's more difficult than being brave for someone else."

He leaned forward, bracing his elbows on his knees. "Do you know, I agree with you. My brother Harry died for his fellow guards, and for the dull metal that the world says is worth more than a man's life. What would it have taken for him to walk away, to give up his post and say, 'Damn what everyone else tells me to do, I'm going to look out for myself'?"

"I wish for your sake that he had. Yet when you put the matter in those words, it sounds so selfish."

"Not at all." He edged a boot forward, bumping the toe of hers with his. "Miss Wallace is fortunate in your guardianship. Most people don't have anyone who looks out for them. Not even the people who love them. It's hard for them to think outside of their own wants and wishes."

"And what about you?"

"It's my job to think outside of that. Otherwise I'd never solve a case."

"Why is it your job?"

He leaned back, pushing up the brim of his hat to regard her with wary eyes. "Because it is literally my job. I get paid to do it."

"*Callum.*" She knocked his boot with hers. "*Why* is that your job? Rather than working at the family grocery, or . . . or being an opera singer?"

"I can't sing a note. Other than that—I wanted to be like Harry, maybe. Protecting people. And I didn't want to work in the grocery, because my family expected me to." He smiled thinly. "Just being contrary, I suppose. Though it worked out all right."

"Who looks out for you, though?"

He tugged his hat back down and settled against the squabs, arms folded. "So many questions."

"Hazard of your profession, isn't it?"

"I'm usually asking, not being asked. And I look out for myself."

Pat. A raindrop slapped the window. Isabel turned toward it, watching a second fall, then another. As they ran down like tears, she watched the city change around her. The buildings grew taller and narrower, the streets spiderwebbed into lanes and alleys. Rain grayed the sky, dimmed the light.

Into the silence, Callum added, "I'll look out for you, too. That's why I'm here."

Brows lifted, she turned back to him. "Why will you look out for me? I suppose it is because I summoned you, and I hired you to help me."

"You tried to hire me. But I can't take payment for breaking the law. Besides, looking out for you seems like the right thing to do."

Was he *blushing*? It was difficult to tell in the shadowy carriage, where his face was half-hidden anyway. "Thank you," she said simply, not wishing to embarrass him. "I am glad that you came here, and that you want to be sure I'm safe."

"You've been through enough. Shouldn't be involved in another case without help." He sat forward again, craning his neck to look out of the window. "Can't tell if we're getting close yet."

Isabel was struck, as she ogled her surroundings, by how much of London she didn't know. She'd never had to know. And how swiftly a street could alter! One side of a street might be in genteel poverty, one side might be comfortably well off. At any place, a dank alley, from which a human form peered and lurked, could shoot off, and it gave her a most unpleasant prickling feeling.

When she mentioned this observation to Callum, he said, "It depends on the landlords. And on the Watch in the area.

Places have personalities, as people do, and that determines what sort of people want to live there."

The observation rang true. Certainly her own house had a personality: Andrew's. "I never realized that before. It's a privilege, isn't it, never to have to think about how other people live?"

"It is," he said gravely. "But I wouldn't wish it away from you. I'd only wish there was less for you to be shielded from. Fewer people who lived in desperate circumstances."

They passed by the tanneries, close enough for Isabel to catch the stench of rotten urine. Thankful for the rain and the quick-stepping hackney horse, she held her breath until they were past. As the rain continued to fall, the crowds thinned—though in these narrower streets away from Isabel's plummy borough, they merely drew aside. In each alleyway, people looked and lurked. Buildings tilted forward or to one side, as if whispering about each other to their neighbors. *Did you see . . . Can you believe . . .* The pavement was broken here, ragged and uneven, and filth trickled down the middle of the street in a makeshift gutter.

It smoothed out a bit shortly before the hackney pulled to a stop. Callum opened the door, then assisted Isabel down.

"I don't wait by the docks," the jarvey called down. "Good luck to ye, gov, if you wants a ride back."

With a snuffle, the black horse shook its harnessed head, sending raindrops flying.

"We'll sort it out," said Callum. "Thank you."

The hackney departed, and they turned to face their surroundings. The docks were a long and narrow portion of the city, with streets that dived down to the Thames in stone staircases of great anciency. The city's lifeblood, the river was endlessly busy with everything from barges to one-person punts. It smelled of oil and old fish and refuse.

Butler's residence was in a set of rooms near the West India Docks, a neighborhood still respectable by virtue of being new. They found the right building after asking one of the warehouse guards. When they stepped inside, shaking off rain-damp hats, they were greeted by a tidy entryway with neat whitewashed walls and a sharply angled staircase. Up one floor, then another, then another still, until they were just beneath the attics.

Following Butler's direction, Isabel located the correct door. When Callum shot her a questioning look, she nodded. "Go ahead, knock. Please."

He gave a sharp rap at the door. In an instant, it was flung open, and the doorway was filled with the massive form of Andrew Morrow's artist acquaintance.

Isabel had met Butler in passing once or twice, as she had many of Andrew's circle. Though it had been more than a year, probably closer to two or three, he looked exactly the same: light brown skin, short-cropped black hair with long side whiskers, a luxuriant mustache that curled up at the ends. This afternoon, he wore a paint-stained smock over his coat, shirt, and trousers; the unmistakable heavy odor of linseed oil and the sharp scent of turpentine revealed that he'd been painting.

It was like being in the hidden room again, cramped among blank and covered canvases everywhere and the sense of being at a great height. But the rain made the place cool, and great windows opened the room to a view of the river traffic.

"Lady Isabel! So good to see you again. It has been too long." His voice was low and gentle, with flat vowels that hinted at time in America. "And you've brought a friend to meet me as well!"

As he ushered them inside, she was reminded of his size. He was easily four inches above six feet, and broad and blocky, with hands that swallowed hers as he shook them in greeting.

"Yes, I have. Though he's more than a friend."

"Congratulations!" Butler beamed. "You were far too young to remain a widow forever."

Callum cleared his throat. "I'm an associate as well; that is what the lady meant."

"A friend *and* an associate *and* a romantic partner. Well chosen, Lady Isabel."

Suddenly bashful, she couldn't look at Callum as she corrected Butler's misunderstanding. She then completed the introductions between the two men.

"Is it just Butler, then?" Callum asked.

"Like Angelus," Butler confirmed. "One name. More intimidating." After a beat, he laughed. "Not really. It's Ignatius Butler. But I even made my parents call me by our family name."

"Callum's not my favorite either," said that man. "Call me whatever you like."

"Butler. Jenks." Isabel frowned. She didn't really want to be called Morrow. "Just Isabel for me. We're to be a team now, I hope. Ca—Jenks will help me to retrieve one of your paintings, and I hope that you will assist us as well."

Butler looked disappointed at the lack of a romance, but moved along to business. He began to perch on a high stool, but was caught by the long length of his smock. "Sorry about that." With a roll of his eyes, he untied it and draped it over a handy bit of furniture. Then he seated himself, awaiting further explanation.

"You recall," Isabel began, "that Morrow had you copy original pieces."

"Of course." Butler's brows knit. "I must have painted dozens for him. He never paid me on time, but when he finally got around to it, he paid well." An incline of his head. "*You* paid well, my lady, to be accurate."

"I would never let his final debts go unpaid." She hesitated again. "I must ask you, now, if I can go into your debt. You see, there's a matter with which I want your help. Perhaps you know Morrow sold your copies as the originals?"

She wasn't sure what he'd known, or when, and so she probed carefully. Butler sighed, his great shoulders sagging. "I didn't ask what he did with them, and he didn't tell me. But I suspected as much." A corner of his mouth crimped. "Especially when I saw one of my works hanging in the Pall Mall Picture Gallery."

Callum slid to the edge of the seat, alert as a bloodhound. "I saw that painting too—and thanks to Lady Isabel, I have now seen the original. I could not tell it from your work. I haven't an expert eye, of course, but how do you tell?"

Butler's hands spread wide, as if he were seeing the canvas in his mind. "In that one, there's a drop of blood that wasn't in the original. Just one extra, and I know where. In others, it's a drop of wine, or a tear. Or I put a B in the background somewhere."

"You always leave a clue," Callum mused. "Clever. Sir, you are very talented."

"I know I am," he said simply. "I don't like seeing Botticelli take credit for my work, the old bastard, but money is money. What I really want, though"—he slid from the high stool to pace around the room, dodging canvases—"is to have my art known for my own. I'm more than a copyist. I'm an artist. Here, look at this portrait."

He drew a cover from the canvas on an easel beside the window. Isabel had an impression of vivid color and bright joy that leapt from the canvas. She blinked, wondering, and the lines resolved themselves into the chalk-sketched portrait of a woman from the shoulders up. At an angle from the viewer, her face was tipped roguishly. A stunning blue fluff of a hat and a brilliant lapis-blue gown set off her dark skin. Her lips were soft with pleasure, or maybe a remembered secret. The background was naught but a blur so far.

"Who is she?" Isabel breathed. "She is beautiful. And so real; she looks as if she might speak to us."

"My wife. Angelica." Butler looked proud yet wistful, and he drew the cover back over the painting. "She lives in New York with our daughters. I came to England first to earn their way, and for five years, I've saved what I can to bring them over here. I've almost enough now."

"Morrow was a villain to delay payment to you," Isabel said. "I am sorry for that. Of course, I will pay you for taking part in this plan."

"Oh? How much is she paying you, Jenks?"

Callum met Butler's dark gaze with his own. "Not as much as I'm worth. But then, she couldn't afford what I'm worth."

"It's true," Isabel said primly.

At first, she'd been surprised that he wouldn't accept any payment from her, but now she was glad. It made their every meeting a choice rather than a transaction, and how lovely it was to be chosen.

Butler's laugh began low, then built. "All right." He stuck out a hand. "All right. I'm in. Whatever you have planned, I'm in."

"Hold that promise until you know the details," Isabel said. "This has to do with the Duke of Ardmore."

Butler pulled back his hand, sucked in a deep breath. "So it's true? The money troubles? The deal he struck with Angelus to erase his debt for a painting?"

"There's not a corner of London that doesn't know the duke's private business," Callum noted. "The greater the secret, the quicker the gossip spreads."

"So. It's one of my paintings," Butler guessed. At Isabel's nod, a smile spread over his face. "One of my paintings is set to haul a duke out of debt. My Angelica will be so pleased."

"Best not let that happen," said Isabel. In a rush, she explained her reasoning: the possibility the painting's true provenance would be recognized; the scandal; the destruction of Andrew's reputation; the death of Lucy's chance at a good marriage.

"Pity, though," Butler mused. "I'd like to see all those copies destroyed. Botticelli wouldn't like someone else's work pretending to be his any more than I like the reverse."

"But that would involve going public about Andrew Morrow's fraud," noted Callum. "Or trusting to secrecy and bribes for each family that owns a Butler painting. Or carrying out numerous swaps."

Isabel slumped. "Each suggestion strikes more terror into my heart than the one before. Can we think on the potential scandal later, perhaps after Miss Wallace is happily wed?"

"We should wait," agreed Butler. "It's not the young lady's fault her former guardian set up this tangle."

"*Thank* you," Callum burst out.

At Butler's puzzled look, Isabel explained, "Officer Jenks has told me something similar in the past."

Isabel outlined their plan for a swap that would go undetected by the ducal family.

"But we've got to act quickly." Callum drummed fingers against his knee, thinking. "Two nights from now, the moon will be ideal. We can't wait much longer, or we'll lose the painting to Angelus."

"And there are two dogs to consider," Isabel piped up.

"Large ones," said Callum.

"Loud ones," Isabel added.

"Then we'd best get on with the plan." Butler stood. "Let me order us some tea and sandwiches, and we'll have this out."

He excused himself, thundered down the stairs to speak to the charwoman.

At Callum's side, Isabel sat silent and straight-backed. A little nervous, a lot eager, and with a strange fizzle of something she didn't understand at first. Something buoyant that had nothing to do with the room, or the river winding outside, or even the plan.

No, it was the pleasure of the company, accepting and eager. It wasn't only like righting a wrong. It was like . . . belonging.

Chapter Seven

By the time they left Butler's rooms, the rain had stopped and the daylight was fading. Callum was more relieved than ever that he had happened upon Lady Isabel as she'd left her house. Despite the guards on patrol around the warehouses, the lanterns that winked on one by one as the sky darkened, the London docks were not the sort of place a woman ought to be alone.

"How are you?" he ventured as they began to walk in the direction from which they'd come. Callum scanned their surroundings not only for activity, but for any signs of a hackney.

"Fine. Why? Am I too conspicuous?" She tugged the hood of the dark cloak over her light straw bonnet.

"No. I only wondered about the dark. You mentioned that you have not liked it since the time you were trapped in the hidden space in your house."

"Oh. Thank you." She almost choked on the words. "I am perfectly fine. I am not trapped, you see. And I am with you."

He caught a foot on a loose cobble, taking a great step forward to catch himself. "How you knock me off balance." The step gave him some excuse for the words.

"Stay upright," she teased. "We mustn't draw too much notice."

No, they mustn't. This was the city that existed outside of the gaslights and carriage-lanterns of the ton. The night was loud and roiling with life, with light, laughter, and the occasional drunken man spilling through the door of a public house. From alleys, prostitutes beckoned—and if Callum had his guess, there'd be a man waiting right behind most of them to bop a cully over his head and take his purse.

Nothing he could do about that, unless he wanted to leave Isabel to her fate and go marching into every alley. Nothing he could do about most of the everyday trespasses against the law and civility. The worn-out mothers who shouted at children crying from hunger, the girls from the country who could make no living except on their backs. The street was narrow and crowded, with black smoke turning the sunset bloody and dark.

"How do you make any progress," Isabel wondered, "trying to watch everything as you do? There are so many pie sellers alone, I can't imagine how one would notice— oh!" She halted. "That boy."

So. She'd seen it too: a boy no more than waist-high, nipping food from the wagon of a pork-pie seller occupied with a customer.

"Good eye," Callum said grimly. "According to the law, we could collar him and have him tossed into jail. He can go before a court tomorrow."

"Oh, no! For stealing a pie? No, please. He must be hungry." Isabel hesitated. "Yet the pie seller is probably scraping by on every penny he earns." She turned to Callum. "What would you do if I weren't with you?"

"I'd walk on. I don't get angry at boys who steal food." At the adults who drank away their money instead of providing for their children, yes. At the Prince Regent, who spent hundreds of thousands of pounds a year and had never known a moment's want, certainly. Though such anger helped the city become safer as little as throwing a hungry boy into jail to await a sentence for stealing a pork pie.

"Well, *I'm* not going to walk on. Hold a moment." Isabel rummaged beneath her cloak—digging into a dress pocket, he assumed—then strode over to the pie seller. "Sir, I think you dropped this half-crown. See that you hold tight to your purse."

It was well done. She sniffed as she said it, so it wouldn't sound anything like charity, then stalked back to Callum.

Another child followed her, doubtless trying to sort out the best angle for picking her pocket. Callum caught the lad's eye and gave him an unmistakable signal to shove off.

When Isabel reached his side again, she took his arm as they resumed their walk. He pretended not to notice, and not to think it was the loveliest gesture he'd encountered in some time.

"So many everyday crimes you must encounter every time you venture outside," she mused.

"Sometimes I wish I could stop noticing them. But if I didn't, I couldn't help. Then what good would I be?"

"I know the answer to that question, but I don't suppose you care about anyone's answer but your own." Her voice was quiet and low, cutting beneath the sounds of the city street. A breeze blew at the black smoke overhead, revealing a star that winked before it hid again. "So much to overlook or respond to. How do you decide?"

"I keep in mind the law. Next, I keep in mind my sense of what's right."

She mulled this over. "That makes sense. I wish they always went together."

"The law always goes with someone's sense of what's right. Sometimes that person was a king a few hundred years ago, though. Doesn't do a pie seller or a hungry boy any good."

"Jenksie! Hoo!" A hoot echoed from one of the alleys, and a familiar figure sashayed forward.

"Janey. How do you do?" Callum greeted his informant politely. She surely looked odd to Isabel, draped in any number of shawls and puffed up with petticoats. Sometimes a prostitute, more often a cutpurse, Janey also did a brisk business in stolen clothing and often wore her wares. All the better to hide coins and purses, Callum suspected. He had done his best never to learn the details. If he knew too much, he'd have to arrest her. *Again.* Too much of that and a good informant was lost.

Janey did no more than wave, then return to her conversation with a pair of young men. They looked put out by the interruption, which was likely the point.

Isabel looked rather put out too. Once they'd passed out of hailing distance, she said stiffly, "That was a very pretty young woman."

"Did you think so?"

"Of course. Anyone would think so." A pause. "Do you know her well?"

He suppressed a smile. "As well as I need to. Janey's one of my informants. London is full of people with sharp eyes and ears who could use a coin. We make use of their skills, and they dip into our pockets. Usually we know about it." He darted a glance back over his shoulder. "She was probably too far away to try a dip this evening."

"Are all your informants young and pretty?"

"I'd love to hear you say that in the presence of Toothless Jim. Or old Rance McGillivray, who can't hear a thing without his ear trumpet, but whose eyes are as sharp as a much younger man's. Or Ellen Church, who used to be a mudlark, and who—"

"All right. I take your point."

"Which is that prettiness has nothing to do with being a good informant."

"Maybe not for Toothless Jim." Isabel sidestepped a pile of droppings. "But for Janey, prettiness helps. She'll gather far more information from men if they like the look of her."

Callum craned his neck, looking for a damned hackney stand. "Will she, now. Is that the way of it in high society?"

"Of course it is. Prettiness brings unwarranted advantages."

"You'd know." The words slipped out before he thought better of them.

Isabel choked. "Why, sir, was that a compliment?"

He clamped down on the ragged edge of feeling. "I was calling you pretty, if that's what you're wondering. I don't know if having unwarranted advantages deserves a compliment."

"Nor does the way my face looks, then, as I had nothing to do with its construction. Ah! There is a hackney. Let us hire it, if no one's picked my pocket."

No one had, probably thanks to her long cloak or whatever complex arrangement she'd fashioned with a pocket and a purse. Callum gave the hackney driver an address a street away from Isabel's house.

Her smile was approving. "So we can return as inconspicuously as we left."

Once they descended from the carriage, the walk to the Lombard Street house was quiet, the air startlingly clean, the pavement uncrowded. He wondered if she noted the difference, and what she thought of it if she did.

Waiting at the bottom of the steps, he watched for her to mount them and be let in by the butler. As soon as the door opened to her . . .

Noise. A cacophony of crashes and yips and barks rolling down the steps into the street.

What the devil? Callum pounded up the stairs, ignoring the butler, who held the door, and took Isabel's arm. "Hold, please. Let me see if it's safe."

"Miss Wallace," intoned Selby, "is in the morning room. She is quite safe."

Wordlessly, Isabel and Callum looked at each other—then strode after the sound, following it to the morning room. Why didn't the butler seem bothered? Maybe butlers never seemed bothered. Strange creatures.

When the door opened: chaos.

Yes, this room—specifically, the dog Brinley—was the source of the noise. He ran from one side of the small room to the other, baying his heart out. His path was unobstructed by furniture, as the table had been pushed to one side of the room, its chairs in rude disorder around the edges. Broken cakes and biscuits were scattered across the tabletop, while other dainties remained on silver platters. A young blonde woman, hair falling in disheveled hanks from its pins, was tossing bits of food at the running dog. Candles were lit against the fall of twilight, throwing grotesque moving shadows over the walls.

Above the tumult, a large painting of fleshy nudes peered down curiously. They were spattered with wine from the god Bacchus, but the inhabitants of the room were the ones who truly appeared drunk.

Isabel cleared her throat.

"Oh!" The blonde woman turned as she threw the next object, and it hit Callum on the sleeve. It proved to be an almond.

"Aunt Isabel! I didn't know you were—that is, look! I have been training the dog."

This was the ward, then. The famous Lucy, for whom he had agreed to right a wrong perpetrated by a dead man. She looked young and innocent, with a great fluff of pale hair and the unconcerned movement of one who hadn't yet got used to minding her every word and manner.

The almond fell from Callum's sleeve to the floor. With a *yip* of delight, Brinley darted for the almond and crunched it in his doggy jaws. And then, of course, he began sniffing around Callum's boots.

Callum had polished them, not that the results were impressive. He was never going to achieve a fine gloss like a gentleman's valet could with champagne. But they looked a little nicer, he thought. Or they had before this afternoon's excursion.

Brinley gave a final sniff to the boots, then lifted a leg.

"No, no!" Isabel swooped for the dog, clutching him belly-forward in her arms and aiming him toward the hearth. "Brinley! How could you?"

The beagle looked proud, his tongue lolling from his mouth, as he piddled a stream over the spent coals from the morning fire.

"That's one way to ensure the fire is out." Callum's mouth twitched. "As all seems well, I'll bid you good night."

"Ca—um, Officer Jenks." Isabel set Brinley down carefully. "Please, don't go. You are most welcome." She performed the introductions between Callum and Lucy Wallace.

"I was trying to coax Brinley to be silent and still. But it didn't work, and so I . . ." Lucy trailed off, tucking fallen locks of hair behind her ears and resettling hairpins.

"And so you had a bit of a battle," said Callum. "With cakes and nuts. I understand perfectly. I thank you for the almond. Generally any food thrown at an officer is rotten and inedible."

"Um. You are welcome?" She looked befuddled.

"Have you any ideas for getting a dog to be silent?" Isabel untied her bonnet and cloak, laying both on one of the disarranged chairs. Callum doffed his hat and set it there too.

"That depends on the dog," Callum said.

"This dog," Isabel called over the bark of triumph Brinley emitted when Callum bent to pet the little dog's head. "The loudest dog ever. Surely not even the Duke of Ardmore's dogs are as loud."

Lucy looked quizzical, but only popped a cinnamon biscuit into her mouth.

Callum stood again, dusting his hands against his breeches, and let Brinley resume sniffing about his boots. "The scent of anise seed will make a dog follow. We've had some fun at the Bow Street court tossing anise oil on a fellow who's about to make his rounds."

Isabel looked much struck. "Do they follow calmly?"

Brinley barked. Callum frowned. "No. Not calmly. They become . . . spirited."

"I don't suppose it bears thinking of," decided Isabel. "Though I should love to see the effect on stray dogs when one of your fellow officers passes by with anise trousers. Ah—Lucy, would you take Brinley from the room before he eats our guest's boots?"

This was not an idle question. Brinley was showing his teeth, tilting his head to gnaw at the smooth surface of the boot. Callum shifted his foot back, drawing a mournful yowl from the dog. *Too bad, dog.* He hadn't cleaned his boots for Lady Isabel only to have them consumed by a beagle.

"Of course I will. Brinley! Brinley! Officer Jenks, it was good to meet you." All of this was spoken in a single breath. Then, heedless of Callum's protest, Lucy Wallace brandished a biscuit in each hand and backed from the room, drawing the dog after her.

"She is an agreeable girl." Isabel pressed her hands to pink cheeks. "Dear Lucy. I am glad you made her acquaintance at last."

"You didn't have to send her away," Callum said. "Or Brinley." He felt an interloper in this household, where fine eatables were thrown around like waste and he had blundered into a game that halted because of him.

"I didn't *have* to, no. But I did. Do sit, will you? If we could just retrieve the chairs—there. I do apologize. And would you like some tea?"

Callum shook his head again, but he gingerly accepted a seat beside hers. The chairs were still all askew, and some were scattered over with crumbs and almonds.

And then he recalled himself, patting at his pockets. "If you truly would like tea, I've a parcel of a new variety." He'd got it for his landlady, a robust elderly female who also served as his charwoman. No matter; he'd get more for Mrs. Sockett tomorrow.

The excited lift of Isabel's brows was reward enough for his offer. "Is this from the famous Jenks family grocery?"

"It is." He had escaped from the grocery today with the tea, yes, but also with the usual heavy complement of errands to complete.

Ever since Harry's death, the Jenkses didn't seem to know what to say to each other. The hope of Sir Frederic's trial had glued them together for a while, but that was gone now too. So Callum didn't say much of anything, and his parents needled him for favors.

This time, his brother Jamie had too. That was interesting. Wanted to know about the tea shop next to the grocery, and whether the man selling it was in debt, and to whom. Callum didn't need to be an investigator to suspect that his brother was considering a move toward independence. Yet he was the last son in Jenks and Sons.

The potential for familial awkwardness was not small.

Isabel opened one corner of the parcel and breathed in the scent of the tea leaves. Her smile was a ray of light. "What a fine fragrance. I will ring for Selby, so we can have some of this brewed."

She suited her actions to her words. Once Selby had come and gone with the parcel, she added, "I must meet your family. I have never met a grocer before."

He stuck out his boots, examining the finish. Really, it was just as rough as ever. "Grocers are but ordinary people. They do not perform feats of acrobatics in their shops."

She went slightly pink. "That sounded dreadful, didn't it? So rarefied. I meant rather that I realize how many gaps there are in my life." Then she lifted her chin. "Besides that,

I should like to meet your family. Not because they are grocers, but because they are your family."

"To what end?"

Stretching out a hand toward the table, she dug in the bowl of almonds and whipped one at him. "What is the end, ever, in knowing someone?"

"I'm not the person to answer that. Are you as eager for me to meet your relatives as you are to meet mine?"

She pulled a face. "I wouldn't want anyone to meet my brother."

"Is there some chance I might?"

"I doubt it. He lives in Kent, where my ailing father is still." She folded her hands into a tidy shape in her lap. "Lord Martindale—Martin, I call him—is not a bad man. But he is much my elder, and certain that what he believes right is in fact so."

Oh, for the impenetrable confidence of those born into wealth and high status. "Are you in his disfavor, or is he in yours?"

"Everything has put me into his disfavor since my birth when he was twelve years old. I ought to have been a boy, he thought."

Callum hid a smile. "I heartily disagree."

Her smile was faint; then her gaze shifted to the exuberant painting of Bacchus. "When I married—well, Andrew was rich, or so we thought. Still, Martin thought the family bloodline deserved better. My father is perhaps more practical. He considered a married daughter better than a spinster."

Isabel, married. Callum had met her only at the violent end of her marriage; it was odd to realize she had lived with Andrew Morrow for nearly a decade.

"I've never wed," he said. "But surely it's sometimes better to be a spinster. It depends on the identity of the husband."

"An incisive observation." Isabel unfolded her hands.

"Not all husbands are created equal. Martin did consider a wealthy but untitled man better than a debt-strapped nobleman. He wasn't well pleased, though, that we left England at once after our marriage."

That winking star had granted the wish he'd made the day before, over a mug of porter. He wanted to know everything about her—and wondrously, she seemed in a confiding mood. Perhaps planning a minor criminal assay had that effect on some women.

"During wartime? Where did you go?" All right, that was two questions.

"The Kingdom of Sicily." She took up a single almond, then began scraping the fuzzy brown skin free with a fingernail. "It was under British control, so Andrew was sure it would be safe. And it was convenient for arranging the secret sale of artworks by nobles on the Italian mainland. I won't use the word 'smuggling' since I am in the presence of an Officer of the Police."

"Wise of you."

"Also, because I don't know exactly what went on. I was very young and not very worldly." The almond was nude now, and she set it aside and took up another one.

He wanted to ask more about this, but a servant entered just then with a tea tray. "That poor almond," he settled for saying.

Once they were alone again, and after Isabel had poured out, she shoved the plates of dainties along the table to Callum. "Have some . . . whatever we have left here," she said. "It looks as though Brinley ate all the aniseed cakes, but there are plenty of sweetmeats left."

"That's all right. I'm full enough of the sandwiches we had with Butler. What will you have?"

"I don't usually eat between meals. Morrow thought it unladylike."

He allowed his expression to communicate exactly what he thought of this.

"I know, I know. Another habit from the days of my marriage that I haven't yet shed." Isabel plucked at the long sleeve of her tidy gray gown.

Callum took up his spoon, stirring his cup of black tea unnecessarily. "I like you no matter how you behave."

She was silent long enough that he ventured a searching glance at her features. She looked distant. Considering.

"I beg your pardon," he said.

"No, no." She blinked back to the present. "I thank you. That was kind of you. I was only thinking of some things."

"Did you come to a conclusion?" He took a sip of tea. Well-brewed, hot and strong.

"Never." She attempted a smile. "Never mind. Forgive my wandering mind. I should recall Lucy to this room; she would make far better conversation than I. Even Brinley would, for that matter."

"Both are fine companions for you." Her nudge to turn the subject was unmistakable, so Callum obeyed. "You've told me how you came to own Brinley. How did Miss Wallace come to be your late husband's ward?"

Isabel pressed a fingertip to a crumb on the tabletop; then another, and another, tidying them into her saucer. "Lucy's parents died."

"I assumed."

She grimaced. "They were murdered during a robbery. But they weren't wealthy; only one good piece of jewelry was taken. A pearl brooch, Lucy told me, that had been in the family for generations."

"I am sorry to hear it." Murder for jewelry was dreadful. After all these years with Bow Street, he still found it difficult to accept that some people held life so cheaply.

"The greatest pity was losing her parents, of course. I don't mean to imply anything else." Crumb, crumb, crumb.

Tidy, tidy, tidy. "But not to have any legacy from them was a cruelty on top of a cruelty."

"The culprit was never caught?"

She shook her head. "There was no Callum Jenks to take on the case."

He waved this off. "There are plenty of good investigators. Often a good one is not even needed; only open eyes to note the sloppy bits of evidence left behind."

"I don't know if the Wallaces had even that." Isabel sounded apologetic. "It was all in Gloucestershire, and Morrow didn't attend the inquest or the funerals. I don't know if he knew of any of it until Lucy turned up on our doorstep."

"And that was shortly after you returned from Sicily? Quite a busy time."

"It was an easy move." Evidently satisfied that she had cleaned the tabletop to perfection, she shoved away her teacup and saucer. "In Sicily, I lived as I would have in England, surrounded by servants and seeing only other English people. When we returned to London after Napoleon surrendered for the first time, I could hardly have told this house from the one in Sicily. They were both so . . . Morrow."

There had been something odd about the marriage between Isabel and the late Andrew Morrow. Callum couldn't quite determine what.

Didn't want to, really. If his thoughts turned to Isabel, there were other activities he wished to imagine.

Again, Callum's face must have shown what he thought of Morrow, for Isabel hastened to add, "He was not unkind or ungenerous in the slightest. He wanted me to have everything I wished for. There was always someone around me, watching to make sure my needs were met. And if there was anything I wanted to do, why, he would see it done for me to save me the trouble."

As she spoke, her expression flickered. It was sad, it was annoyed, it was rueful, it was resigned.

He wondered if she realized what she had admitted. "He saved you the trouble of getting to make any choices on your own."

"You noticed far more quickly than I did," she said softly. "A nobleman's daughter in a gilded cage. I didn't see the bars until after Morrow died. Now I realize I always lived within them. Before I wed, they were forged by my father and elder brother.

"I sometimes wonder if I accepted Morrow's hand just to disoblige my brother, Martin. But that's not flattering to the dead, is it, or to me?"

"I would not presume to judge your motivations," Callum said.

"Which means you think I'm awful, but you don't want to say so."

"Not at all." She didn't seem to believe him, so he said it again, more quietly. "Not at all."

The room was warm and close and messy and full of odd smells from Brinley. Callum crossed to the window, unlatched it, and slid up the sash, letting in a puff of cool air heavy from the earlier rain.

"Callum." A pause. "Are you available this Sunday? I am considering a small dinner party to introduce Lucy to some friends."

"And you want some of these guests investigated?" Remaining at the window, he fiddled with the latch. Flipping it back and forth with the sash still open, so it locked upon nothing but air.

"Not at all. I want you to be a guest." She sounded amused.

The latch pinched his finger. He muttered a curse. For the first time today, he felt ill at ease. He turned to face her. "Thank you, but I wouldn't suit. Not at a table full of the elite, all dressed in their best, using a fork for this and a spoon for that, tossing in French phrases here and there."

He stepped closer to her, drawing near the middle of the small morning room. "You cannot pull me into your circle, my lady."

"Maybe I would rather pull myself out."

Playfulness would have wounded him, but her tone was nothing of the sort. She sounded considering, her words slow, as if the idea were being knitted only as she spoke.

Her offer still unnerved him, but he liked that she had asked. "Thank you, but I will be working overnight on that date."

"Oh." She tipped her head, looking as if she didn't believe him. Wise woman. He hadn't been planning to work overnight until this moment. "That is the night after we—um, visit the Duke of Ardmore. You will be tired out."

"It's for the best if I'm not at a dinner. Most people don't like me. Or police in general. It reminds them that everything isn't as perfect as they'd like to think."

"I know that only too well," Isabel said. "Although being around you makes me feel safer. But I mustn't pull you away from your work; the city needs you too."

Her fingers drummed at the wooden arms of her chair. "It's not really about work, is it, though? Your refusal? It's about money."

Money, yes. Her elevated birth; his solidly low one. Families such as his were in-between, never good enough for the Quality, but always above someone they looked down on, and gratefully so. There were many layers in London society, and the only people who didn't care were those at the top and those crushed beneath all others.

"Yes." He dropped into his chair again, knees almost touching hers. "You're right. It's about money."

She drew in a breath, doubtless readying an attempt to persuade.

"It's not personal. Everything is about money," he said. "The reason that boy stole a pie: he didn't have the money to pay. The reason my brother was killed: for money, stolen from the Royal Mint. The reason the Duke of Ardmore is selling a painting he believes to be valuable: money, and his lack thereof."

"Not the reason Morrow died, though."

"Maybe not. But money was the reason for the forgeries."

"It wasn't only money," she said. "It was covetousness. He wanted those paintings like he never wanted—" She cut herself off. "It doesn't matter now."

He ought to say something understanding. Profound. Comforting.

Fool that he was, he was only staring. She was running a finger around the edge of her china teacup, and the gesture was captivating. Thoughtful. Erotic, in its deliberation.

With her hands, she had taken his arm. Taken all of him once, yes—but it had been a pleasure of an entirely different sort to have her lean on him as they walked together on a London street. Or to see her smile when she turned and recognized him.

Two nights from now, their odd mission of illegal justice would be completed, and she would be done with him again. And maybe that would be for the best. Everything was about money. She had a lot, he little; they did not belong together.

But for now, they sat in the same room, and she had welcomed him. And he did not have to leave just yet. Not just yet.

"You are looking at me so oddly," she said.

"I should practice my expressions in a mirror," he said, "if my regard looks odd to you."

Her hand lifted to her cheek. "Nonsense. After everything to which I've subjected you today?"

"I'm not wily. I'm blunt. I can't possibly deceive you about my own desires."

This convinced her better, he thought, than fine words would have. She lowered her hand, then looked at it as if it were an ornament she did not know where to place. Slowly, she extended it, following it with the line of her body. Leaning toward him, slow and inevitable, until her hand lay warm against his cheek.

He shut his eyes. Her fingertips traced the side of his face. The lines of bone, the faint stubble. She found the little scars from thrown rocks, from razor nicks; as many inflicted by others as by himself. There were so many tiny ways to draw blood from a man. Her touch trailed over them all, soothing.

Then she drew a fingernail around the edge of his ear, and he shivered like a green youth.

"Lady Isabel, I—"

"Just Isabel," she breathed, and it was impossible not to kiss her. Eyes still closed, lips to lips, a gentle brush of intimacy. A thank-you for all she had told him; a thank-you from her, maybe, for absorbing her honesty. For being on her side.

When she pulled back, her nose nuzzled his; her lashes touched his face. His every muscle tensed, fighting the wish to gather her into his arms, to enfold her and keep her safe, here, in this rare space where they could both exist.

"You told Butler you weren't fond of Callum," she murmured. "But I am. The name and the man."

Blinking his eyes open, he saw her before him flushed and starry, and he copied her own actions. Touching the beautiful lines of her face, learning them in soft candlelight. He took her shoulders in his hands, drawing her nearer, and found her lips again with his. Like that, each in their own chairs, they kissed, and they kissed, their hands sedate and their lips saying everything they had not been able to speak.

Later, they would talk more about the plan. Later still, he would leave.

Two days from now, she might never care to see him again.

But for today, she had welcomed him. Touched him. Invited him. Kissed him.

Trusted him with her person, her reputation, her truth.

By the time he departed the Lombard Street house, though he knew full well he'd no place in her life, she'd left him feeling as lofty as a lord.

Chapter Eight

To what end? Callum Jenks had said to Isabel. To what end? The question preoccupied her.

To what end had she kissed him—or he kissed her? The night that followed his unexpected visit had been a confused one of broken sleep. But it was not the insomnia of recriminations Isabel had struggled with so often since finding Andrew's hidden room. There were no *shouldn't haves* and *should haves*, not with kisses. There was only a sweet recall, a yearning for . . . what? For more?

To what end?

Maybe the closeness, the pleasure, was the end in itself. For there must be an end. He was work, all work on London's roughest streets, and she was a proper widow in a bubble of funds and fashion. A proper widow who would find herself new lodging. A space of her own, maybe to become a person of her own too.

Only after a broken night's sleep were manners and mores faded enough for a daughter of the ton to think in such terms.

She arose early and wrote busily at the small desk in her bedchamber. Not invitations to the dinner party she had suggested to Callum. No, the dinner had been nothing more than a nebulous inkling, so she would place it on hold.

Instead, she seized upon the promise idly made to the Duke of Ardmore that she intended to move houses. That was something she could do, to fill the time between invitations into society—or until the time she became a thief and housebreaker. A note to Septimus Nash, the house agent the duke had recommended. Lady Isabel had a desire to move households and would await Mr. Nash at his earliest convenience.

Next, she wrote her father, knowing that the letter would instead be opened and read by her brother. Lord Martindale would be annoyed that she was moving households; he cultivated normalcy as gardeners cultivated roses. But if one acted like everyone else—wasn't that ordinary, rather than normal? Isabel was not sure of the difference.

She was not sure she wanted to be either one.

By the time her lady's maid had clucked over Isabel's breakfast and helped her into another gray gown, a reply had arrived from Mr. Nash. He would be pleased to meet her ladyship at a certain address in Russell Square at a late hour of the afternoon, should that suit her. The property was most attractive and would be an excellent situation for a friend of the Duke of Ardmore's.

"Hmm." Isabel knew she sounded like Callum Jenks, her brow creasing as she read this reply. Russell Square—surely that would be a stately, costly address.

But she might as well look. She returned a note of agreement to Nash's reply.

She spent the early afternoon paying calls with Lucy. To Lady Teasdale, of course, and to Mrs. Roderick and the Dowager Lady Mortimer—all women with sons of marriageable age. So often, a mother was looking harder for a possible bride for her son than he was looking for himself. Lucy conducted herself quietly—always so quietly!—but with pretty manners. If they were not striking, at least they did not offend.

Perhaps she was regretting her failed attempt at training Brinley, though Isabel had assured her she thought it was quite funny.

They returned to Lombard Street briefly to refresh body and clothing, then retrieved Brinley and clipped him to a long leather leash. The coachman, Jacoby, brought around Isabel's landaulet, and women and dog clambered in.

The journey to Russell Square was not long by foot, but in the crowded London streets, it took some minutes for Jacoby to thread the bays through the clutter of carriages and street sweepers and servants on foot. When they approached Russell Square, the accustomed noise of the city dimmed gradually, filtered out by the trees in the central garden.

The landaulet pulled up before the given address. Brinley leaped out, yipping, his short legs a blur of hops and jumps, as Jacoby aided Isabel and Lucy in climbing down.

Septimus Nash awaited them at the front door of the house, keys in hand. He was tall and spare, and he had a raven's way of tipping his head and regarding one with skeptical eyes.

"Lady Isabel. Miss Wallace." Once the ladies had ascended the steps to join him, he made his bow, all the time regarding Brinley with a look of distaste. "The animal should remain outdoors while I escort you about the premises."

Isabel had intended to leave Brinley with the groom, but Nash's nasal certainty set her teeth on edge. "The animal," she replied, "will be accompanying my ward and me, as he is to live here too." She caught up the end of the leash, wrapping it around her hand, and ignored the fact that Brinley had lifted his leg beside one of the gray stones framing the tall wooden doors.

"Very well. Doubtless you noted the desirability of the

neighborhood? The garden square? We could tour it if you wish."

"I do like the garden square." Raised in the country seat of her father, Isabel sometimes felt starved for the sight of growing things in the city. "And there is no question that the neighborhood is fine. But let us have a look at the house first." She took up another loop of the leash as Brinley sniffed circles around Nash's patent-leather shoes.

"Ordinarily I wouldn't show this house to two females," Nash confided as he unlocked the door. "But I have made an exception for a friend of the Duke of Ardmore."

Lucy darted a sideways glance at Isabel. *Is that all right? Are you going to let that comment pass?*

Of course it wasn't. And she wasn't.

"The dog is male, if that helps," Isabel replied. "And why would you not show this house to delicate females such as ourselves?" She leaned in, eyes wide, and whispered, "Is there something improper about it?"

"Heavens, no!" He pokered up. "But it is a large house and will require a steady hand with staff."

He wasn't wrong about this; she could tell by looking at the broad stone façade. Three stories plus an attic, and who knew how many rooms?

"If you *swear* it's not improper," she granted, "I suppose we will have a look."

With a sniff from Nash and the satisfying silence of well-oiled hinges, the door opened on a spacious entryway. It was at least three times the size of the one in Isabel's current house, marble-tiled and silk-papered and pleasantly scented of beeswax and lemon oil. Bare of furnishings, it looked even larger than it truly was, and the staircase that lay ahead loomed just as wide and grand.

Isabel knew at once she wasn't going to take this house. "It is lovely," she said over the sound of Brinley's claws clicking over marble. "I am not certain, though, that it will suit."

She would bring a dog inside to disoblige Nash, but she wouldn't purchase a house.

"I understood you to want a tonnish neighborhood." Beside her, Nash tipped his head and fixed a beady dark eye on her.

Isabel handed Brinley's leash to Lucy. "Tonnish, yes, with the emphasis on the *ish*. I don't mean that I wish to have Angelus as a neighbor, but I don't mind if I'm outside of Mayfair."

Nash waved a hand. "Of course you want to be in Mayfair. Now, have a look through this door. I believe you will be pleased at the size of this drawing room. I say *this* one, because there are several, all elegantly appointed. Come, come! Do not hang back. You must have a look at the house you intend to buy."

Lucy dropped the end of the leash. With a yelp and a skitter of claws over smooth stone, Brinley took off—first for Nash's shoes, then, after he'd rejected them, into the drawing room to sniff about its perimeter.

"Oh, dear!" Lucy clapped a hand to her mouth, looking almost genuinely distressed. "I am so sorry, Mr. Nash. I was overcome at the sight of the room. Truly, it is beautiful."

The house agent made a strange noise.

Isabel fought to keep a solemn expression. "How embarrassing," she cooed. "I must apologize, Mr. Nash! Truly, we should have let you hold the leash. You have the firm hand that we ladies lack."

Nash looked suspicious, as if he suspected he were being led by the nose but could not see the rope.

Crossing the drawing room—which really was elegant and spacious—she took Brinley's leash in hand. He whined a protest as she marched him back across the room, away from what had evidently been a fascinating smell. "Mr. Nash, would you mind holding him while we tour the remainder of the house? Excellent! I do appreciate it. You will know just how to handle him, I am sure."

The house agent looked at the leash in his hand, and the little dog winding it in a circuit around his legs, with some dismay. "Lady Isabel, I cannot—that is, it's not done for you to look about the house without my supervision."

Again, she widened her eyes. "Oh, dear! But you assured us it was not improper! What ever will we find? Oh, Lucy dear, come take my hand."

Lucy's mouth was twitching as she obeyed.

"No, it's not—I assure you, my lady, there is nothing improper in the house. Nothing that will offend your sensibilities in the slightest."

Isabel let out a great breath. "How you relieve my mind! Thank you, Mr. Nash. We should not have known what to do without you. Shall we meet you here in—let us say, fifteen minutes? Only I do not have a watch, so you must let me know when it has been long enough."

And with Lucy's hand in hers, she turned about and swanned up the stairs, not much caring in which part of the house she wound up. Behind them, Brinley barked and whined. Nash called after them once, but she pretended not to hear.

"Aunt Isabel," Lucy breathed as they reached the first story and stepped onto a floor of polished wood, "you were marvelous."

"I can't imagine what you mean. All I did was act in the way he expected. Dim-witted and helpless." Isabel paused, looking about the corridor. Good lines. Wide, spacious. Far too many rooms for her needs. "Perhaps I took it farther than he expected. But you know, Andrew—Mr. Morrow—used to treat me as if I were helpless sometimes. I wish now that I'd turned it about on him, instead of lodging a protest to which he didn't listen in the slightest."

"But you're so brave. You traveled all those places with him, and you were so young."

Isabel smiled at that, but it was wry. "It was easy to agree and obey. Not to mention it was good manners, and above all I'd been raised to have good manners." She turned around, looking at the dimensions of the house. "Do you want to look about anymore?"

"Not if you don't."

"It would be more entertaining to poke around if there were still furniture and belongings. In truth, I knew as soon as I saw the place that it wouldn't suit, but we mustn't let Mr. Nash know we females can make up our own minds. Not just yet."

The upstairs was pleasant enough, with filtered sunlight and the same clean scent of lemon oil. But there was not a chair in sight; not a stick of any furniture. So Isabel plumped onto the floor at the top of the stairs, setting her feet on a step as if it were a stool, and patted the floor next to her. "Come, sit by me, and I shall tell you the terrible truth about husbands."

Lucy looked wary as she sat. "I thought you wanted me to marry."

"Not if you don't," Isabel teased, repeating Lucy's own words.

"But I do." Lucy caught one of her blond curls between thumb and forefinger, tugging and twining it about her finger. "Are husbands truly terrible?"

"No, I was being dramatic. Though some are. It depends on the husband." Her brows knit. "It depends on the wife, too. Some men will take exactly as much power as they're given, and they'll give as little respect as is demanded of them."

"But Uncle Andrew—" Lucy halted; she didn't often speak his name.

Isabel didn't either. "I was meant," she explained, "to be an adjunct to his career without asking too many questions. But once the wedding was done and we were alone on our honeymoon, I had nothing to *say* for myself. So much was drilled into me in order to get me ready for my come-out in society, I had never thought about what would come afterwards."

Lucy looked much struck. "You knew how to run a household."

"Does that fill a person's days? It could, I suppose. But it felt like treading water. I never accomplished anything of my own." She traced a vein in the marble of the top stair. "I knew how to paint a pretty watercolor, but I couldn't discuss paints and shading as Andrew wished. And what good was needlepoint when our home was fully furnished? What use cards when there was no one to play with?"

As if he heard her questions, a fit of yipping from Brinley echoed up the stairs.

"He is enjoying himself." Lucy frowned. "So what did you do?"

"I read everything I could. I wanted to learn, because if I didn't learn, I wouldn't be useful. And if I wasn't useful, who would I be? I was useful to my parents when they thought I'd train up well and make a good match. But then what?"

"It's awful to be uncertain," Lucy agreed. "But men in the ton don't want useful wives, do they? Lady Teasdale's son is in politics, and Mrs. Roderick's son hunts all the time."

"They don't want their wives to *have* to be useful," mused Isabel. "But a pretty face fades over the years. A sharp mind doesn't dull. Though as long as I was pretty and sweet, that was all Andrew expected of me."

Lucy drew up her knees, folding her arms around them. "Then why did you care?"

Isabel rolled her eyes. "Ugh. I couldn't imagine spending the rest of my life being nothing but pretty and sweet."

"Yet you can't help it," laughed Lucy.

"Dear girl. I should give you more pocket money."

"You give me more than I could wish for." Lucy's brow puckered. "I should like to learn more too. About art. Do you—do you think I could learn enough to teach it someday? If I don't marry?"

Unspoken was the question: *What if no one wants to marry me?*

"I think you could. Likely you already can." *I will watch over you.*

"If you wish to teach private lessons, we must look for a house with a fine studio space. Or you could teach at a girls' school."

Lucy was shaking her head already. "Too many people." She unfolded, sat up straight. "I think—I should like to get married. To the right sort of person."

"I would not want you to wed any other sort." She couldn't look at Lucy when she said this. A husband and wife's private life was their own, and she hoped Lucy knew nothing of the realities behind Isabel's marriage. Andrew Morrow had been Lucy's cousin, and one never wished to speak ill of the dead. Or think it.

With a ringing bark and a whirl of little churning legs, Brinley rounded the curve of the stairs. The leash trailed behind him, loose.

"Brinley!" Lucy shot to her feet. As the beagle ran up the steps and skidded past them, she snagged the end of the leash. He halted at once, quivering with delight, and yipped again.

"You imp," said Isabel. "You've been leading Mr. Nash on a merry chase, haven't you? We might as well descend now and relieve the poor man of his anxieties."

Lucy kept hold of the leash, and as a sedate trio, they descended to the ground floor. At the foot of the stairs, Nash awaited with disheveled hair, his breath coming in quick pants. "Little fellow . . ." He strove for good cheer. "Got . . . away from me. Never seen . . . such a little . . . animal move . . . so fast."

"He is part thoroughbred." Isabel smiled pityingly, as if this made any sense at all. "You mustn't blame yourself, Mr. Nash. But I don't think this place would suit him, and I am sure it will not do for us."

Color rose in his cheeks. "Lady Isabel! I urge you to reconsider."

"All right." She tapped at her chin with a forefinger. "No, my decision is the same. I am afraid we have wasted your time. So sorry. Two women, you know, we are doing our best."

"Do you not wish to set up your own household after all?"

She dropped the feather-witted act, lifting her chin. "I already possess my own household. I merely wish to move it to someplace smaller."

"Because it is too much for you." Nash was all sympathy at once. "I could show you a set of rooms in Cheapside. They are over a linen draper's shop. Most respectable."

"Mr. Nash, come now. I haven't the income of the Prince Regent, but I needn't live in a set of rooms. I would prefer a house."

He was smoothing his hair, regaining his composure word by word. "You might consider the rooms, truly, if you seek to economize. The rent is most reasonable, and the widow who lives in the attic rooms is quite willing to cook and serve as charwoman."

"I am not in financial difficulty," Isabel said. "I wish to move households because my husband died in the house I live in now."

Lucy looked embarrassed by this. But then, Lucy often looked embarrassed.

Isabel knew this reason would satisfy Nash. Let him believe her sentimental and fearful—though in truth, Isabel had rarely entered Andrew's bedchamber before his death, and she had no reason to now. The physical signs of his death were entirely gone.

No, it was the physical signs of his *life* that bothered her. The fussy, fragile antiques on which one had to sit gingerly; the silks that could not be touched; the paintings that turned the house into an art gallery curated by someone whose tastes differed entirely from Isabel's.

"I understand." Nash looked pitying, which was a sliver better than condescending. "I shall inform you if anything suitable comes on the market."

They parted ways outside the house, descending the steps to the landaulet as Nash relocked the door. At the carriage, Brinley sat on his haunches on the ground and looked up mournfully.

"Hop in!" Lucy patted the carriage step. "Come on, boy. You love to ride in the carriage."

His long tongue lolled out of his mouth. He flopped over and lay on his back with his legs splayed out, looking as if he'd been pressed by an iron.

"Oh, *now* you're quiet," Isabel groused. She clambered up and took her seat, then asked the groom to pick up the dog and hand him in after her and Lucy.

As the bays set off at a trot, and Brinley rolled into a sleepy ball at their feet, Lucy turned to Isabel. "He's not barking. He's not even jumping. Have we found the answer to training him?"

"Sheer exhaustion, after he runs away from everyone all morning and most of the afternoon?" Isabel laughed. "Perhaps we have."

It didn't help her determine how to deal with the Duke of Ardmore's dogs. And she hadn't found a suitable house. But at least it meant the afternoon had not altogether been a waste, even as the time remaining before the switch of the paintings was growing assuredly short.

Chapter Nine

When Callum pushed open the door of Jenks and Sons Grocery at half seven on a Friday, his mother didn't even look up from her cash book when she greeted him.

"Hullo, Callum." Davina Jenks dipped her pen once more, added a figure to the total, then bade a good evening to the well-dressed servant who had just selected dry goods on a household account. "Whit like are ye, son?"

In all her years in England, she'd never shaken the comfortable old Scottish greeting, or the soft remnants of her burr.

"I'm fine, Mum. Also a creature of habit, if you know it's me without looking up." Callum dutifully crossed to the huge shop counter, stretching across it to embrace his diminutive mother.

"Had to look up to know it was you yesterday, didn't I? When you came in for the tea."

He granted this was true.

They had fallen into this routine of regular visits when he'd begun working for the Bow Street Public Office. Each week was, for him, completely different from the one before or the one that would come after. But every visit to the grocery was the same. Friday evenings, the same greeting, the same goods for sale, the same staff. For year on year, since the days his grandfather owned the shop, Jenks and Sons had been redbrick outside, wood-floored within, with a close plaster ceiling that somehow made the space seem pleasantly cool.

A wooden counter both wide and long cleaved the space, with shelves on shelves climbing the wall behind. On those, bins and baskets held every sort of good imaginable—except for the sorts that were stored in barrels, like flour, or in great hanging ropes, like the pungent onions with their tops braided together.

There were baskets, too, of dry beans and peas and of nuts in their shells, scooped out with Davina's grandmother's wooden ladle and sold by weight; spices and tea and coffee; pickled vegetables in jars; candles in great bunches; and a ladder tipped against the wall next to the shelves for fetching the high-up items. Little loaves of sugar and cakes of soap made attractive pyramids on the counter.

Callum picked up a bar of soap and sniffed it. "Lavender?"

"Indeed it is. And you're dependable, that's all." Blotting the cash book, Davina tucked it away open beneath the counter. "Every Friday thirty minutes before we close, you're here certain as sunset, unless you're on a case. And glad I am to see you today."

His brows lifted. "Truly?"

"Whisht! Of course. I've so much to—ah, just a moment." She interrupted herself as the bell over the door jingled, signaling the entrance of another customer.

Rare was the visit that didn't bring a spate of tasks for Callum to complete "just this once." He suspected this was why she was glad to see him. In exchange for the packet of tea the day before, he'd not only taken on Jamie's queries about the tea shop for sale next door, he'd also agreed to ask at any fire-damaged businesses he passed whether they were selling off their stock.

So it went. With a shrug, he turned away. Near the

window, but not so near its inhabitants would suffer in the sunlight, hung a wicker cage in which hopped and twittered a pair of linnets. The male was just coming into his summer plumage, his reddish breast and wings fluffed proudly as he hopped from woven bar to bar of the cage.

"Hullo, George," he said. "Hullo, Charlotte."

The Jenkses' linnets were always named after the king and queen, a dubious honor considering the little birds' brief lives. But they were sunny and sweet, and customers loved to feed them seeds. A cloth in the bottom of the cage to catch their messes was changed daily and shaken outside— as Callum knew from past experience. If the shop was shorthanded or particularly busy, he was likely to be pressed into service doing any one of a thousand everyday tasks.

But other than this late shopper, the grocery was quiet. One of the shop assistants—Lionel, a stocky man around thirty years of age—was sitting on a sealed barrel marked FLOUR, braiding the dry tops of onions together so the vegetables could hang in tidy ropes. He and Callum exchanged nods, then Callum settled onto one of the ladder-backed chairs around the Franklin stove. The stove sat where one might have expected a fireplace in a home, merrily boiling kettle after kettle of water for the shop's teas and coffees, offered as samples for shoppers to taste as they sat on one of the little stools scattered amongst the bins and barrels.

He'd lived in the quarters above this shop from the day he was born until the day he'd turned twenty-one. It was familiar as ever, but how quickly it had lost the feeling of home. Though James Street was no more than a brief walk from Callum's lodging or the Bow Street court, stolen purses and bullet-shot corpses were a world away from the grocery's cookery and coziness.

Maybe that was why he'd chosen to work for Bow Street.

Next to the shelves behind the shop counter, a door led to the family's upstairs lodging. The door opened just then, revealing the oldest Jenks sibling: Anna, as red-haired and blue-eyed as Callum's brother Jamie and their mother. With a smile for the customer and her mother, she lifted the hinged bit of counter and stepped into the shop—then halted.

"Lionel! I didn't know you were down here."

Lionel turned red. "Miss Jenks." He fumbled his braid, sending an onion tumbling to the floor. It rolled across the smooth wooden planks, jerking to a halt a dozen feet away. "I—I am down here."

"Let me get that for you." Anna darted forward, picking up the fallen onion. As Lionel sprang to his feet, she rose and handed him the vegetable. For a long moment, they stared at each other over the onion as though it were a magical pot of gold.

Callum could only roll his eyes. At age forty-two, Anna must be at least ten years older than Lionel, but the difference in their ages had never stopped the two from bashfully flirting. When, or whether, they'd ever move beyond handing each other produce and giving each other hungry looks, he couldn't guess.

Callum's own progress with Isabel was a bit better. Slightly? Greatly? She *had* kissed him. Or he her. Perhaps it didn't matter.

As Anna turned away from Lionel, cheeks flaming as red as her hair, Callum stuck out a boot. She shrieked at the unexpected thump, then darted over to cuff him. "Rascal and rogue! I didn't know you were here."

"People are always here. If you had the place to yourself, it wouldn't be much of a business."

She pulled a face at him, then sweetened her expression to dart a look back at Lionel. "I know that. I only—oh, never mind. Mum's got some things to ask you about this week."

"I expected as much." Callum dragged his foot back,

setting it beside its twin. He got to his feet, glared at the stove, and glared at Anna for good measure.

She arched a brow. "Grumpy as a bear, aren't you? Must be you need feeding."

"Sure," he said. "That's it. I need feeding. I'll get a pie on my way home."

She looked puzzled. "You're not going to eat with us?"

"No." At her hurt expression, he softened his reply. "Jamie and Dad aren't even here, are they? It'll be a while yet before you eat. I need to get home; I've work early in the morning." *And late at night tomorrow.*

"Right." She looked mollified. "If you insist. But I think—"

"Ho, ho, hullo!" The door's bell jingled to let out the latest shopper just as his father and brother walked in. Alun Jenks, dark like his youngest son, was bandy-legged and ever-cheerful, while Jamie . . . well, Jamie was a stern grump who always sat too long at the best table in the Boar's Head.

Though Jamie would probably describe Callum the same way.

The thought made him smile as he greeted his father and sole living brother.

"Ah, it's a Jenks party!" said Alun, as if this gathering didn't happen almost every week. "All we need is our Edward and Celia, and we'll be set."

"Edward's still haggling with the tea merchants," Jamie said of the other shop assistant. "I told him he was doing a bad job of it, but he would continue. Still. Brought another sample of the newest sort from Ceylon." He patted his coat pocket, then looked around, eyebrows raised. "Ah . . . where's Celia?"

The casual note in his voice would not have fooled a baby. No one, Callum was quite sure, missed the longing in his eyes or voice as he asked this question.

Celia Lewis, the late Harry's fiancée, had moved into the

family quarters on the upper floors after Harry was killed since she had no family of her own. She shared a chamber with Anna, taking over the family's sewing. At twenty-five, she'd been widowed before she was wed, and she was sweet but faded. There was no ring on her finger to justify her grief to the world.

Jamie had fallen for her the first time he'd seen her, though he hid his feelings—poorly—under the guise of brotherly tolerance and gruffness.

"Celia is upstairs, of course," said Anna. "Mending the heels in your old stockings."

Jamie blanched. "My stockings? You're joking, aren't you?"

"Never mind that, never mind that." Mrs. Jenks drew out a cylindrical object from the capacious storage built into the back of the counter. "Callum! Look what we've come into."

Callum crossed the floor to peer at the object on the shop counter. "Very nice. A metal barrel too small to be of any use."

"No, indeed! It's not a barrel. It's called a tin, and it's full of beef. The container's made of tinned iron and sealed closed."

He poked at the side, then the top. "How do you know there's truly beef in the can, then?"

Davina looked much struck. "We canna open it to see, for then it'll be spoiled."

"In that case, you could say it's full of unicorn meat and charge ten guineas. If no one's ever going to check."

"And you half Scottish!" She swatted him on the arm. "Never say you'd cut up a unicorn."

"I never will," he said dutifully. Honestly. Meat in a can—the world was a strange place. "So. What do you need from me today?"

"Ah, you're a good son. That's what I was meaning to tell you when you walked in."

"That I was a good son?"

"That I needed a few things. But ye are a good son." She

tugged a pencil from behind her ear; she always kept one there and another in the knot of her graying red hair. Pulling a list from the pocket of her apron, she ticked off each item. "Last night, Edward got a fine for being drunk in front of the Bow Street court. He canna pay it until the next quarter day when he gets his wages. If you could talk to the magistrate—"

"Fine." Callum picked up the scoop in a basket of lentils, digging it deep, then letting the dry little beads rush back down again. "Fox will probably forgive it, as long as he doesn't see Edward again for a few months. What else?"

"A bit of pork from that butcher you know two streets over? He always gives you the best price, since you found the thief who was stealing from his—"

"I know what I did. That's fine. I can probably get seven pence the pound." He knew he was being terse, but he didn't care.

"Make it forty pounds, then." She hesitated.

"What? Is there something else?"

"There is," Jamie said as he slouched over. "Leave the lentils alone."

Deliberately, Callum dug the ladle in again, then let lentils stream from it. "Surely that's not what you wanted to tell me."

"No, no. It's nothing, really." Alun was looping the braided chains of onions about his arm. "Just that the building next door is for sale. Your mum thought you'd be interested."

Jamie jerked. "You know about that?"

Callum shot him a hard look. "Of course *I am interested*," he said through his teeth, stressing the last few words for Jamie's benefit. *Shut up if you want me to poke about in secret.* "You mean the tea seller, I'm guessing, and not the confectioner?"

"The tea seller, yes. Morrison hasn't the sense of a baby." Davina clucked. "Giving credit for everything, never keeping records! One trusts one's neighbors, ay, but a man can't live on promises to pay soon, soon."

"Might be we could buy 'un," said Alun. "If there's anything we like." He hung the tidy lengths of onions over a hook, beside the potato barrel.

"Buy the shop?" Jamie's head snapped up. "You want to buy the shop?"

"Nae, o'course not," said Davina. "What would we be wanting with a tea shop? But his stock would be worth a look. Callum, I want you to find out what happened there. Was there a crime, and can we get his goods cheap?"

Business as usual. Callum let another ladleful of lentils dribble down. "There's no crime in a man wanting to sell his building."

"Aye, I know. But if there *was* a crime, we'd like to know. Being his neighbors and all."

"Hmm."

"So ye'll find out?" she pressed.

"Fine." Near on eight o'clock. He could go now, having done his duty to the family for one more week. He flung the ladle back into the lentils. "I have to leave now. Give my love to Celia, Jamie, won't you?"

His brother flushed, then caught his arm. "Look. Callum," he said in a voice pitched low. "I want you to check into the building next door."

"For God's sake. I told you yesterday I would. And I just told Mum I would, too."

"Not like that." He bent even closer, his close-cropped beard brushing Callum's ear. "I want you to find out how much it would go for. Not what Morrison's asking, but the least amount he would take."

"Let me guess. You still don't want Mum and Dad to know." A needle of tension crept into his voice. It always seemed to poke out when he and Jamie spoke. They'd never got along with each other the way Harry had with both of them.

"Are you going to help or aren't you?" From Jamie's tone he might as well have been saying, *Are you going to bugger off or aren't you?*

Callum sighed. "You're in a better position to find out than I. Talk to the shop assistants. Or the servants."

"The creditors would have a better idea."

"Well, you know them too."

Jamie rolled his eyes. "Be reasonable. I've a shop to run."

"And I've a city to police." He peered over his elder brother's shoulder. By now, their mother was watching them curiously. "I've got to go."

"Callum. Please. It's just you. Your time is your own." Jamie's blue eyes were sincere. Pleading.

Shit.

As the youngest in the family by far, Callum had grown up running the errands everyone else thought too unimportant to handle themselves. If they only flung him a kind look, he'd fly to do their bidding.

Because it was only Callum, after all, and he ought to be doing what he could to help.

It seemed his weekly visits weren't the only family tradition.

"I'll help you if I can, Jamie. But my own work comes first."

"Taking care of strangers before your own family." Jamie's manner was as bristly as his beard. "Never thought I'd see the day."

"Everyone in London is family to someone." As Jamie granted this with a shrug of his shoulders, Callum had an idea. "Let me have some more of that new Ceylon blend, will you? I know someone else who'd like it."

"*I'd* like it." But Jamie relented, tugging the small parcel from his pocket. "Fine. Here. Let me know what you learn, all right?"

"I will. Probably next Friday, unless you want to come by

court before then." As he headed for the door, George the linnet fired a trill of song at him.

"I could use help with a few errands meself," Alun called after him. "If you don't mind. Will ye be in the East End for—"

"Just make a list. Whatever you need. Make a list, and I'll fetch it next time." The jingle of the bell over the shop door saw him out.

He turned his steps toward Bow Street, to the magistrate's court he knew as well as the building he'd just left. Which one felt more like home? Which one *was* his home?

Maybe he didn't have one, at that. But maybe he didn't need one. There were streets aplenty to pound up and down; questions to ask of informants and criminals—and those who were a bit of both.

That was the blessing and the curse of being an Officer of the Police: since his work was never done, there was nothing he needed besides work.

"Cass, you never forget a bit of gossip," Callum said to his friend. "What do you know about the Ardmore line?"

"Cass hasn't worked with them," Charles scoffed. "But I have, a time or two. Unofficially." He winked. "The duke pays well when he's got something that needs doing, or something someone needs not to notice."

"Charles!" Cass's admonishment cut through the hubbub of the courtroom, which at this hour was more subdued than usual. Fox held regular hours, yes, but the officers came and went all day and night.

Callum had been hoping to encounter his friends in the courtroom, and here they were, having just dragged in a pair of drunken lordlings who had dropped their trousers during a theatrical performance. Charles was none the worse for wear, but Cass's hair was decidedly disheveled. She sat on one of the long benches with a dazed expression. Maybe one of the drunken men had tried to kiss her. It wouldn't be the first time she'd been pawed in the course of her—really, her brother's—duty.

"I don't mean anything serious by it." Charles flicked a falling lock of his sister's coppery hair, then slouched onto the bench beside her. "It's not as if the duke chops up people and puts them in a pickle barrel. But he enjoyed smuggled brandy for years. Think he lost his taste for it when it became legal to ship brandy into England again."

"Oh. That." Who didn't trespass against the law a bit in the ton? It was still wrong to accept smuggled goods, but there was so much that was wrong-er, like Sir Frederic Chapple leaving his plush cell in Newgate.

Or Andrew Morrow selling forged paintings as genuine articles, holding the reputations of two women in his dead hands.

"And then there was a bit of procurement," Charles mused. "A woman or two for the duke. But only occasion-ally."

"Charles!" Cass exclaimed again.

"Joking, joking." Benton rolled his eyes, and when Cass turned away to answer a question from one of the Watch, peering in as he went about his rounds, Charles whispered, "Not joking. Ardmore likes them buxom."

Cass turned back just in time to see her brother holding his hands before his chest, palms flat and fingers curled as if to indicate enormous breasts. "I'm not even going to ask."

Callum shook his head. "Best not. So. What needs doing tonight?"

"Slow night for criminals," Charles sighed, putting his boots up on the back of the bench in front of him.

"You could join the foot patrol," Cass said brightly, stabbing pins into her tumble-down hair. "We'll put you in one of those pretty red waistcoats."

"Not my best color. Thanks anyway." Callum had a better idea.

There wasn't much he could do, or needed to do, about the Duke of Ardmore right now. So instead, he would probe the other matter that occupied his mind. He would scratch for more information about Andrew Morrow's sudden death.

So many investigations began with questions to the city's prostitutes. They went everywhere, they were ignored by the elite and so overheard much, and they met everyone from rag-pickers to nobles.

And two benches away, sitting in the courtroom as if it were the finest place in the world to locate a cully, was his old informant Janey.

"Excuse me," Callum said to the Bentons, and sidled away from their seat to find one beside Janey. "How goes your day, Janey darling?"

"Jenksie again!" She grinned, showing crooked but clean teeth. "Today's a good 'un. Found me this apple right on the street, like, and not a bruise on it!"

She polished the fruit with the fingerless gloves she wore to her wrists in summer. Just as she had been the night before, she was all but covered in clothing: head scarf over brown hair, shawl, pinafore, round gown, high-topped boots. All the better to hide her take—not that he asked about that.

"Found an apple right on the street?" Callum lifted a brow. "That was lucky. It was nowhere near a costermonger's cart, I assume."

"Nowhere near," she sniffed, as if the idea of her pinching a fruit from a peddler were inconceivable. She took a great bite of the apple, crunching it as she asked, "Wha's on your mind, Jenksie?"

"Since you ask . . ."

She laughed. "I always ask, because there's always something."

They had known each other for the nine years he'd worked for the public office, since he was young and she far younger. Janey—he had no idea of her last name—had taken to the street for her living at a horribly young age. Unlike many women who did the same, she'd kept most of her teeth and, as Isabel had noticed, even some of her youthful prettiness. Stealing was easier on the body, and probably on the spirit, than selling oneself. Selling information might be easier yet.

Callum asked her, "Do you remember the death of a man named Andrew Morrow? It was about a year and a half ago."

"Lot o' death goes by since then." She took another bite. "Who was 'e?"

"An art dealer. Rich man, lived on Lombard Street. Died from a shot to the head."

Janey looked interested. "Murder?"

"Officially, an accident."

"Right. Like them *official* answers is worth the breath it takes to speak 'em. You think it was murder after all?"

"I don't know."

Janey swung her legs, chewing at another juicy bite. "What's he to you?"

Callum hesitated. That wasn't an easy question to answer. Sir Frederic Chapple's release had been a personal matter, a wrong against a loved one that had gone unpunished. But the death of Andrew Morrow . . .

He had wronged Isabel in everyday ways, every day of their marriage. But what had that to do with Callum? If he cared for Isabel's well-being, shouldn't he let the man's reputation alone?

He *did* care for Isabel's well-being. But he cared for the truth, too. And there was something wrong about that house, that death. It was like a rotten tooth that still looked fine and white on the outside. He had warned Isabel: he was blunt by nature. He wanted to crash through that pleasant surface and learn the truth of what lay below.

He wanted, too, to knit himself into Lady Isabel Morrow's

life. Had wanted that since the moment he saw her; had
never managed to stop.

Already, he'd been silent too long. Janey narrowed
shrewd eyes. "Never mind that," he said. "Keep your ear to
the ground, will you?"

"If you give it a shilling to weight it down." Her grin was
cheeky.

He almost smiled at that. "Got to look out for yourself,"
he agreed, and pressed the coin into her palm. "Oh, one
more thing. Have you heard anything unusual to do with the
tea shop on James?"

"Morrison's? Nahhh. He's a good one. Gives a girl a cup
of tea, like, in winter when the whole world seems froze."

Consistent with Davina Jenks's opinion that the shop
owner was no kind of businessman. "Thanks. Good to know.
Here, Janey—another shilling. Keep both ears to the ground,
all right then?"

"Flat as they get," she agreed.

After this, Callum left the courtroom and headed for his
rooms on James Street. Not far from the heart of his work;
closer still to the hearth of the family that had raised him.

He imagined that, miles away, on Lombard Street, Lady
Isabel Morrow roamed an elegant house with a hidden room.
Readied herself for bed. Dreamed.

For approximately the five hundred fortieth time—only
approximately, for though he'd met her eighteen months
before, he was neither a mathematician nor a besotted
fool—he wondered whether she thought of him. And what.
And why. And for how long. If she was worried about the
plan for the following night. If she would agree to see him
again after it was carried out.

Questions, so many questions, raced through his mind
until he fell asleep.

Just another tradition.

Chapter Ten

"Lord Martindale has arrived, my lady."

Selby's voice broke into Isabel's reverie. Her fingertips, which had been dancing silently over the keys of the drawing room's pianoforte, crashed over the notes discordantly.

Martin? Here? Today, of all days, when she had friends to charm and a painting to steal? Under her breath, she cursed.

Then, pasting a smile on her features, she turned to face her butler. "I was not aware that his lordship was planning to visit. Did he send word?"

Selby paused. For him, this was a sign of thunderous disapproval—though whether of Isabel or Martin, she was not sure. "His lordship indicated only that he was in receipt of troubling news."

Her brow puckered. "Is it to do with our father? Is Lord Greenfield well?"

"Indeed, my lady. The matter does not pertain to your father." Selby's already correct posture grew even straighter. "Lord Martindale is available to speak with you at any time. I told his lordship I would ascertain whether you were prepared to accept callers."

"He must have loved that," she said under her breath.

Martin hated being thwarted. "As a matter of fact, Selby, I am only waiting for Miss Wallace to come downstairs; then we are to walk out with friends."

The first step in the plan to relieve the Duke of Ardmore of his false Botticelli: a long walk with Isabel, Lucy, and Brinley as well as Selina, George, and the duke's two hounds, Gog and Magog. Bringing dogs along on a casual promenade was an odd request, but Isabel had made up some ridiculous excuse about Brinley being lonely for friends, and the Godwins were too polite to demur. In truth, she hoped to tire out the hounds enough to subdue their aggression. Exercise, more than any food, had worked to calm Brinley.

"Have his lordship settled in the Chinese bedchamber," she decided, "and we shall see him when we return."

"No need for that. For making me wait or packing me off to a bedchamber." Aloysius Newcombe, Lord Martindale, pushed past Selby to enter the drawing room, then strode toward Isabel. "I'll see you now, as you've time. You'd put your own brother off merely for a walk? Disappointing."

Selby withdrew, the picture of silent tact.

All tailoring and exactitude, Martin drew up short as he reached the pianoforte. "Were you playing? Why didn't you raise the lid?"

Because she could feel Butler's letters gummed under it, obvious as a lit candle in a lantern. "It would be too loud if I raised the lid," she excused. "I didn't want to overpower your welcome in case you happened to call unexpectedly at an odd hour of the day."

Martin was a creature of great literalness, so he accepted this. "Excellent foresight. That was thoughtful of you."

"Sit, sit." Isabel pushed over to one side of the bench, then regarded her brother. He was a male mirror of herself, medium in build and with the same dark hair and eyes. Twelve years her senior, he had wed young and sensibly and filled the nursery of the family's estate in Kent.

True, Lady Martindale had done most of the difficult

bits, but Martin took full credit for the health and successes of his children. It was a year after Andrew's death before Martin ceased looking expectantly at Isabel's midsection, as if wondering how anyone who shared his blood could fail to take the proper steps in progressing through life. Marriage, children, widowhood. Careless of Isabel to skip the second.

He settled onto the bench beside her, taking care not to sit on and wrinkle his coat. "Isabel. I heard you were planning to set up your own household. That cannot be true."

Gossip. Miraculous gossip—the only thing in the world that traveled faster than a horse. "I *do* have my own household. And surely it was too early for my letter to reach you? I only sent it yesterday."

"What letter?"

"You didn't receive my letter? How did you know about my plan?"

"I've been here in London since yesterday, conducting some business for Father. Stayed at Greenfield House, of course—that's why you wouldn't have known I was here. Ran into Ardmore at the club last night, and he said he'd put you on to the scent of a house agent."

She sifted through his words, found a troubling grain. "You weren't planning to call on me otherwise?" Though she'd joked of their distance to Callum, the realization stung.

Martin pokered up. "I told you, I am here on business. I have been much occupied." To his credit, he didn't look her in the eye when he said this.

"All that the duke told you is accurate," Isabel granted. "This was Morrow's house. I should like my own instead."

He pressed a key at random, doubtful. "It's not usually done for a woman to buy a house of her own. But I suppose there is no harm in it, if the address is good."

"I did go over a house in Russell Square yesterday."

Martin looked mollified. "Excellent choice."

"But I decided it didn't suit, so I looked at a few rooms over a shop in Cheapside."

His jaw went slack. "You are joking."

She poked him in the side, enjoying his startled expression. "I am. The house agent did offer, but the second would suit me no more than the first."

"I am relieved to hear it." And he truly did sound relieved, as if he'd just learned she'd made a narrow escape from a rampaging lion.

She laughed. "I am spoiled; I want a comfortable home. You needn't fear that I will choose against my own preferences."

He poked another key on the pianoforte. "I do worry about you, with no one to look after you."

Callum Jenks said he would. She hid her smile within, warm like the memory of his gruff, calm words.

"Thank you for that. Do forgive me, Martin, but I cannot visit longer just now. Lucy and I have an appointment to walk out with Lady Selina Godwin. Is that not an *excellent choice* of company?" She repeated his own phrase.

He was blinking rather a lot and did not reply.

"You are welcome to order whatever you like of the servants, of course. Or come walking out with us. Lord Northbrook is coming too—you could talk about masculine things."

Now Martin looked interested. "Is he courting Lucy?" As a rule, he didn't approve of Lucy, who had neither birth nor fortune to recommend her. But interest from a ducal heir would repair these faults.

"No, George is not looking for a wife as yet. But I hope Brinley will make a friend of his father's dogs."

"Isabel, you are growing odd in your widowhood. And what is this you are wearing?"

She looked down. "It's a walking dress."

"I mean your pelisse."

"It's a pelisse. As I mentioned, I'm preparing to walk out."

"It's *blue*."

"Quite right." It was a subdued sort of evening-ish color, but it was, if one wanted to be quite specific, blue.

"But you are in mourning!"

Had she been hurt that he hadn't planned to call on her? Ha. That would have been preferable. Exasperated, she slid from the bench, forcing Martin to spring to his feet as well lest he demonstrate unmanneliness.

"Brother. Dear. Morrow died more than eighteen months ago, and you never liked him while he was alive. To twit me now for wearing a blue pelisse over my gray is unkind."

"Isabel!" He sounded shocked.

"Mar. Tin. Dale." She punctuated each syllable with a rap on the lid of the pianoforte. "You mind only that I am not allowing you the polite fiction of concern anymore."

"But I have need of it! You have lost sight of proper manners."

She rubbed at the sleek finish of the instrument's lid, marred by her touch. "I am a wealthy widow. Must I have proper manners?"

"You are a marquess's daughter. I should be ashamed if you had anything but."

"Oh, Martin." She sighed. "Could you not be ashamed of more substantial crimes than my telling you the truth?"

"You are not yourself anymore. Grief has addled your wits." He flicked his gaze over her clothing, frowning. "And you cannot just *invent* fashion. You should follow it, so you do not draw undue attention to yourself."

He was stuffier than a taxidermied elephant. "I am myself, I believe, more than ever. Perhaps my wits have been sharpened. And what is undue attention?"

"Any attention."

"I thought so." She shook her head. "Martin. I am a grown woman. I shall not behave as if I am a shadow any longer."

All this over a dark blue pelisse! What a sad little rebellion, if it were even intentional. But she'd put it on innocently, not meaning to start a battle of words with her brother. Now he had awoken a wondering in her. What sort of attention would she like? What sort of fashion ought she to favor?

So deep she was in her wondering, she almost missed his next words.

"Our mother never—" He pressed his lips together, cutting off the sentence.

"What?" It came out harshly, so she asked again—gently this time. "What did our mother never do, or say, or think? I don't know, Martin. I honestly don't."

At this appeal to his greater knowledge, he softened like wax worked in friendly hands. "Poor mite. You never knew her, and I got twelve years with her."

Poor mite. Honestly. "I'm a grown woman, for the second time. But yes, if you're to hold her up as an example, you must tell me what she's an example of. I suppose I knew her on the day I was born, but as she passed away just hours later, I cannot recall."

He looked grave, his eyes turning sad. "It was difficult. She was docile, always doing what father wanted. There were so many babies lost between my birth and yours. It wasn't your fault when she died."

"I know that it wasn't. I was a baby, and I didn't choose to make myself."

He hadn't chosen to make himself either, she realized. Son and heir, only child of a noble couple, their sole comfort as child after child was lost. They must have heaped more expectations upon him with every passing year, until he all but ossified beneath the burden.

"Thank you for calling on me," she said. "Truly. I know you act out of concern." For his own reputation as much as her well-being, certainly. But it didn't much matter. The effect was the same.

Her gracious words softened the stubborn line of his jaw. "You are most welcome. I return to Kent in the morning, but I shall call on you again before I go."

"Come for breakfast," she offered recklessly, and he agreed.

If all went as planned, tomorrow morning she'd be sleepless and euphoric after switching the Duke of Ardmore's painting. The idea appealed, facing her brother and Lucy over toast and marmalade, neither of them knowing what she'd done. Yet both of them would benefit. Her small trespass would prevent a greater scandal.

"I must go now," she said. "I've plans, and it's time to get on with them."

Each member of the team had his or her part to play that afternoon. Isabel walked with the others and the dogs until everyone was footsore. When she returned home, she burned all of Butler's letters, for they were all to become moot.

As none of them had found a way to force a window latch from the outside, Butler was to ensure that a window at Ardmore House was broken. He intended to press a street urchin into service. For the excessive price of a half-crown, they would buy his silence as well.

As evening fell, the boy was to come onto the rarefied street and throw stones at the house, being sure to hit the windows of the study that were pointed out to him. If the job were completed late enough, there would not be time for a glazier to make a repair until the next day.

This would be the way in.

Isabel passed the rest of the day in one task after another. She collected the necessary supplies and put them in a small black satchel with a long string that could be slung over her shoulder like a pack. She sent Celeste, her lady's maid, to buy a youth's mourning clothes from a secondhand shop, as "I know someone who has need of them." It was becoming a common excuse for her.

The most important task, of course, was retrieving the

original Botticelli from the hidden room. The process was hardly distasteful at all this time. She remembered sidling up the hidden stairs with Callum and imagined he was there again.

When she reached the room and laid hands on the painting, relief flooded her. Relief that this bit of Morrow's legacy would be undone, that this particular reminder of her failures as a wife would be gone. Many more remained, their painted eyes accusing as she slipped from the room with the priceless painting under a cloth. She took satisfaction in turning the key on them before she headed back down the stairs with her parcel.

And then it was only necessary to wait. Wait through dinner and make pleasant conversation with Lucy; wait for the long late-spring day to end and night to fall. It must be night, full night with only a moon to guide them, before they ventured out.

At midnight, Isabel was waiting behind her house with the painting. She saw nothing, heard nothing—and then Callum's voice was a whisper in her ear. "You don't look the slightest bit like a man."

She jolted, almost dropping the painting, then turned toward him. He was all in black, his face shaded by a brimmed cap. Until he appeared, she had almost doubted that he would. That any of this would happen. That she, Lady Isabel Morrow, proper widow who had never worn anything more scandalous than a dark blue pelisse, was now wearing cheap boys' clothing and carrying a mourning-shawl-wrapped painting of three nude women.

"Hullo to you too," she whispered. "You do look like a man. What of it?"

"Your—" He waved a hand at her hips. "You aren't the right shape. No one will be fooled."

"I'm not trying to fool anyone. I only want to be able to climb without a bunch of skirts getting in the way."

He considered this. "Since we don't intend to be noticed

at all, your point is well made. Shall we?" He stretched out a hand to the painting, and she released it. Another flood of relief, to have it out of her own hands.

"I couldn't think of doing this with anyone else," she said.

"I couldn't think of doing this for anyone else." She thought he smiled, but with his face shadowed and the moon behind him, it was difficult to tell.

"Thank you. I hope we shall make things right."

"That is the whole reason for my career," he said. "And for this unusual outgrowth of it."

The walk to Ardmore House was not long. At this hour of the night, traffic was light, the tonnish revelers who had left for the evening not yet on their way home. The air was cool and petulant, with yellow fog twining around lamps and buildings, disturbed by breeze and the threat of rain. It jaundiced the moon, turning the crescent of silver light to sooty dullness.

As much as possible, they slipped through mews, an unfamiliar world at night. The weight of the pistol was heavy in her pack. If she needed it, she wouldn't be able to reach it in time. Callum's hands were full of the painting, so he was helpless too.

She thought all this, eyes wide, heart racing, as they slinked from street to street—but then, before she had made up her mind to take the painting back from him, they were there: in the mews behind Ardmore House. Butler awaited them, also garbed in black.

Callum collected them into a huddle. "This is a tipping point," he murmured. "We can all still leave. We could leave the duke with the painting he believes to be real, and you can leave with a clear conscience, having committed no crime."

"I won't have a clear conscience unless I do the right thing," she whispered back. "It's not for Morrow's memory. It's for Lucy."

"I already hired a boy to break a duke's windows," Butler said mildly. "I'm in."

As he was too large of frame to fit easily through a window, he had agreed to take up watch. First, though, he helped to boost Isabel over the wall that separated the house and yard from the mews. Once she was over, landing quiet as a cat in her kid half-boots, Butler and Callum slid the cloth-wrapped painting over the wall; then Callum climbed over and followed her.

The yard was pitted and cluttered with a kitchen garden, a chicken coop, a wash area. At night, the plants were shadowed skeletons, the coop a great looming blackness. No wonder the Quality walled off the backs of their houses: the perfect façade would be spoiled by revealing all that it took to maintain it. They picked their way cautiously across the yard, pausing when the moon popped from behind a cloud to shine extra light. All was silent, though, the servants asleep in their beds save for the unlucky ones who had to wait up for their gallivanting master and mistress.

Callum went before, carrying the painting in the dark lee of the house. Isabel veered to the other side, following the line of the wall and searching out their entry point. The wall met up with the house behind the second set of windows. Fortunately, the study was near the rear, so they could enter from this hidden area. There was the fifth window back, and the fourth . . .

Oh, hell.

Taking care to be silent, she crept to where Callum stood. "Butler's boy couldn't count," she whispered. "Or he couldn't aim. He broke the third window back, not the fourth or fifth."

Callum said something unprintable, then apologized. "What will the third window lead us into?"

Isabel thought about the windings of the house. "The music room, I think."

"Nothing for it. That's where we can get in without causing further damage, so that's where we'll go in."

She agreed. He set the wrapped painting down gently next to the house, then undid his own pack and pulled out a rope with a sort of metal hook at the end. Stepping back, eyeing his target, he spun the rope in a quick circle—then flung it high. The hook hit the window frame with a *thunk*, then slid, moonlight glinting on its silvery surface, and bit down hard into the wood.

Every sound set Isabel's nerves on edge. *Andrew, if you weren't already dead, I would kill you for putting me through this.*

They waited, pressed against the house, for an endless few minutes. When no one and nothing appeared, Callum tugged at the end of the rope. Satisfied that it would hold, he whispered, "You can wait down here. Less trouble for you that way."

"No, no. Butler is keeping watch from out here. I can keep watch from indoors. One person to carry the painting, one person to drug the dogs." She didn't have enough faith in the day's walk to keep the dogs sleepy and silent throughout their time in the house.

"Fine. But I'll go up first," he insisted.

"In that case, take several of the cakes." She opened her satchel and took a packet of wrapped aniseed cakes. She'd estimated the weight of the dogs and carefully droppered in just enough laudanum to give them a peaceful night's slumber.

Callum slipped them into his pocket, then drew on a pair of black gloves. He laid hold of the rope and began to climb, bracing his feet against the side of the house, aiding his arms as he drew himself up hand over hand. His progress was swift, almost effortless. Isabel swallowed. Nerveless and nervous though she was, she appreciated the sight of his firm backside, his strong legs, the inexorable grasp and climb of his hands.

At the top of the rope, he studied the window. They had wondered if it would be covered with something on the inside, and from the way he gingerly poked at the hole in the window, she guessed that a board was blocking it. Still grasping the rope, braced against the wall with his legs, he poked at the broken edges of the glass—then put a gloved fist through the hole in the window and pushed out the board. He contorted himself wildly, arm jutting and angling—trying to catch the board as it fell forward? Oh, she *hated* being below and helpless. Her pounding heart made her eager to move.

Finally, he undid the latch and slid up the sash, then swung a leg over and climbed inside. Isabel strained her eyes, her ears, for a few seconds that took years—then Callum leaned from the window and silently motioned her up. Wrapping the painting in knots of rope, she settled it gently on her back like a cape. Then, bracing her feet on the wall, she climbed up, half pulling, half being pulled. It felt good, so good to use her muscles in this capable way.

Then she was at the window. She swung one leg over the sill to steady herself, loving the freedom of her boys' trousers, and leaned forward flat. Callum's hands worked over her back, a series of silent pressures undoing the rope, and he drew the painting free and eased it through the window. It was a rare feat, taking some coaxing on his part and some wiggling on Isabel's, but then it was through and he leaned the painting against the wall.

Taking her hands in his gloved ones, he tugged her through the window. When she placed both feet on the floor, she let out a soundless, belly-deep breath. Swiftly, firmly, Callum gathered her into his arms. For a moment, they stood thus with their heartbeats tripping against each other. Body to body, silent in relief and partnership. Isabel breathed him in, the scent of his neck, his hair. *I couldn't think of doing this with anyone else.*

He bent his head to her ear. "Boots off," he said in a tickling voice that was little more than breath. They were in the music room, as she'd expected: there was just enough light from the moon for her to spot the large instruments.

Releasing each other, they removed boots, and he stripped off his gloves and tucked them away. Every movement seemed as loud as the stomp of an elephant. Her breaths were shallow scoops of air, silent and quick. But it was all right. They were done; ready to move to the study.

Then outside the closed music-room door, they heard footsteps—and a dog began to bark.

Chapter Eleven

Callum's heart thudded, too loudly. The footsteps were drawing close, then closer. Too close upon the floor of the corridor. The dogs were a riot of sound, bark after bark. To shield her, Callum pushed Isabel behind him. Each movement was silent as a breath. Each breath was caught, trapped, stifled.

The barking continued—but the footsteps went past the doorway. Their owner spoke up at last: "Quiet now, ye damned beasts! Wouldn't be no need to check all the doors if it weren't for you shoving 'em open with yer great dirty bodies."

The accent was too thick to belong to any member of the family. So, one of the servants, keeping vigil while his fashionable employers were about their entertainment.

"There! Eat it and be quiet." A *rrruff*, then clicking claws as the dogs evidently pounced upon some treat. "Don't be wakin' the whole house." Keys jingled. Heavy-soled shoes shifted, headed back the way from which they'd come.

It was like attending a play with his eyes shut. Callum strained for every noise, every clue, even as he held Isabel still and taut behind himself. Was that it? Could they proceed?

The footsteps crossed before the music-room door

again—and the barks and snarls resumed. Callum gritted his teeth. If the servant opened the door, there might be just time to hide in the shadows behind the pianoforte. Better that than coshing the man. He was innocent, only doing his job.

No, not even that. Whatever he was supposed to do for the dogs, he gave up on it. "Ahh. Be damned to ye, then. Hobbes can lock you away himself. I've no wish to lose a finger."

A whistle and a throw, then an object struck a wall down the corridor. "There!" called the man over the noise of the dogs. "Fetch, and if ye break yer necks, all the better."

It was impossible to track the sound of his steps after that. Had the man gone away? The dogs returned to the music room, pacing before the door. Whining. Scratching at it. The servant, whoever he'd been, said no more. He must have returned to his bed.

"We were lucky," whispered Isabel, "that the servant hated the dogs. If he'd noticed they were interested in this room . . ."

"It's the aniseed," muttered Callum. "I told you they don't follow calmly."

"Nor will they resist it." With nimble fingers silvered by moonlight, she teased open the satchel she carried and pulled out a paper-wrapped parcel. The clawing at the door intensified when she unwrapped it to reveal a half-dozen small cakes.

"Any one of these should cause a dog to fall asleep," she whispered.

Would one fit under the door? He wasn't eager to open it, exposing them to the large dogs. Maybe it would fit, if he squished it flat. He re-folded the paper about the cakes and pressed them between his palms. Isabel made a sliding motion, her brows lifted: she understood.

"Two cakes at a time," she suggested. "No more than that, in case one dog gobbles everything."

He crouched before the door, thankful for every bit of the solid wood between him and the great hounds Isabel had told him were called Gog and Magog. The door was bearing the brunt of their attention. Someone would have a job painting over the claw marks marring it.

Again, he unwrapped the cakes. Set one before the door, then shoved it with fingertips through the narrow space beneath. Hot canine breath touched his fingertips as he withdrew them, and the clawing stopped. *Sniff sniff.*

He did the same with another cake, then stood, wiping his fingers on the paper wrapping. Then there was nothing to do but wait.

As an Officer of the Police, Callum was comfortable with waiting. With letting a pause stretch out awkwardly long, so his quarry felt the need to fill it. With keeping a quiet watch on a person or a piece of property.

Waiting with Lady Isabel Morrow? That was no hardship at all.

They were alone here. More alone, in the dark and soundless room, than they'd been at the grotto in Vauxhall, where fireworks exploded overhead as they took their pleasure of each other. How had that night led them to this one?

Thank God it had led to something; that that had not been the end of Lady Isabel Morrow in his life.

With only moonlight behind her, her hair was night-black as her clothes. The gentle light made her features glow.

"What is it?" she asked softly, eyeing him with some trepidation. "Do you hear—"

"Nothing," he said. "You are beautiful to look at."

At once, she turned away. "How can you say that at a time like this?"

"Because it is true. At any time, it is true."

"Silver tongue." She shook her head. But she must have believed him, for she closed the distance between them, fitting her head onto his shoulder. Her hair tickled his neck, his chin. Her breasts pressed his chest; her arms linked about his waist. And here he was, still holding the ridiculous but necessary parcel of aniseed cakes, unable to take her in both his arms as he wished.

He had one, though. One free arm. He placed the hand at the small of her back, enjoying the slide of his palm over the fabric of the odd shirt she wore. Like that, he held her, stroked her, fit her against himself. And they waited in the silence, aware of its pressure, of each other.

And then: *snore*.

A sleepy sound had issued from before the door. Then a snuffling sound, a half-hearted *ruff*.

Isabel pushed away from Callum, instantly on alert. "Sit," she hissed, loudly enough to carry.

A click of canine toenails. Another animal snore.

Was it one dog? Was it both?

Slowly, he pressed the door handle and eased the door open, inward. Every little creak made him wince. The dim outside light picked out one large form on the floor: a hound stretched out on his side, breath whistling as he slept.

One sleeping dog. Where had the other one gone?

Callum eased a flat cake out of the packet and left it by the sleeping dog. "In case the other one comes back," he said below his breath into Isabel's ear. "We can pick it up before we go." Isabel nodded, and he returned the cakes to her to put back into her satchel. He retrieved the painting in its wrapping, hoisting it under one arm.

Leaving the door ajar, they left the music room. Already it had come to seem safe and familiar to Callum. Isabel linked index fingers with him, making a chain of themselves so as not to lose each other in the dark.

Callum's eyes had adjusted well enough to see in the windowed room. In the corridor, he was walking almost blind. The silence was oppressive; darkness lay heavy on his eyes. His eyes and ears were full of nothing at all, though he strained to see . . . was that a darker rectangle amidst the darkness? A doorway? Isabel stretched out a pale hand, brushing her fingertips downward—and found a door handle.

Gingerly, he let out a caught breath. This was the study. As slowly as he had opened the music room door, she now did this one. Painting in hand, Callum stepped inside.

Isabel's drawing hadn't prepared him for how cramped it was. A huge desk, a darker shadow among shadows. Heavy draperies over each of two small windows. He tugged one aside, just a little, and the crescent moon silvered the dark.

Not much light, but enough to spot their quarry. Centered behind the desk was the painting. It was not especially small, but too small for all this trouble.

He uncovered the genuine Botticelli. Held it up. There they were: three scarcely clad women with firm, pale limbs and joyless faces. In the moonlight, the two paintings looked exactly the same to Callum's eye. But in bright light, would one with greater knowledge notice Butler's clue? Or did one have to know the real painting as intimately as the fake?

No matter. The fake would vanish, and Botticelli's Graces would be the only ones to survive.

So. He set aside the old painting and lifted the forgery down.

Now came the tricky part of removing the fake from its frame. He had filled his pockets with tools, hoping against hope he wouldn't have to use them. How could one hammer in a bunch of tiny tacks without being heard? If it came to that, Isabel could slip back outside and have Butler cause a commotion to distract the wakeful servant.

On the desk, he laid out the tools. Pliers. Tacks. Hammer. A small knife. He flipped over the fake, and here was a bit of luck. There was no heavy paper over the back to protect the picture from dust. The stretched canvas was held into the frame by tiny nails through the stretcher into the wood of the frame. With his pliers, Callum yanked them all straight out, finding it as satisfying as if he were drawing out rotten teeth. As he tugged the last one free, the painted canvas tipped backward, falling right into Isabel's waiting hands.

She steadied it with one hand, slid the Botticelli to Callum with the other and tied the covering cloth around her waist. He fit the centuries-old painting into the frame, blessing Butler's accurate eye when it slipped neatly into place. Now for the nails. He would re-use the old ones if he could. He picked up the hammer, gritted his teeth.

Isabel tapped him on the shoulder. When he looked up, she handed him a . . .

"A thimble?"

She indicated he should put it on his thumb, then shove the nails in silently.

Easy for her to suggest. But if he could find old nail holes and use those, perhaps it would work. Dubiously, he put the thimble over the end of his thumb. It looked like a too-small hat, and when he pressed at a nail head with it, it flicked off and struck the front of the desk with a tiny *ping*.

Never mind that. He tucked the thimble into a pocket, then stripped off his coat. Laying it flat on the floor to muffle sound, he laid the framed painting on its face atop the coat. With the hammer's head, he shoved silently at each tiny nail.

Isabel took up the discarded painting by Butler, turning it too onto its face. She kneeled on the floor beside Callum, pliers in hand, and yanked free the fastenings holding the canvas to its stretcher bars. They had planned this ahead of time. Off its wooden skeleton, they could roll the copied painting small, dispose of the wood bars, make a quick escape.

It was an odd partnership, switching paintings in silence by night. For an Officer of the Police, it ought to have been unacceptable, but he found he rather liked it. Perhaps he would have liked any task done at the side of Isabel.

He paused when he heard claws clicking in the corridor. The first dog awake? The second returning? Isabel, too, froze.

A snuffle. A growl. A gulp. More claws on the polished floor, steps receding.

In a crouch, moving with the sinuousness of a cat, Isabel rounded on the door and eased it open a fraction. One eye pressed to the crack. When she turned back, shutting the door again with a slow turn of the handle, she pumped a fist in silent triumph.

Still asleep, she mouthed. Which meant the second dog had returned to eat the remaining cake. Good. Gog and Magog would be sleeping like baby giants by the time Callum and Isabel completed their task.

Back to work, then. Infinitesimal bit by bit, he forced the nails through the stretcher bars of a canvas once touched by Botticelli. Through wood they went, into the frame. He did not use as many as had held Butler's painting, but time was short. Every minute made the return of the family possible, the wakefulness of a dog likely.

Silence was key, speed only slightly less so—yet maintaining either was impossible. Each time Isabel separated one of the wooden bars from its neighbor, there was a *crack*. Callum ventured a *whap* with a hammer occasionally, deadening the sound by working beneath a tent of his coat, then removing it to examine his work by moonlight.

Before he was done, Isabel had completed her task, creating two rolled bundles. One was the canvas, tight-wrapped and tied like a scroll. The other, the stretcher bars, was a collection of smooth kindling the size of two fists together.

"Good work," he whispered.

"Ready?" she returned. He nodded.

She eased her bundles atop the duke's desk, then laid hold of a corner of the bulky framed painting. On his fingers, Callum counted off, *one—two—three*, and they heaved it upright. Isabel eased her side of the picture into his grip, then guided him by the elbow. Forward, sideways, up—all in silence, all by touch. Her fingers were warm through the thin cloth of his shirt, making his skin prickle with sensation. Every sense was heightened, on alert.

As he hung the picture back on the wall, letting the frame settle into its accustomed spot, triumph rushed through him. It was done, and they'd managed it together. Once they were on the ground, he would kiss the devil out of her—or into her.

The last steps were drawing on his gloves again, then closing the draperies. Then, a moving shadow in the night-dark room, Isabel took hold of the door handle. Slowly, she eased the door open. The doorway across the corridor showed paler with moonlight from the open window, beckoning them forward. Out. To safety.

Then it happened, faster than he could understand.

A dark blur whipped by on the floor. Hit the door, knocking it free from Isabel's grasp. It smacked the wall heavily, the sound resounding down the corridor.

A dog whined. Growled, close at hand. Further away came another growl, feeding the first. And then—the yowl of an angry cat? Where the devil had a cat come from?

The barking grew louder, the groggy dogs fighting off their slumberousness.

Callum caught Isabel's eye. "Back. Go. Quickly as you can."

Sidling along the wall, she whipped across the corridor in her stockinged feet. Shit! They hadn't their boots on. He scrabbled for the bundles of Butler's work from the desk, his coat from the floor.

A human voice rang out. "What now, ye bloody beasts?" The servant again. Callum swept his tools up from the desk, wadding them in his coat. Did he have everything? They must leave nothing behind. The need to hurry was like ice in his fingertips.

"Caught something, did you?" Now the servant sounded awake. Close as he had been in the music room, when only

a door and his ignorance of their presence shielded them.
There was no time for secrecy, for stealth.

Clutching everything against his chest, Callum kicked
back, finding the edge of the desk. His foot made a hollow
thud that he, with a great leap, was nowhere near. A distraction, he hoped. Enough of one?

No, the air stirred behind him. Teeth snapped. But the
dogs were slowed and sleepy, and he was safely across, in
the music room. Already Isabel had tossed their boots out the
window. As soon as Callum entered, she shoved the door
closed behind him, fumbling at the lock. No key! No help
for it; they had to go, go, go, as the dogs snarled at the door
and scratched it with their paws.

By this time, Butler was waiting below the window. Callum
shoved out the whole bundle: coat, tools, painting, stretcher
bars. With a quick squeeze of Isabel's hand, he swung her
through the window frame. She met his gaze, dark eyes
wide in the moonlight. Quickly, he pressed a smacking kiss
to her lips. "Go! I'll be right behind you."

Isabel shimmied her way down, looking up at Callum all
the while. From half a story up, she jumped, not waiting for
Butler's helping hand or the support of the rope. She landed
heavily, awkwardly.

Callum gritted his teeth, then swung out after her. As he
disappeared through the window, the door burst open, and
the room was full of hounds swaying on their feet. Snarling.
A man, light glinting off a weapon.

Callum slid down, the rough rope heating through his
gloves and shredding the leather. As soon as his stockinged
feet touched the ground, he snatched his boots in one hand
and took hold of Isabel's shoulder with the other. With
Butler's help, he pulled her to her feet, then tugged at the
rope to bring it down and slow their pursuers. The hook
that had sunk into the window frame took a chunk of wood
with it.

A man's head stuck out the window, shouting something unintelligible. If they were lucky, he'd think he had surprised housebreakers in the act of entering, scaring them off before they got far.

Callum hoped.

He had hoped to go entirely undiscovered. He had hoped the servant wouldn't carry a weapon. A blade? No, a pistol—and he was aiming it at them.

Butler and Isabel were hidden in the shadows; Callum was a step behind, slowed by pulling down the rope. As he turned away, a shot rang out—and a stripe of fire slit the cloth over his calf. Callum left it all behind on the ground: tools hidden in the turf; the rope a pale, sharp-headed snake in the dark. And they ran.

The frantic flight from the Duke's house carried them for a few streets, Isabel wincing as she ran in her stocking feet. Yet the moon smiled on them, pleased with their night's work. Clouds drifted over its bright face, bringing welcome darkness as they slipped away from the gas-lit street, then drifted on to give them a faint light once they reached a safe distance.

Butler had taken charge of the painting, his own rolled-up work. When they paused in their flight, he stretched it out to admire it.

"There's the B." He showed Isabel and Callum, pointing to a spot Isabel had taken for naught but greenery when she'd looked at it in the duke's study. But there it was, picked out by the touch of his finger. The only signature Butler had been able to place on his work.

Satisfied, Butler rolled the canvas tightly and slipped it into a hollow cane. Likely there had been meant to be a sword stick. This painting was an even greater weapon against the duke, against Isabel, against Morrow.

Butler took the stretcher bars too. "Might put them back together," he said. "Or I might kindle a fire against the nighttime chill."

She hoped he would burn the copied Botticelli with its own stretchers. "Be safe," she whispered.

He handed over her boots and wished her the same, then melted off. Isabel and Callum retreated into the deeper darkness beside the building. Several houses back—only a few minutes back?—the Duke of Ardmore's dogs snarled and bayed their frustration. Dogs couldn't climb down ropes, thank heaven. But as soon as they could run down the stairs, they could sniff out Isabel and Callum's trail.

Impatient, she crammed her feet into her boots without bothering with the fastenings. Callum shoved his arms into his coat, his feet into his boots. Odd how undressed they'd become.

Hoping to confuse the dogs, she took out the remaining aniseed cakes from her satchel. Hard as she could throw, she flung one here, one there, and watched where they landed.

But there was something more on the pavement: drops, trailing black on the surface where everything was black or gray or silver. With her eyes, she followed them to the source—then gasped.

"You are bleeding! Were you shot?"

Callum cursed. "I was. It's not bad, but we can't leave a trail."

"We've got to bind your wound." From about her waist, Isabel untied the cloth that had wrapped the Botticelli on their way. It was a shawl, sturdy and black. She crouched, wrapping it around his leg once, then again, then tucking in the loose ends.

"That might be tidy enough to get you back to my house," she whispered. "We can fix you up there."

"What about you?"

"I didn't get shot."

"You fell. Hard."

He was right. Her ankle had hurt like the devil when she'd collapsed onto it, but as she'd run, she'd forgotten it. Now a warning twinge returned.

"I'm fine," she said. "Let's go."

Callum took the satchel from her and ripped it along the seam, making of it two dark and anise-fragrant rags. With them, he wiped up a bit of the blood, then tossed the rags in different directions. "That might confuse the dogs a bit longer."

He put out an arm for Isabel, then asked, "What was it that tripped us up? There were only two dogs."

"Titan." Isabel snarled the name as if she were one of the duke's hounds. "All our preparations for the damned dogs, and the creature that ruined our plan was Lady Selina's cat."

Callum chuckled, the unaccountable man. Hobbling and limping and skulking and sneaking, they made their labored way back through the mews. To Isabel, the journey back to her house seemed to take forever. Surely each street stretched out long and longer, like a sweet only half-boiled.

By the time they reached her back garden, tears sprang to her eyes with every step, and her right ankle and foot were nothing but a weight to be dragged along by her upper leg.

With all the servants asleep before they had left, she prayed that the servants' entrance would still be open. She had a key, of course, but the easier the better. Every second, every step saved was a boon.

"Come in and we'll see to your injury," she told Callum.

"I'm all right. Come in and we'll see to yours."

Once they were inside, he added, "I didn't intend to stay, but you can't fool me, brave woman though you are. Your ankle is all but broken. Have you any more laudanum?"

"No laudanum." She gritted her teeth. "There is port in the dining room sideboard."

She pointed him in the right direction. For a few minutes, he was gone; when he returned he held a cut-crystal decanter.

"You carry this," Callum whispered. "I'll carry you."

"No, really, you needn't—"

"I want to," he said. And she was in his arms, cradled sideways as if she were small and light instead of an average-sized woman with a useless foot that surely weighed a hundred pounds. His arms gripped her about her thighs, her back; his chest was a wall of support. As soon as he lifted her, the throbbing in her ankle eased a little.

In a low tone, she directed him to where he might find rolled bandaging. From there, she told him how to reach her bedchamber. The words were strange and intimate; she blushed as she spoke them.

With his hands on her, the frantic flight over, the switch of paintings a success, she was swamped with buoyant eagerness—a physical awareness she could never remember experiencing before. Every inch of her throbbed or tingled or was caressed by closeness. She was all a jumble, her thoughts and feelings in confusion.

But there was one thing she was sure of. Something she knew she wanted.

As soon as they reached her bedchamber, she said, "Lay me on the bed, Callum. And then lock the door so we won't be disturbed."

Chapter Twelve

She raised herself up onto her elbows, watching as he turned the key in the lock. "I am so sorry you were hurt in helping me. I should never have involved you."

"Probably not." His footsteps crossed the carpeted floor to the window, where he tugged open the draperies. In the faint light of the moon, he became a broad, strong shape silhouetted against the window.

"There is a lamp on the writing desk," Isabel said. "And though I meant what I said, now I am even sorrier that you agree with me."

"I'm being honest." He laid hands on the tinderbox, struck a spark, then lit the lamp on her desk. It flung warm light on his features, showing their wry expression. "I wasn't telling you how I feel about the matter. I'm glad you involved me."

He carried the lamp to the table at her bedside, then set it down. There, he hesitated.

She shook the decanter at him. "Sit with me. Have a drink."

Gingerly, he sank onto the bed. His feet remained on the floor as he tested the ropes of the mattress, bouncing his weight. "Good bed," he commented. "But how are you?

Besides your ankle, did you come through all right?" He hiked up one knee onto the mattress, twisting to study her. "Are you afraid? Shaken?"

She tugged out the crystal stopper, then handed it to him to set on the table. "Why are you asking about me?"

"I want to know everything. Hazard of the profession." His mouth crimped. That trying-not-to-smile look.

She tipped the decanter to her lips, imbibing courage as well as sticky-sweet port, then traced a fingertip over the line of his lips. "I want to know everything too, and I'm no Officer of the Police."

His eyes lowered, lashes shadowing his cheekbones. "Ah, you got the name right this time. And tonight, you were as much one as I was."

"Which is to say, not at all?" She took another sip. The decanter was heavy in her hand, expensive lead crystal. "Don't use your profession as an excuse, you wily man. You'd have been just as blunt and prying if you were a grocer."

"You make me sound like a crowbar." He tugged at his boot, wincing.

"Look at your leg! Oh, I'm so sorry." She sat up, all but flinging the decanter at him. "Let me take that ridiculous shawl off of your wound."

He set the decanter on the table beside the lamp. "It hurts like the devil, but I'll be fine if I bind it. It's not the first time I've been shot."

"Don't say that. Don't tell me that. Now I'll just worry about you more."

"I'm honored." His tone was so dry that he made it sound like a jest—but when she looked him in the eye, his gaze was serious and stark.

Unknotting the shawl from about his calf, she quickly made a cushion of it to cradle the injured leg and protect the coverlet. "It's ruined your boot," she chided. "That's just annoying."

Callum frowned at the hole in the thick leather. "Shame the duke's servant wasn't an even worse shot. But I've faith that Brinley will still adore my footwear."

"You and that dog." Isabel shook her head. "He did take to you uncommonly quickly. Will it hurt you if I pull off the boot?"

"Maybe. But I can't live forever with it on."

That was fair enough. She seized the heel and tugged hard. When the boot hit the carpeted floor of the bedchamber with a *thump*, she ventured a glance at Callum. He wore a tight expression, but said nothing; he only took the roll of bandage they'd brought upstairs. Tugging off his ruined stocking, he wrapped a band of gauze around the raw scoop the bullet had taken from his calf. Once around, and the bandage turned red; around again, and it stayed white. A third time around, then he tore it and tied it off. The shawl that had served as a bandage, he shoved to the floor.

"All better." He dropped the remaining bandage onto the table beside the lamp.

"I wish you were." Isabel swallowed. "I would have been so scared without you. I was scared all the same, but without you . . ."

"It wouldn't have been wise to go alone," he said gravely. "Investigators often have partners. Or informants, or consultants. It's more than twice as easy to work with the help of another."

"Is it? Well, I'm trying to thank you. So, thank you." She rubbed her lips together. "The port isn't strong enough to dull pain, but it's quite good. You ought to have some too."

"I will, then. We ought to celebrate our success." He took up the decanter, waving it before his nose. His brows lifted. "Why, Lady Isabel, you lay in a fine port."

As he tipped it back, sipping, she hissed, "It's not a celebration! We can't celebrate your bullet wound!"

"It's only a scratch." He darted a sideways glance at her.

"I mean—you are right. It is very severe. I am in incredible pain. You should minister to me with your kindest attentions."

She snatched the port from him, suppressing a smile, then sipped from where his lips had touched. The port was sweet on her tongue, warm in her throat and belly. Yes, her ankle still ached, but she didn't care as much as she had. Callum Jenks was ample distraction.

"You"—she reached over him to return the heavy crystal to the table—"are a rogue. But I won't protest at all. Any sort of bullet wound is worthy of kindest attentions."

He arched a brow. "And how do you define those?"

"Much the same way you would, I imagine." When she again traced the line of his lips, he nipped at her finger. Startled, she laughed—and then leaned forward, brushing a kiss against his jaw. The muscle jumped beneath her caress, so she had to kiss it again, then back around to his lips to sip the sweet, heady taste of port, the headier heat of his mouth on hers. Tenderly, he brushed the tip of her tongue with his, then he pulled back.

"You are intoxicating," he said. "But you're also injured. You need kind attentions too." Without waiting for agreement or protest, he nudged her back so she lay flat on the bed. For a moment, he merely looked upon her. She would have given a great deal of money to know what he was thinking.

Then he turned away to remove his other boot and stocking, letting them fall to the floor beside their mates. He slid to the foot of the bed then, crossing his legs atop the coverlet with a hiss of discomfort. She raised herself up on her elbows. "Callum, please don't hurt—"

"Please don't hurt my feelings," he said dryly. "I've never taken the boots off a lady with a sprained ankle, and I don't want to muck it up."

At that, she had to smile. She sank back again and let him minister to her. What would his kind attentions be?

At first, they didn't feel particularly kind, though they

were necessary: as she'd done for him, he removed her boots. The left one was not a problem, but the injured right ankle protested his slow, tender movements. She moaned as the tight kid slid free from her swollen ankle. A pulse beat in the injured joint. How was that possible?

"May I go on?"

"I'm still waiting for the kindness," she grumbled. "But yes, whatever you think best."

She sucked in a sharp breath, prepared for another pain, as he slid his hands within her trouser-cuffs to find the tops of her stockings. They were tied just below the knees. Gently, he untied them. The left one first, he rolled down and off, leaving her foot bare. Then the right, slowly and carefully.

She exhaled, wondering. His fingertips on her skin were a tiny pleasure; even over her ankle, he did not hurt her. With the stocking off, her foot up on a pillow, he pressed at the sides of the joint, then up, down, around again.

"It is not broken," he said. "But you will not dance a cotillion for some weeks."

"It was not in my plans."

He asked for the bandage; when she handed it to him, he wrapped the remainder of the roll about her ankle. Around the arch of her foot. Back, looping, again, then tucked the end under. "I confess," he said as he worked, "I am eager to know your plans."

"At the moment," she said, "they involve you."

Everything she had done was to please someone else. Only in Vauxhall had she turned the situation about, making a decision solely for her own pleasure.

And Callum, here, now? He was her choice, and hers alone. There was something about Callum Jenks that made her want more.

"It was the day I found the hidden studio," she admitted. "That I went to Vauxhall. I didn't know what to do. I didn't know the man I'd married, or what sort of secrets my house had been hiding. Were there more? Who was I grieving? Was I even grieving anymore?"

"That is a great many questions." He tweaked one of the toes on her left foot, tickling.

"It was, and my head felt so full of them that I had to get away. Vauxhall was having a masquerade; my lady's maid had mentioned it. So I slipped out and . . . and once I was there, I met you."

Met. Ha. She had done far more than *met* him. She had flung herself recklessly, passionately, at the Bow Street Runner who had impressed her, during their brief acquaintance, as someone she could rely on. *Be honest. Be true.* How hungry she had been for something genuine.

He was silent for almost a minute, stroking the sensitive arch of her foot until her toes curled. "That was the day of my brother's funeral," he said at last. "My head was overfull too."

"Your brother who was the guard," she remembered.

"At the Royal Mint. Yes."

"I am so sorry for your loss." She heard it in his voice, the resonance of how it still bothered him.

"And I for yours."

"They are not to be compared, surely." She folded her arms behind her head, the better to study him. "You lost a loved one; I lost only my illusions."

"You lost a person too."

Oh. Yes, of course she had. A person who had murdered himself rather than . . . what? See the evaporation of all he'd worked for? Rather than return the paintings in the hidden studio? Rather than watch his wife become other than what he'd wanted?

For she was becoming something else, wasn't she? She was asking questions, and not only of herself. She was making plans, and not only for other people.

"Andrew and I did not have the sort of marriage I expected." Was she really going to tell him? She had never told anyone before. But his face was open. Listening. He wanted to know everything, he'd told her. "It was a true marriage, but not often. He preferred painted women to the real thing, I believe. Palest skin. Smooth limbs, hairless all over. I did not live up to the art."

"Those pictures." Callum's jaw clenched. "The ones in which he had a 'private interest.' Damn the man."

"I don't blame myself." *Anymore*, she did not say.

For she had, once. Hers wasn't the sort of body that appealed to Andrew. The hidden room had been proof upon proof again, falling like a blow when she'd thought she was healed from the pain of his suicide. Painted Venuses, flawless and seductive; sweet-faced maidens both innocent and bare-breasted. Perfect in paint, endlessly naked before a lascivious gaze.

"It's not right to speak ill of the dead," said Callum. "So I won't tell you that he was a villain to marry you, knowing he could not treasure you as you deserved."

He took her toes in his hands, a touch that could have been casual save for the burn in his dark eyes. That look made it intimate, prickling and pleasurable, a reminder of what had passed between them, and what might happen again if she dared.

Did she want to dare?

Of course she did. She had ever since he'd taken her against his chest; ever since, maybe, he had accompanied her to Butler's flat. Her life took odd turns when Callum Jenks was a part of it, and when it did, he would not be shaken from her side.

"Do you think . . ." She hesitated. "Do you think you might make love to me again?"

He never looked surprised. Ever. "I might, at that. But the circumstances would have to be ideal."

"Such as?" Her cheeks burned. "I don't worry about conception. It has never happened for me."

"It's always a possibility, though I do take precautions.

But that's not what I was thinking." Slowly, he rolled up the legs of her odd boys' trousers. "Before I could make love to you again, I'd have to have a title and a fortune."

"Do you think so little of me, to suppose that I expect such a thing?"

The right leg was rolled to mid-calf; the left was almost to her knee. "No, Lady Isabel. I think so much of you. You're a proper widow and the daughter of a marquess, and that's the sort of man you deserve."

"I'm not the daughter of a marquess tonight," she said. "And I'm certainly not a proper widow. I'm a thief."

"Ah, I can't go to bed with a thief either. I'm an Officer of the Police. I ought by all rights to drag a thief before the magistrate." His hands belied his words, stroking the tender skin behind her knee. Dancing over her calves.

"Is that what you are tonight?" He was raising shivers in her, delicious ripples of sensation. "If I've laid aside my roles for a while, perhaps you could too."

"And then who would I be?" He looked serious, when she'd intended to tease him. "If I'm not an Officer of the Police?" The question seemed to trouble him.

She raised herself on one elbow and caught one of his hands, rubbing his calloused fingers with her own. "You're just Callum. And I'm Isabel."

"Isabel," he murmured.

"What we've done, we've done together. And I hope we'll do more." *God.* She was throwing herself at him—or would be, if her sprained ankle permitted such exuberant movement.

When he met her eyes, he smiled. It was a wry expression, and a sweet one. "Do you know why I helped you tonight?"

"For justice?" she guessed. He shook his head. "Because you find me irresistible?"

"You are not wrong. But I am very good, madam, at re- sisting things I don't want to resist."

"Why, then?"

He looked at where their hands were laced, then wiggled his fingers to knit them more tightly together. "Because I failed Harry. And the law failed Harry. So I know how it hurts to fail, and to feel trapped within the law you thought would save you. I wanted to spare you that."

She was missing something. "But why?"

He shut his eyes. "I am not the cold man I might seem, Isabel. Nor am I unfeeling."

"So you did it for me." Her tone was wondering. "Because . . . you care about me?"

Streets away, in the Duke of Ardmore's study, Botticelli's three Graces danced. Wrapped in a sword stick, or maybe smiled upon by Angelica Butler, three much younger Graces made an endless circle.

Antique and new, none of them smiled as they danced.

Amazingly, though, Callum *did* smile. Not his usual crimp of lips, of duty fighting for control over amusement. This was real. Sharp and sweet and happy.

"I like it when you smile," Isabel said.

His smile fell away, heart in his eyes—and then his lips were on hers.

Head spinning, she remembered something puzzling. "What about"—she let herself be taken in another kiss—"all that nonsense about wanting to be different?"

"If you don't want me to be different"—he undid the laces fastening the boy's shirt she wore—"then I'd be a fool to wish myself anywhere else in the world, or with anyone else."

"Silver tongue," she laughed.

"You have no idea." The flame-gold of the lamplight turned his dark eyes to fire.

This was no stone bench, no stolen moment. They had trespassed in a duke's house, and the hidden room remained full of other paintings that lacked proper homes. Yet that didn't matter now: it was night, and this was a bed, and there was nowhere else she ought to be, and nowhere else she wanted to be but with him. Here they could be bared to each other, completely. They could take their time.

"Your ankle." He eyed it, and many other parts of her too. "Best not to put weight on it."

"Oh," she said vaguely, distracted by the slow stroke of his hand beneath her shirt. "Right. We can't hurt your leg either."

A feral sort of grin crossed his features. "You'd better get atop me."

"Atop?" Her face flushed. "Yes, good idea."

In a hungry fumble of hands and mouths, they kissed, unbuttoned clothing, stripped it off.

There were so many ways he had seen her, and yet he still seemed to tease out something new from her each time. Never had she kissed her way up a man's naked body; never had she settled herself over his torso, chest to chest, heartbeat to heartbeat, flesh to flesh. Two halves of a shell being eased shut. A perfect fit. His skin was warm against hers, the hairs of his chest dark and ticklish on sensitive skin.

"Sure, torture the wounded man," he groaned. "If you wanted me dead, it would have been less cruel to shoot me again."

She laughed, then pushed up onto her wrists. Seated almost in his lap—not quite, still an enticing space away—she was bare above him. Like one of Morrow's pictures, but she was spare in some parts and fleshy in others, and there was hair at her woman's parts, and—

And Callum had grown impatient with waiting, for he was testing her readiness with one fingertip. Slicking her own excitement over private parts, finding and testing the hard nub of pleasure. A flick that made her gasp, a stroke that made her moan.

"Shhh," he said. "Silence. Don't want to draw the attention of the police."

She pursed her lips together, smothering a laugh. But silence was difficult when he touched her so cleverly, when he lifted his head to capture one of her nipples between demanding lips. A nip of his teeth, and she shuddered and could bear it no more. Rising up onto her knees, she guided him within her. She was tight and he filled her, deeper and deeper as she sank until she was seated fully against him again.

His eyes were startled and wide. She surely looked no less stunned.

"Good God," he choked. "You feel . . . you are . . ."

"I know," she said. "I know. You feel, and you are."

That was the heart of it: they felt, and they were. They were together, and she leaned forward again to take some of her weight onto her hands. Like this, she rocked upon him, letting him slide almost free, then reseating herself to draw a groan from him. He sucked in a hard breath, the muscles of his neck corded and tight, and drove upward with his hips.

"Your mouth," she gasped. "Use your mouth on me too."

"Anything you desire." He curved up, grabbed a pillow and shoved it behind his head to hold him at this wicked angle where he could hold her hips in his hands, could take her nipple between his lips again. He suckled as he guided her, using one hand sometimes to pinch at the other nipple.

She buried her face in his hair, breathing deeply of his scent. Port wine, heavy and sweet; a simple soap; the hot scent of sex. He filled her body, her senses, and there was naught she could do but surrender utterly. As she ground against him, shocks of pleasure sparked, caught, flamed until she was licked all over.

Then there were no more words; nothing from their mouths except kisses, moans, a guttural chuckle when one of them found a new place to kiss or touch. Sweat-slicked and sex-drenched, they drew each other on. Further, tighter, harder, faster, until pleasure was a great crashing wave that swamped them, leaving them gasping in each other's arms.

Together. As she had in the music room earlier that night, endless ages before, she settled against his chest, tucking her head atop his shoulder. He was the right size to lie on, to lie with. To scheme with, to steal with, to trust, to kiss.

He wrapped his arms around her. Pressed a kiss to her lids, to the top of her head. "I've got you," he said. "Sleep, Isabel. I will stay as long as I can."

"Longer," she murmured, drowsy from success and sex, and plummeted into sated dreams.

When Isabel woke, Callum was gone.

It was for the best, she knew, since her lady's maid came in at the usual time—just after Isabel hopped across the bedchamber to retrieve a dressing gown, then tied it about herself. Celeste would have been shocked to find a man in her ladyship's bed. Thoroughly English and proper, the maid was about a decade older than Isabel. They were fond of each other in a quiet way, though Isabel shared no confidences with her as she knew other women often did with their maids. For years, Isabel had not had any confidences to share.

Instead, there was no sign Callum had been there at all. Her boots were tidied away. The blood-soaked shawl and strewn boys' clothing had vanished. Even the bottle of port was gone—though she must remember to have the decanter washed.

He must have noticed every detail of how her room was, then returned it to the expected state.

"Officers of the Police," she muttered under her breath. Had she imagined it all? She might almost think so but for the pleasurable throb between her legs, the lamp on her bedside table.

"Your brother is here for breakfast," said the maid. "And then he will accompany you and Miss Wallace to church. Oh! My lady, you have hurt your ankle?"

Isabel sank onto the edge of the bed, regarding the still-bandaged joint dubiously. "Yes. So clumsy of me; I turned it as I climbed out of bed this morning. I found something to wrap it with. I'm sure I shall be fine soon."

The flesh was tight and hot this morning, swollen, but not visibly bruised. If she kept it bound well, she might be able to hide the injury. If she had to admit it, she would say again that she'd turned it getting out of bed and would let the world think her a ninny. With Celeste's help, she dressed in a severe gray gown suitable for a morning church service, then slipped on her loosest shoes.

It was for the best that Callum had left without a word, she told herself again, as she made stilted conversation with Lucy and Martin over breakfast in the morning room—a nod to Martin's preference, since the women often ate in their own chambers. Though as absorbed as her brother was by the *Times*, Isabel might as well not have been there at all. So much for his fraternal fondness of the day before.

She pushed her toast and marmalade around, crunching at it between sips of tea and reminiscences of the night before. Already it was retreating into unreality. Perhaps that, too, was for the best.

Just as the meal concluded, Selby glided into the room with a note on a silver tray. "Lady Isabel," he intoned. "A messenger has brought this for you."

She thanked him as he withdrew. Her brows knit as she cracked the wax. The seal was familiar as belonging to the Duke of Ardmore.

The letter was a few lines only. His Grace requested the honor of Lady Isabel's presence as soon as it was convenient, for a business matter of interest to them both.

Toast caught in her throat. Her ankle fired a warning shot of pain. And it was not for the best that Callum was gone, because this note could not be a coincidence. The duke *knew*, he *knew* what they had done, and how was she to respond? Callum would have known what to do, but she did not.

She stood, walked to the door, walked back to her chair again. Stop. She must think.

"Something amiss, Isabel?" Lucy was regarding her with some concern.

"Of course not." She managed a smile. "No. I was merely surprised that the Duke of Ardmore took the trouble to remind me of something I'd forgot at the house last time I called. So kind of him."

"Oh. I was wondering not because of the note, but because you are limping."

"Clumsy of me." Isabel forced a chuckle. "I turned my ankle as my feet first touched the floor this morning."

"Mmm," said Martin, clearly not listening.

"I shall call on His Grace after church, I think." She strove for a casual tone. "Since he was kind enough to send over a note so early."

Lucy sawed at a grilled kidney. "When we walked out with Lord Northbrook and Lady Selina yesterday, I didn't notice that you forgot—"

"Douglas." Isabel interrupted Lucy to speak to the footman at attention beside the sideboard. "If His Grace's messenger is still here, ask him to wait."

Already standing straight, Douglas snapped still more upright. "My lady! He departed, my lady, without waiting for a reply."

Dukes. So sure that everyone would do their bidding. And rightly so.

She sighed. "All right. Then tell Jacoby to have my landaulet readied as soon as we return from church."

Lucy shoved back her chair, abandoning the remainder of her breakfast. "Do you want me to go with you? Or Brinley too, so he can get tired?"

"Not this time, dearest. You can stay with Martin. He gets frightened if he's left alone."

"Mmm?" Martin's face emerged over the top of the paper. "What's that?"

Isabel raised her voice. "I said that Lucy gets frightened if she's left alone, and you're to stay and play cards with her while I call on the Duke of Ardmore."

"Oh, excellent!" Lucy grinned. "I haven't played cards with you in ages, Martin."

Martin shot Isabel a disapproving look. "Cards are not an appropriate pursuit on a Sunday."

"Do not worry," Lucy said brightly. "You might win this time!"

This was the true reason for his hesitation—and after a moment, he relented. "Only find the cards, Miss Lucy, and I shall be at your service."

And so, after an hour spent hiding troubling thoughts behind a placid, pious face, Isabel would be at her leisure to visit the Duke of Ardmore. The scene of the crime, she might rather say.

No, she mustn't say that. Anything but that.

But what *would* she say in place of the truth?

Chapter Thirteen

Isabel reached Ardmore House at the quiet hour between church and luncheon, when most servants were at services or taking their leisure, and the family of the household was occupied with quiet pursuits. Reading, letter-writing. Music.

She wondered if anyone had yet entered the music room that morning.

Favoring her right ankle, Isabel made slow progress up the stairs. She glared when she passed Titan on the stairs, the cat's plume-like tail waving with silent arrogance.

She entered the study yet more slowly, though she attempted to look stately. The long dove-gray sweep of her skirts hid her fat bandaged ankle, but the duke's eyes missed nothing. He rose from the chair behind his enormous desk, extending a staying hand to Gog and Magog, whose hackles had raised upon her entry.

"Do I detect a limp?" His Grace's blue eyes were hooded. "Dear me. You have hurt yourself, Lady Isabel."

"Clumsy of me." She forced a laugh, trying to look, without appearing to look, at the painting centered between the study windows. Had they done well switching it? To her eye—well, to the corner of her eye—it looked the same as the false one had. "I turned my ankle this morning as I was arising."

"Really? That seems an unlikely way to hurt one's self." He escorted her into a chair, then retook his own. He shushed the dogs as they showed their teeth.

Perhaps they recognized her scent from the night before. Or perhaps this was nothing more than the ordinary sort of hatred they bore toward every living creature who was not the duke.

Never mind the dogs. The duke could hardly allow a visitor to be torn apart in his home. She pasted a polite smile onto her face and replied, "An unlikely injury indeed. I cannot think how I managed it. I was most displeased with myself."

In case she was not a good liar, and she suspected she was not, she had returned to her bedchamber after breakfast to stumble from her bed in truth.

He only watched her, but did not reply. If he and Callum ever had a staring contest, it would last until the end of time.

"But you did not invite me to inquire after the state of my person, Your Grace." Isabel made use of all the manners that had been drilled into her: keep a pleasant smile, never show a gentleman that your mind is wandering. The same method worked well for not showing apprehension. Wariness. Dread. "I am perplexed as to the reason, I admit. What business matter of yours can involve me?"

"I was visited by housebreakers last night. They left behind their tools and a rope."

"Dear me," she murmured. "Have you contacted Bow Street?"

"I have not. You do not ask me what they took?"

"If I thought it any affair of mine, I would. But I cannot see how it is. The housebreakers are not a business interest either."

"Not precisely, no." He leaned back in his chair, tucking his chin to look at her sharply. "Then again, they might be. I have summoned you here—thank you for coming so promptly—to discuss the painting you see behind me."

She could almost hear her own heartbeat, thumping beneath her prim bodice of gray frogged and trimmed with black. "Oh? It is a lovely work. A Botticelli, of course. I enjoyed having a look at it the last time I was in your study."

But it wasn't the last time she'd been in his study, and some flicker of expression must have betrayed her.

"I recall your interest. Do tell me everything you know about it, Lady Isabel."

"Surely you learned all you required when my late husband sold it to you? He was the expert, not I."

"Indeed." The duke smiled. It was not a pleasant expression. "But this is not the painting your husband sold me."

Her heart halted, considered its options, then began to sprint. "Of course it is! Why, it's a genuine Botticelli. Look at the fine brushwork, the cracking of the paint that proves its age." She had learned the vocabulary well enough. "It's an Italian masterpiece."

"Exactly." Ardmore leaned closer. "As I said, this is not the painting your husband sold me."

Gog and Magog, the two great hounds, stared at her like gigantic carvings from either side of his desk. She had the impression they were waiting only for the duke's signal to tear her to pieces. Or were they? A faint smell of anise lingered, and their eyes were drowsy.

She attempted to arrange her features into an expression of polite confusion. "I don't understand your meaning, Your Grace."

"This. Is not. The painting your husband sold me," he replied slowly, each word ground out heavily like a stone being fitted into a wall.

"That cannot be. I'm not the expert he was, but it appears perfectly genuine."

A hard look from the duke. "Exactly."

"Are you displeased with it?"

The duke considered. "It does not serve its intended purpose. I should like the other one back again."

Now this was odd indeed. He intended to use it to settle a debt *knowing* that it was worth little? Knowing that Andrew Morrow had once defrauded him?

But if he knew, why had he never revealed the truth? How could he have been satisfied to receive less than what he'd paid for? Unless he had never paid for it at all, and Morrow was just another in the line of people to whom the duke was in debt.

She bit her lip. "Why should you think this isn't the same painting?"

"A dodge, Lady Isabel?"

"Mere curiosity," she laughed. "Though of course for it to be other than the same painting you bought from Morrow is impossible."

"Is it? You see, I stamped the back of the painting when I brought it into my home."

She gasped, a reflex from her years as the wife of an art collector and dealer. "You *stamped* an *original canvas*?"

The duke looked taken aback by her disapproval, but he soon recovered. "In this case, I rather think it was not Botticelli's original. But I *am* in the habit of stamping my acquisitions. If you'll indulge me? Come, look at this picture in the corridor."

They stepped out of the study, and the duke lifted down the nearest artwork at hand. "You see? This one is stamped." He replaced it, lifting down a Restoration-era portrait to its left. "And this one too. I trust you'll believe me that all of my paintings are stamped. And the one in my study, which I intended to sell, is not."

Of course he was telling the truth. In the dark, she had not noticed that Butler's painting was marked by a stamp, which took the form of the Ardmore crest. The duke used a brown ink scarcely darker than the canvas backing, like weak tea spilled on vellum.

"I cannot believe you stamp directly on the paintings themselves," she said again. "But if you're convinced it's a real Botticelli, then there is no problem is there?"

"Only if one doesn't want to sell a real Botticelli." The duke's smile was humorless. "Something your late husband knew something about, I'll warrant."

The smell of aniseed was stronger in the corridor. At her back, she felt the presence of the music-room door like a pressure between her shoulder blades. "I am sorry, Your Grace. I was never a part of Morrow's business dealings before his death."

"But what about since?"

"Your Grace, I really cannot say."

He looked tired, suddenly, and she wondered how old he was. Not as young as his energy led one to believe. "Come, let us sit down again." They returned to their chairs in the study. Gog and Magog eyed them beadily, quivering against the command to sit.

"Lady Isabel, I did not summon you here idly. My questions apply to far more than one painting."

"I can't imagine what you mean." This, at least, was honest.

"Fortunate you." He seemed disinclined to say more, and for a minute they merely blinked at each other across the desk.

"Well." Isabel cleared her throat. "If there's nothing more, I'll—"

"Father, you'll never believe it!" George had approached the study, unheard, and now stood in the doorway. "Since Knotwirth vanished, the betting at White's is up to—oh! Hullo, Isabel."

Gog and Magog had sprung to their feet when George appeared, and his voice was all but drowned out by their frenzied barking. A tiny portion of Isabel was relieved at this return of their usual temper; she hadn't wanted the laudanum-laced cakes to have an ill effect on the duke's beloved hounds.

"Sit," she ventured. The dogs looked at her with almost human annoyance, then plumped their haunches onto the study floor in their accustomed spots.

"Well done," George approved.

"You told me it was the only command they obey."

"From other people it is," said the duke. "I can get them to r-o-l-l o-v-e-r and p-r-a-y and play d-e-a-d." Spelling the words so as not to set off a flurry of tricks, Isabel supposed.

"George." She turned her attention to her old friend. "You look well." The polite words were truer than they usually were. He looked more alert than the last time she'd seen him—could it have been only the morning before?—with no circles under his eyes.

"I slept last night. First time I haven't fallen asleep in church since I was a schoolboy." He shrugged. "Might even make a habit of it, and stay awake during the day. It's making a world of difference."

"What, spending the night asleep? Why would you go to such an extreme?" she teased.

"Realized I wasn't enjoying myself as I used to. And my waistcoats don't lie nicely anymore." He rubbed at his abdomen, looking mournful. The gold-shot blue silk of his waistcoat bulged, the buttons tugging at their holes instead of lying flat.

"Ah, there's the real reason."

"Indeed." He leaned against the doorframe, all lazy unconcern. "Not even I could have two wardrobes made in a single Season. The excess." He winked.

In truth, George was far less of a dandy than many young men of society. The clothes, she suspected, were an excuse to cover his lack of enjoyment. A young man of fashion couldn't simply say he'd had enough, could he?

It was too bad George wouldn't do for Lucy. He was

not steady enough, though, and Lucy would wilt having a terrible duke for a father-in-law. That was one of the nicest things about being married to Andrew: he had no family whatsoever.

Which reminded her of her own brother, dutifully playing cards with Lucy while she conducted her mysterious errand. "You must excuse me," she told the two men. "I have to return home. My brother, Lord Martindale, is visiting me."

George held out an arm. "See you out? Unless you two are still talking."

Isabel forced herself to meet the cold blue eyes of the Duke of Ardmore. "I think we have said everything that is to the point."

"For now," said the duke. "I will not keep you any longer."

It ought to have sounded like a mannerly farewell. Was it unreasonable, therefore, that Isabel perceived a threat?

When she returned to her house, she found Martin in the drawing room. Cards had been abandoned atop a table, and he was holding a note and pretending not to be picking at the seal.

He jumped to his feet. "Just arrived for you. I was checking to see whether it was properly sealed."

"Thank you. How thoughtful. And where is your fellow card player?"

Martin glared at the cards. "She won all my pocket change, then lost interest in the game. She's off playing with Brinley, maybe, or doing some sort of sketch."

"Good guesses. She spends ninety percent of her waking hours in one of those two activities." With her thumb, she cracked the seal and skimmed the letter's brief lines. It was a new communication from Septimus Nash, the house agent.

"News? Something you need help with?" Martin was

crowding her, trying to read over her shoulder. He never could be convinced that she handled her own affairs perfectly well.

"Yes to the former, no to the latter. The house agent has located another property in which I might be interested."

The owners want to let it, said the note, *but I do not believe they are in a financial position to decline a good offer of purchase.*

The house was in Bedford Square. It was not a tonnish part of London, but she knew Bedford Square to be the home of success nonetheless. Wealthy tradespeople, nobles closely involved in politics rather than land-holding, scientists and reformers and writers. They would make for respectable neighbors, and interesting ones.

Well done, Nash, she thought. This time he had deigned to consider Isabel's preferences. Perhaps being saddled with an incontinent beagle in an unsuitable house had done him good.

Martin tugged the note from her hand in the most irritating elder-brotherly way. "Bedford Square? Ah, you're still pursuing this scheme of moving households."

"It's not a scheme. It's a plan."

Martin's hand, still holding the note, dropped to his side. With his other hand, he scrubbed wearily over his eyes. "Look here, Isabel. You needn't put yourself through the trouble of moving to a smaller place. If you want more money, I can arrange it from our father's holdings."

"It's not a matter of money. It's a matter of choosing where I live."

"How could you want more than this? You have a fine home." He spread his hands, looking about the drawing room. Elegant, elegant. Andrewish, Andrewish. The house was a showplace, not a home.

And besides that, there was the secret studio. The stacked-up paintings of women, naked in every way.

Isabel replied coolly. "Would you like to live in a house where a man had shot himself?"

Martin blinked. "Er. It wouldn't appeal to me, I suppose. Though his death was an accident. Wasn't it? There's no shame in that."

She had thought it an accident—though Martin was wrong; there was shame aplenty in the circumstances of their life together. The death was but the epilogue to a story she had never much liked.

But if Callum wasn't certain Andrew had died from an accidental gunshot, the remaining possibilities were disconcerting.

"Accident is a tragedy," she said. "Suicide is a scandal. Which would you prefer to live with?"

"Why, neither of them—oh. Yes. I see what you mean." He understood, then, in a way that was meaningful to him.

She wasn't sure which it was better to live with now that time had blunted shock. What if the accident was a lie, a suicide the truth? A tragedy brought one pity; a scandal brought one notoriety.

None of it should have been hers. But a man and wife became as one flesh once wed, and anything Andrew Morrow did reflected on her as well. The Duke of Ardmore had proved that once again.

Managing a smile, she drew Nash's note from her brother's hand. "I would like to see this house. I will make an appointment with Nash to view it tomorrow. You may come along, Martin, but you will not advise me in any way."

"I'm returning to Kent in the morning, so I won't be able to join you." He looked at her askance. "Isabel, you seem different."

"So you told me yesterday. Surely it would be unconscionable if I wasn't, after being widowed so suddenly."

"No, it's more recent than that. You're surer of yourself

now." His expression was considering. "You don't blush so much."

She had certainly blushed the night before. The memory made her smile genuine. "I know now that I have done nothing to be ashamed of."

"That's the sort of thing I mean." Martin paced, rumpling the nap of the expensive carpet. "Everyone has done something he is ashamed of."

"Why, Martin! You hint at a most interesting tale."

And now he was the one blushing, and she laughed. "Please give my love to Father when you return to Kent."

"Ah. Well. Could you write it in a note? It'll mean more coming from you." Which meant that he didn't want to utter the words of embarrassing emotion.

"I will. And one for your lady and my dear nieces and nephews, too."

By the time she had penned the notes, and Martin had departed for the family's town house, Isabel was tired and her ankle was aching like the devil. She thought of Gog and Magog, the constantly enraged hounds made peaceful by laudanum, and wished for a drugged cake or two for herself.

Callum did not consider himself a superstitious man. Based on observation, *not* superstition, he had concluded that if Monday began quietly in the Bow Street magistrate's court, the rest of the week tended to be quiet as well.

This would not be that sort of week. When he pushed through the door of the familiar old building, the whole courtroom was thronged—and not with the usual sort of petty criminal or weepy inebriate. No, today's crowd was well-dressed and sober. Indignant and puzzled. All male, mostly elderly, with the ascetic look of scholars. More than one wore a flannel waistcoat at odds with the already-warm day.

Callum scanned the crowd, found the Benton siblings. He made his way toward his friends and asked, "What brings the Royal Society to our door?"

He'd meant it as a joking reference to the appearance of the crowd, but Cass shook her head. "Wrong group. It's the Royal Academy. Not all of them, of course, but the president's here. Benjamin West."

She pointed out an elderly man with wiry gray hair and a thin, suspicious face. He was small and stringy, with a puffed-up look of self-importance.

"I don't know if we deserve the honor." Callum frowned. "Why are they all here?"

"Not for us. For a man named—what was it, Cass? Butter, or Butler, or something like that."

"Butler," Cass confirmed. "An artist. West says he's committed some sort of crime."

"But Fox disagrees," Charles said of the magistrate, who wore a harassed expression along with his usual wig. "And all the artists, if they *are* all artists, are going to stay here until Fox changes his mind."

"Or until they get hungry. They've been here for quite a while already," Cass noted. "And men who wear flannel waistcoats aren't accustomed to going without creature comforts."

"The orange sellers ought to be here any time," Callum said. "Unless . . . you bribed them to stay away, didn't you?"

Charles grinned sheepishly. "Can you blame me? I feel for the man, Butler. All he did was copy a painting, and that's not a crime."

"Right," Callum said, using a vague tone to cover the unpleasant swoop taken by his insides. He looked around the room for the artist's familiar dark face. *There.* Butler sat calmly on one of the benches, looking beatific to be awaiting his turn in court.

"Think I'll talk to Butler, see what's happened with the

Royal Academy," Callum told the Bentons. "A cool head can straighten this out, surely. We'd like our courtroom back."

"And our orange sellers," sniffed Cass, elbowing her brother.

"What happened to your boot, Jenks? It looks even worse than usual."

Damn. He'd been hoping no one would notice the slice in the leather. The bullet's track on his calf was a ropy scab now, bandaged and shoved into the boot. For the boot itself, there was no remedy.

"Met with a misadventure," he grunted. "Part of the job. It still covers my foot well enough."

This had Charles laughing at Callum's lack of fashion, all questions dropped. Just as he'd intended. With a nod of farewell, Callum made his way through the throng. One hand slipped into a pocket; with thumb and forefinger, he worried at the silver thimble he'd taken from Isabel.

He had put it into the pocket of his black clothing the night before. After leaving Isabel's house in the dim dawn hours of the morning, he'd abandoned the torn and blood-soaked clothing in a dark alley near his rooms on James Street. Let the rag-pickers make of the fabric what they could.

The thimble he had kept, transferring it from his damaged clothes to his everyday breeches. It was silver, worth enough that he could have been transported for stealing it. He ought to return it. But he knew that he wouldn't. Isabel had given it to him, and even though it didn't fit and was far too fancy, it reminded him of her.

He slid onto the bench also occupied by Butler. "Mr. Butler, I believe?"

Butler grinned. "You hear correctly, stranger. You remind me of someone I know; can't place him, though."

"Best not, no." Callum looked up at the front of the room,

where Fox would ordinarily hold sway. "Our magistrate's busy with some of your friends. What's on with them?"

The pleasant wide face folded into lines of disappointment. "They're no friends of mine, as you see. I went to the headquarters of the Royal Academy this morning, taking a painting I'd done. One that was recently returned to my keeping."

"I know the sort of work you mean," Callum said dryly.

"Right. I was proud of it and told West I wanted it in the Summer Exhibition. They let anyone enter, did you know? Anyone from the public, and if your work is accepted, it goes up in Somerset House."

"That would be a coup," Callum said. "Though if the painting in question were a copy of a painting notable in society, there might be . . . well, questions."

"Right you are," Butler sighed. "Old Westie spotted a stamp on the rear of the picture. Duke of Ardmore's stamp. Right on the back of the canvas!" He sounded shocked.

"You don't say." Callum's insides pitched. "I'd no idea the duke stamped his artworks. Though that's not the sort of thing someone like me would commonly know."

"I should have known. Noticed, that is." Butler looked grim. "Faint it was, but the stamp was there. West called in a bunch of his cronies and they all marched me over here to see me arrested for theft."

"As you haven't been arrested, Fox must disagree with the charges."

"Ah, well, that's interesting." Quickly as it had appeared, the grim expression vanished in favor of a sly look. "A lady was here just a short while ago. I didn't know her, of course, but she said her name was something like . . . Lady Isabel Morrow? I think that was it, yes. She had popped in to leave a message for one of the Runners—"

"Officers of the Police," Callum corrected reflexively. *Isabel?* She had come here with a message? "What message?"

"Police. Right. You'll have to ask your magistrate about the message. *If* it's for you, which it might not be, as you don't know the lady. Or do you? I don't know either of you, so I don't know who you know."

"You're enjoying this."

Butler held up one huge hand, pinching his thumb and forefinger together. "Little bit, yes." He grinned again. "So when that lady saw all the to-do and asked what it was about, she looked at my canvas, and she said there couldn't have been any theft, because she'd visited the duke only yesterday and seen his original painting in his study. And if it had been stolen, surely he'd have reported the matter."

"Bold," Callum murmured. "Very bold. I wonder if she really did call on the duke yesterday." Why would she have done so? Unless they'd left some clue behind. The tools and rope dropped outside couldn't be traced to anyone. Had there been some other sign?

"Everyone will find out, because Fox sent a messenger to the duke to confirm what the lady said. If Ardmore's still got his painting, I get to leave."

"How do you explain the stamp, then?"

"My fault." The artist adopted a pious look. "It was unwise of me to try such a perfect copy. After I painted the picture, I thought to put the sort of stamp a collector puts on the back. As an artist, I've seen many paintings the Duke of Ardmore has loaned to museums and galleries."

"It's as likely a story as any alternative I can think of," Callum said.

"I wonder what will happen if the duke says his painting has been stolen," Butler said idly.

"He won't," Callum realized. "He can't do that. If he hasn't got a Botticelli painting, he hasn't a way to pay his debt to Angelus. Which ought to be a private matter, but somehow everyone in London knows."

With this, the unsettled tilt of his stomach righted itself.

Perhaps Angelus circulated the information about his debtors, to ensure they'd pay what they owed. However it got about, this fact—that the Duke of Ardmore could not afford to lose his Botticelli—would be the saving of their foolhardy but necessary midnight errand. It would be the saving of Ardmore, too, not that he'd ever know it—and the saving of Andrew Morrow's reputation, and Lucy Wallace's marital prospects.

All in all, it had been a good night's work. And afterwards, a better night's pleasure.

"Paintings in exchange for debts," Butler mused. "I like the idea. If I could sell some paintings of my own, I'd be in fine shape. I'd have my Angelica and our daughters here as quickly as a ship could go back and forth over the Atlantic."

"I've no doubt you'll make it happen. Though why submit a copy to the Royal Academy, rather than an original work?"

Butler drew himself up straight. Even seated, he was a large person, and he drew nervous glances from more than one of the chicken-necked snobs scattered about the room. "You'd think a man like me, big and dark-skinned, would draw notice. But instead, established artists overlook me. They make a point of it. As soon as a man gets ahead a little bit, he can't wait to put his heel on the forehead of the person struggling behind him. All the better if that person hasn't the same color of skin, or accent, or an address in the same part of London."

"You're right, and I'm sorry for it." Callum sighed. "Damned sorry. So you put in the copy because you knew they wouldn't kick Botticelli down. And maybe they'd even be curious about who copied his work so well."

A sliver of a nod.

"I know you don't need me to tell you this," Callum said. "But your painting is the finest I've ever seen. Fox will clear you. If you like, I'll remain here until he does."

One side of Butler's mouth pulled up, making the curled tip of his moustache dance. "It's all right; be off about your work. As you say, I'll be cleared. I only have to wait for a note from the duke, or for the duke himself." His brows lifted with a sudden realization. "I hope it's the duke. I'd like him to have a look at my work."

Callum nodded. "You're a brave man, Butler."

The older man fired a dark glance at the suspicious artists who had dragged him to the courtroom. "Officer Jenks, I am what I have to be."

Chapter Fourteen

With Lucy in tow, Isabel met Nash at the Bedford Square property, hoping to like it. She had set the hour of the appointment with Nash for late morning, before the round of essential social calls to be paid in the afternoon.

The first glimpse of the house was promising. It was one in a row: three stories of gray brick, with a doorway quoined in decorative stone, and dormer windows peeking out from the slate roof. The pavement before it was wide and clean, with trees overhanging the edge from the garden square. And was that birdsong? In the middle of London? The leaves of the trees whispered *yes*. On a bench in the square, a governess attended a baby in a pushchair while a girl about nine years of age chased a butterfly.

Isabel kept her face composed, but she wanted this house with a fierceness entirely unfamiliar.

"I should like to see the inside," she said demurely.

The knocker was off the door, the house's furniture sold off. The servants had been dismissed and the home locked up. Isabel tapped her toes, impatient to get inside, as Nash fumbled through a ring of jingling keys in search of the right one.

Inside, the house was just as she'd hoped. Oh, the plaster-work was damaged here and there, and the paint needed refreshing. But the size of the rooms on the ground floor was good, the woodwork lovely, the floors neat and nice in marble and parquet.

The scent of the morning room was what cemented her decision to take the house. Still sun-warmed at this hour, its wooden windowsills had a musty, baked smell that rang some tiny bell deep within her. It was the scent of the wood-paneled entryway in the home of her grandparents, long-dead people who had treated her with love and kindness the few times she had been taken to visit.

She edged Lucy aside, out of Nash's hearing, and asked, "What do you think of this one? Do you like it?"

"I do if you do." Lucy smiled, her golden hair a halo that peeked out from beneath her bonnet. "It is very nice."

Isabel pressed her. "What if I don't like it? Would you still want to live here?"

"Oh, no!" Blue eyes opened wide. "I couldn't live in a place you didn't like."

You do right now, Isabel thought, but she didn't speak the words. Lucy was financially dependent, and that made her vulnerable. Isabel mustn't press her too hard for an opinion Lucy was afraid to give.

"Run upstairs, then," Isabel said, "and let me know if you see a bedchamber you would like for yourself." While Lucy looked upstairs, Isabel descended into the basement, where the kitchen and servants' hall shared space with the coal cellar, scullery, larder, and butler's pantry. It seemed a good arrangement of the space, with plenty of light from skylights and high windows, and a large modern oven and cooktop.

Yes. This house was the right one. The one in Russell Square might be more fashionable, more elegant, more spacious. But this one was *right*. It was sturdy and pin-neat, half the size of her current house. She could dispense with the liveried footmen that Andrew had found so necessary, and some of the army of maids. She'd have Selby continue as her butler, of course, and would promote the best of the maids to housekeeper. Polly Anne; she knew just the one. And Celeste would remain her lady's maid.

Which would leave Isabel to do . . . what?

She hesitated, one foot still on the servants' stairs and one on the ground floor, and considered the answer.

She would sell the Lombard Street house, that was certain. As soon as ever she could remove her things from it. Maybe before. Nash could sell it furnished if the buyers wanted any of the pieces.

Once she was settled here—why, Bedford Square was closer to Bow Street than the old house was. It would be easier for Callum to make the trip to and fro. Easier for Isabel, too. He must not always be the one making the effort, reaching across great pieces of London. And if the barriers to being together were smaller, the distance shorter . . .

Did she want that? Was he to be a part of her life anymore? It seemed that only crime brought them together. Was there liking enough, esteem enough, to hold them together without an external cause?

She had gone to Bow Street this morning to see him, an impulse she now wished she'd checked. Society said men should be the pursuers of women, not the opposite. Of course, society also said women should remain chaste unless wed, and she had been pleasurably delighted to break that rule with Callum.

When she was finished going over the lower floor, she located Lucy, who had indeed found a sunny chamber to her liking, and then found Nash. He had appeared relieved that they hadn't brought Brinley with them today. Throughout the whole tour of the house, in fact, he had been less supercilious than previously. Wise man. London was full of house agents. If Nash had treated her with arrogance, she would have gone through a different agent to buy the house.

"I have decided that I will have this house," Isabel informed him, then named the amount she was willing to pay. "You will negotiate in good faith with the sellers, Mr. Nash. Convince them that they *will* be sellers, not merely renters."

"That's what you'll do, and what Mr. Nash will do. And what will I do?" Lucy said impishly.

Isabel smiled. "You will accompany me on our errands and calls today. Fashionable ladies must keep up appearances."

Just now, that was all it felt like: an appearance, to be kept up. The shadowed frippery of her current house was like clutter on her soul. The strong, well-kept lines of this empty house, gently gold-soaked by mist and sun, was like an embrace.

It reminded her of someone. Someone who was becoming a part of her thoughts every day, her dreams every night. But as a fashionable lady, she could not, just now, allow herself to speak his name.

Butler had been right: Fox had the note from Lady Isabel in his pocket. It was a few hasty lines, scrawled on Fox's letter paper when Isabel had realized Callum wasn't in the building.

> *Going to look at a house in Berkeley Square today.*
> *Wanted to see if you'd like to accompany me.*
> *—I*

I, she said, as if the initial would be unmistakable—and it was. The short letter was so familiar, so casual. It stung him like water on raw new skin. She wanted him to look at a new house with her? She wanted him in her world?

He had told her she could not bring him into it. But now she was changing her world, and—and maybe she could find a place for him in it after all.

In early afternoon, he was finally able to head in Isabel's direction. With her note in one of his coat pockets and the thimble in another, he loped off to Lombard Street. A rap with the door knocker brought the thin, inscrutable form of Isabel's butler to the door.

"Officer Jenks," said Selby. "Good morning to you."

"Her ladyship sent me a message," he said, "and I bring her a reply in person."

"Her ladyship is not at home."

Callum narrowed his eyes. "Is this the sort of 'not at home' where she just doesn't want to come down the stairs and meet a caller? Or is she really not here?"

The corner of Selby's mouth twitched. "The latter sort. Her ladyship has instructed me to admit you to her presence upon any occasion you might visit the house. At this time, however, she is viewing a house with a house agent, then intends to pay calls upon friends. Will you come in and wait?"

Callum glanced up and down the street. It was so quiet here, with not a cutpurse or pie wagon in sight. The familiar scent of coal smoke pervaded the air, but it was broken by breeze that carried fresh hints of dew. Sky peered blue between dithering rainclouds.

It was less than two miles from his rooms on James Street, yet it was a different city. He hunched his shoulders. "No need. I won't stay. If she's paying calls, she must be done looking at the Berkeley Square house. What do you know about it?"

Selby presented a blank expression. "Her ladyship appeared optimistic about the possibility of resettling in Berkeley Square."

Callum mulled this over. If she took a new house, it would mean *something*. He just wasn't sure what.

But, he realized, he had an opportunity before him on the stoop of Isabel's house. A chance to learn more not about Isabel, but about the man who'd left her a widow. He had vowed to himself, and to her, to sort out his questions related to Andrew Morrow's death. Selby could help.

"What do you recall," he asked the butler, "of the late Mr. Morrow?"

Not with the flicker of a lid did Selby express surprise at this question. "His name, age, height, and approximate weight."

"That's the sort of nonanswer I would give," Callum said. "Well done. What I truly want to know is whether he got on well with the servants."

Selby's brows lifted. "Is there a purpose to these questions?"

"I'm not sure."

The noncommittal answer, far from clamping the butler's jaw shut, seemed to set him at ease. "You're investigating the master's death."

"I am."

Selby stepped outside, shutting the door behind him. His voice was low, hushed. "Has some new evidence come to light?"

Did the old evidence ever get a fair analysis? "Not as such. Lady Isabel said I might look into the matter." Sort of. She'd accepted his insistence, perhaps because she hadn't believed anything would come of it. And maybe it wouldn't.

But after he'd wrapped her sprained ankle and spoken to her of justice thwarted, he wanted to see a bit more justice done.

"I am sure I don't know what sort of information might help," said the butler.

"Why don't you give me something to start with, and I'll decide if it helps?"

Selby's face was admirably expressionless. "The late master paid a generous salary."

"Why?"

"To receive good service."

"You wouldn't have given good service if he hadn't paid more than the going wage?"

Ha. The butler's nostrils flared. "Of course I would have. I merely indicate that he was not a closed-fisted man."

Yes, but it was Isabel's money he was spending. He'd come to the marriage with little but charm and connections—though it seemed to have been enough.

"Officer, can you truly expect to learn more about his death after this amount of time?"

"That's not an answer to my question."

"No, Officer." The butler hesitated. "I have questions of my own."

"I see. Did you have questions when he was alive?"

"I was not paid to have questions."

Callum rolled his eyes. "A butler is a man sometimes. And then he can think of all the questions he pleases."

Selby's storklike frame relaxed. "Just so. I did not always know what to make of Mr. Morrow. He was gracious to the servants, and yet . . ."

Callum knew exactly how the sentence ought to finish. "He was not always gracious to his wife? His ward?"

"As you say."

The breeze whipped up again, forcing Callum to clap a hand atop his head to hold his hat on. "There was no inquest, no postmortem for Mr. Morrow. His death was determined to be an accident."

An inclination of the butler's head.

"Would you tell me," Callum asked, "if you knew how he had died?"

Selby turned toward the door. Taking a handkerchief from a pocket, he rubbed at a smudge on the brass door-knocker. "I do not know."

"You don't know how he died, or whether you would tell me?"

"Both," said Selby, and his usually blank face took on a troubled expression. "Either. I do not know the answer to either one."

Callum squinted up at the first story, as if a memory of Isabel, or of Andrew Morrow, might be made visible in the windows.

There was nothing there, of course.

"That's all right. You've told me enough for now." Before he left, he took a bit of pencil from his pocket, scribbled a reply on Isabel's note, and left it with the butler.

It was a bit of a test. For her, or for himself, he didn't know. There was something about this Lombard Street house that inspired questions but never granted answers.

Chapter Fifteen

At home in my rooms on James Street today. Seven o'clock. Wanted to see if you'd like to call upon me.

—C

This was the note Callum had left with Selby for Isabel. He hadn't been able to resist aping her own breezy style. Nor had he been able to keep from looking out of the window every few minutes beginning at half six, when he returned to his rooms. Until the landaulet pulled up in front of the house in which Callum rented rooms, he hadn't known if she'd come.

But here she was, sharp at seven o'clock. He thundered down the stairs to meet her, pulling up only at the entryway to open the door in a dignified manner. She smiled up at him, her feathered hat drizzle-draggled and cloak beaded with dew, and he had never seen a lovelier sight in his life.

"Shall I tell Jacoby to wait? Is this call to be a proper fifteen minutes?"

Callum suppressed a smile. "As you're visiting a bachelor in his lodgings, there's not much that's proper about this call."

"Why do you think I came?" She grinned, then ran down

the steps to put a word in the ear of her coachman. He nodded, and as she mounted the steps again, clucked at the pair of bays drawing the landaulet.

"I'll find my way home somehow," Isabel confided when she reached Callum's side again. "I've a purse, so I can hire a hackney. Or you can walk me home in the moonlight as if we're courting."

She didn't quite look at him as she said this. Shy? Teasing? He wasn't sure. "I'll see you home safely," he said. "Come on inside."

Once the door was closed and they stood on the landing, he asked, "Why did you come? I wasn't sure you would."

"I tried to get you to attend a dinner party at my house, and you wouldn't do it. I thought maybe you would feed me if I came over here."

"But Lady Isabel Morrow doesn't eat between meals," he teased. "She told me so herself."

She shrugged. "I can always make an exception. And . . . well, I wanted to see you. Where you live, and—and all that."

He took her cloak; she apologized for the rain shaken onto the floor of the entryway. "It only just started spitting when we were a street or two away, and I decided to hurry here instead of putting up the cover of the landaulet."

"Not to worry." Once she unpinned her hat, he took it from her in his other hand. "My landlady is the cleanest and thriftiest sort you'll ever meet. She'll use the water to scrub the floor."

"Resourceful," Isabel commented. "I'm glad she won't fault me."

As if Mrs. Sockett, a widow who had worked almost all her six decades, would cast blame on a noblewoman for dripping a bit of rain on the floor. Isabel took for granted her noble birth; no one without it would do the same.

But all he said was: "Come and have some tea. It's the sort

you liked before." He kept Mrs. Sockett supplied with tea leaves, and she brewed it whenever someone came to call.

Callum led the way into the room his landlady used as a parlor. Despite her pinched financial state, she had a soft spot for bright things. Shawls to cover shabby spots on the chintz furniture, bowls of glass beads to cover a worn place on a table—or just an empty one.

As soon as Isabel had seated herself in a chair, Mrs. Sockett bustled in with a tea tray. She was a sturdy woman, her skin lined and rough. Only since Mr. Sockett's death in a brewery accident five years ago had his widow achieved both peace and financial stability. Callum took three rooms on the second story of her house, a poet lived in the attics, and a trio of day maids shared the servant quarters.

Callum had told her he might have a visitor, and judging from her speed with the tea tray, he had not been the only one looking out the window. His landlady was as curious as she was thrifty.

There was no place to set down a tea tray unless one moved a porcelain doll, a vase holding dried flowers that gave the room a powdery scent, a crocheted sort of star-looking thing that went under the vase, and a gilded tin snuffbox. So Callum did, promising—as he did every time—to replace them exactly where they had been.

Isabel introduced herself to the older woman, then added, "He has a talent for remembering where items go. He has tidied up in my house more than once."

Had he? He had, at that. One time, he'd replaced the fripperies atop her pianoforte. The night before last, he had removed all signs of his presence from her bedchamber. She wouldn't want anyone to know he'd been there, he assumed. They didn't belong in each other's spaces.

But Callum had seen Isabel in an elegant drawing room, in a stony Vauxhall grotto, the prosaic Bow Street court-room, and now a modest parlor on James Street. As she chatted with Callum's landlady as if they were acquaintances of long standing, he could only conclude: Lady Isabel Morrow had the gift of fitting perfectly into her surroundings no matter where she was.

"Shall I pour out, Officer?" Isabel addressed him formally. "Mrs. Sockett, thank you for providing the tray."

"As if I can't find a few niceties for such a caller! Now, I'll leave you alone, even though it's my parlor, for an Officer of the Police always has business to discuss."

"He does." Isabel's eye held a mischievous twinkle. "And he is always so chatty about it. I cannot think when we'll conclude our talk."

"Ha." Callum sat on the one remaining chair, which had a hard wooden seat and a back that would jab one in the spine unless one sat perfectly straight. So he did.

"It is quite true," Isabel said. "Chatter, chatter, chatter, it is all he does. But never mind my woes. I cannot thank you enough for the loan of your parlor, Mrs. Sockett."

With a blush and a bow and a curtsy and . . . a step from a country dance? . . . their hostess departed, shutting the parlor door behind her.

"She's going to listen at the door," Callum said.

"Then what shall we talk about?"

He arched a brow. "Eager as you were to put words in my mouth, you didn't think of something?"

"I'm your guest. You invited me. You should entertain me."

"Well. We don't have to talk at all. We could do . . . something else."

She dropped the sugar tongs. "Surely she would overhear *that*."

"Just making a suggestion," he said.

Since she didn't seem inclined to serve the tea after all, he slid from the chair to sit on the floor before the tea tray and serve himself. Black and strong and almost boiling, the tea poured out just as he liked it into a cup that didn't match its saucer.

"Here's something you might want to know," he offered, and told her of Butler's time in the courtroom. "With your statement about the duke still having *La Primavera*, Butler was certain he'd be released."

She leaned forward, propping her elbows atop her thighs. The angle permitted him a fine view of the tops of her breasts, rounding over the edge of her bodice. "I wish he'd burned the thing," she said in a low tone, to avoid being overheard. "Though perhaps he couldn't bear to. He was proud of his work."

"He's earned his living copying the art of others. I can't fault him for trying to get a bit of notice now. A first step to being recognized in his own right."

"I didn't care for the way the Royal Academy *recognized* him." Isabel laid heavy scorn on the verb. "But he was canny. Ardmore can't admit publicly that he lost the painting. Unfortunately, Ardmore isn't grateful that he gained one of greater value."

She told Callum of the note summoning her to Ardmore House, her conversation with the duke. Callum whistled. "So Ardmore knew he had a fake, and he wants it back—so he can defraud Angelus?" He shook his head. "The idea makes a man need a stiff drink. I wish I had some whisky for this tea."

"It seems foolhardy," Isabel agreed, "to pay one's debts with something without value. I am gladder than ever that we switched the paintings, knowing how reckless Ardmore is. The fakery would be sure to be found out, and Morrow's reputation would suffer, and Lucy through him."

"We can't have that." Callum sipped at his tea, enjoying the mellow heat across his tongue. "I believe all shall be well. You and Butler and Ardmore are in a circle of mutually assured silence."

"And so, on with everyday life?"

"Such as it is."

She smiled, though she looked distracted. "About that, Callum. I am going to buy a new house. The one in Bedford Square that I mentioned."

"Congratulations. Yes?"

"Yes, though before I move households I shall have to clear out the hidden room. I wonder if I could hide the stored items at Butler's."

"Not secure enough." Callum sipped again, thinking over the nooks in his rented rooms. Could he take all those costly paintings? No, no. He couldn't store them here either, for reasons both of privacy and ethics. But maybe Cass could take charge of them, since she wasn't truly an officer.

No, Cass and Charles lodged together. And while Callum trusted to Cass's discretion, Charles was loud as a bugle when he got a drink in him.

"I will let you know," he decided, "if I think of a place that might do."

"Thank you for that," she said. "I envy you your resources."

"My resources? Do tell. I live in three rooms. You are about to own two houses."

She picked up the sugar tongs and snapped them at him like a crab's claw. "I shouldn't have to remind an investigator that there are many resources other than money."

"Such as?" He took another drink of tea, insolently long.

"Information. Experience. Physical strength." Dropping the tongs, she eyed him. "Being male."

He choked, rattling the cup into its saucer.

"I feel I've lived a whole year in the past week," she said. "And it is time. Past time. For I've passed almost eighteen months in which nothing much has happened at all, save for one time I went to Vauxhall."

Idly, he stretched out his legs. The effect would have

been more sensual had his damaged boot not caught on the carpet. "You liked the fireworks, did you?"

"You know I did."

It was clear that this was neither the time nor the place for yet more fireworks. Glad though he was that she'd called on him, this wasn't a good place for private conversation either.

But it was a good opportunity to see whether she could— or wanted to—fit into his life. And there was another such opportunity waiting, only a few doors down.

He bounded to his feet, extending a hand. "Let's go to the grocery instead."

She sat upright at once. "To your family's grocery? You're going to take me there?"

So delighted did she look that he had to lower her expectations. "It's only a shop. It's not a trip to Paris."

"I know, but—you want me to go with you." She put her hand in his, and his fingers closed around hers as if they belonged together. "Let's be off."

Mrs. Sockett withdrew tactfully when they opened the parlor door, busying her hands with a dusting cloth. "Quiet as mice in there, you were! Didn't hear a squeak out of you." She sounded disappointed.

"Officer Jenks is most refined," said Isabel. "He speaks low, yet I am transfixed by his every word."

Callum rolled his eyes. "Lady Isabel is hilarious. That is all."

Mrs. Sockett looked mystified, but she bade them a cheerful farewell as Callum clapped on his hat and Isabel again donned her outerwear. The feathers in her hat were still damp and stringy, and she laughed as she pinned it into place.

"I look like a wet hen. No help for it, though. If you'll lead the way?"

They went a very little distance before Isabel halted,

squinting in the fading light of evening. "This shop is for sale. Look at this card in the window."

This was Morrison's shop. The one Callum's parents wanted to pillage; the one his brother Jamie wanted to own. The sign that hung above the door said simply TEA, white-painted letters deeply carved in wood stained a dark brown.

Isabel had all but pressed her face against the window. Callum's mouth twitched. "Do you want to go in?"

Of course she did.

Inside the tea shop, all was fragrant and dim. It was like being inside a teapot, minus the boiling water. Everywhere were leaves in barrels and bins and packets and parcels; one could buy leaves by the cup or the bushel depending on the depth of one's pockets.

Just now, the shop was empty of customers, and Morrison himself came forward to greet them. Tall and homely, his bald head was fringed by fluffy gray-blond hair. His long nose was almost as good as a hound's, at least when it came to scenting the difference between teas from China and Bengal, tea picked too early or brewed too long.

He had known the Jenks family since before Callum's birth. After a familiar greeting between the neighbors, Morrison and Isabel were introduced as well.

"I noticed the card in the window," Isabel said. "Will you tell me about your shop?"

"Considering a change of profession, is our officer?" Morrison's eyes twinkled.

"Not me," said Callum. "Though I know someone who's interested."

Isabel looked at him curiously, but Morrison was already replying. "Not much to tell, t'be sure. What you see here is what there is to the shop. It's been a delight, but I've been alone since my wife died. Just came into a bit o' money and thought I'd pick up stakes. Move to the seaside, get a cottage near where one o' my daughters lives."

"That sounds lovely," Isabel said warmly. "I am sorry for the loss of your wife, but so glad you will be able to live near family."

Was she flicking a barb in Callum's direction? He didn't know if she yet realized just how close he lived to his family, and how indifferent they were to his proximity.

"It sounds like a happy retirement," he told Morrison, "and I'm pleased for you. Never has there been such a neighbor as you."

"I'll do my best to get a good one for you in my place," beamed the old man.

"About that. I wonder, would you sell the whole shop—lock, stock, barrel, and tea leaves as well as the building?"

"To your mystery person who's interested?" Morrison screwed up his face, then nodded. "Right-o. Tell him to come on by anytime, and we'll talk it over. I've loved the work. Sure would like to see the shop go to someone who'd care for it." He looked wistfully out the window at the carved-wood sign.

"That," Callum said, "I think I can promise you. He'll contact you soon."

When they left the tea shop only to turn into the next storefront, Isabel's brows lifted. "So close?"

"It's farther than it seems," Callum replied shortly. The jingle of the bell at the door alerted his mother, who looked up with a friendly smile of welcome. When she saw who had entered, her smile fell.

"Callum! It's not your day, then. Is something wrong?" Then the smile returned. "You've brought the pork I wanted!"

Isabel looked over her shoulder, then down at herself. "I . . ."

Despite the tension that always tugged at his shoulders when he entered the grocery, Callum fought not to smile. "No, I didn't bring pork. I brought a friend."

Friend wasn't the right word to refer to Isabel, but it wasn't wrong either.

Davina lifted the countertop gate and eased through, almost hiding her disappointment. "Ah, well, we can get along without the pork, right enough. So who's this, then?"

Yet again, there were introductions to be completed—this time, with everyone who worked at the shop, or lived above the shop, or happened to be in the shop, or was walking by the shop and happened to knock against the door. Or so it seemed to Callum.

Jamie was there, flexing his arms as much as possible as he carried a not-very-heavy bag of dry beans past Celia. Yes, even Celia had come downstairs, drawn by the curious clamor. It was good to see her break her solitude.

Callum pulled Jamie aside when he could, told him what Morrison had revealed in the tea shop. "He's not going belly-up. He wants to be nearer family."

Jamie slung the sack of beans over his shoulder. The tips of his ears were red, his color high. "You're sure about that? And he'll take—"

"I don't know what he'll take for it. If he knows how much you want it, he'll probably take less."

Jamie scowled. "That doesn't make any sense."

"He's coming at the sale from a place of fondness, not of desperation. Keep that in mind, and the shop can be yours."

There. One errand done. He'd bring the pork on his usual Friday visit.

He looked for Isabel, smiling at the memory of her confusion when his mother asked about pork. Slim and stylish in her gray, how could she have thought Davina referred to her?

His mother was more than making up for her lapse now. "So good to meet a friend of Callum's! He's so close-lipped, you know. We canna get a word out of him about who he's spending time with."

Did she *bat* her *eyes*? Was she hinting about—oh, good Lord. "Mum," he said. "Mother. Please."

"Whisht, enough. Now, Lady Isabel, you must be hungry. And you're slim as a reed! Eat, eat, have some tea."

Isabel gave the smile Callum now recognized as one of embarrassed politeness. "Oh, no—no, thank you. I'm quite all right."

His mother protested, listing half a dozen eatables she could fetch at a moment's notice.

"Mum," Callum said quietly, remembering. *Morrow thought it unladylike*, Isabel had said. And eating when she wished, what she wished—that was one of her dreams. "Don't press her. She knows what she wants."

"All right, then," Davina granted. "But she must expect notice, beauty as she is."

"Inside as well as out," Callum affirmed.

Isabel pretended not to hear him. Callum pretended he didn't know she had.

When they locked eyes, though, the mere glance went deeper than words. It was a resonant sort of look. Like the bell that rang over the door of the grocery: *Welcome, welcome. You are in the right place.*

He smiled. She smiled back.

Had he thought the store crowded? There was no one else there; no one else in the world.

Then Davina cleared her throat, and Callum's surroundings swam back into his awareness. "Well! You're welcome anytime, my lady, though this rascally son of mine only comes by once a week."

"Does he?" Isabel looked interested. "And what does he do when he visits? How rascally is he?"

"*So* rascally." Davina rolled her eyes indulgently. "Last time he was here, he took a pound of the best tea. If he gave it to his charwoman, I'll have his hide! She takes so much sugar, she wouldna notice if he brought her old ground-up coffee beans instead."

"She would notice," Callum sighed. This was not the first time his mother had spouted this opinion, yet she was happy enough to sell sugar by the pound to Mrs. Sockett.

He looked to Isabel for confirmation about the tea Mrs. Sockett served, but her attention had turned. "Mrs. Jenks. Will you introduce me to the lady in the lovely pink gown?"

Davina turned to follow her gaze. "Bless me, you didna meet her yet? I thought we'd introduced you to everyone."

"I thought so too," Callum muttered.

His mother elbowed him, maintaining an expression of friendly calm. "That's our Celia, my lady. Almost ours, that is. She was to wed our Harry, but he was killed before their marriage, God rest him. She was companion to her aunt, and when her aunt died soon after Harry, she came to live with us."

"She has a kind face," Isabel said. "And a lovely one. Will you introduce me?"

Who could resist such an entreaty? Callum watched as his mother all but dragged Isabel over to the foot of the stairs, where Celia stood—not quite in the store, not quite away from it.

To Callum, Celia had always seemed faded, even before Harry died. Her aunt kept her under a thumb, and the marriage that would have meant an escape had never happened. Instead she was cramped into a corner of the upstairs rooms, given quiet tasks that would not tax her.

Once Davina floated off to attend to a customer, Callum sidled close enough to overhear the younger women's conversation.

"Readily do I believe it," he overheard Isabel say. "And what would you like best to do in the store, do you think?"

"I can't say." Celia retreated a step.

"Please, I'm curious. I've little knowledge of what it takes to run a store."

In her expression was curiosity, but also kindness. Patience. Something he could not put a name to, quite. He only knew that it called to him, a desire to connect. If she turned such a look upon him, he would be at her feet.

Celia was not immune, either. After a long pause, a blush, a stammer, her tongue was unlocked. As Callum listened, the woman he had thought contented with solitude told Isabel of the grocery's great network of suppliers, and how Jamie and Mr. Jenks were constantly negotiating and renegotiating.

"If I worked in the store," said Celia, "I should like to find out what people have enjoyed in the past. Then I could suggest things that they might also like."

"You are a diplomat," said Isabel.

"Oh, no." Celia blushed again. "Jamie's the diplomat."

Callum spluttered. He had drawn closer to the women than he'd realized, for Isabel shot him a warning look. He turned away, feigning indifference even as his ears were still drawn to their conversation.

"But I think I could help, all the same," Celia added. "Though I help with other things now. Mending and whatnot."

So. Not much else, then. How did she fill her time? For the first time, Callum wondered.

"I would be grateful if you would help me now," said Isabel. "What would you suggest as a treat for my ward? She likes every sort of fruit and sweet, but it cannot be good for her to eat so many."

The barest pause. "Perhaps almonds. They are the sweetest of nuts, and if she enjoys marchpane she will already be fond of the flavor."

Davina returned to Callum's side just as Isabel replied, "The very thing. I'll have a pound, and we'll see how she gets on with them."

"Mum," Callum murmured in that lady's ear. "Look at what's going on behind me. Celia is selling nuts to a marquess's daughter. She's not so fragile as we thought."

Davina beamed. "And this marquess's daughter isn't so grand as you believe. She's buying nuts from our Celia, and what do you think of that?"

Callum looked about the familiar shop. Listened to a trill of song from George the linnet. And he decided. "I think," he said, "that it suits them both."

Chapter Sixteen

The habits of duty were strong in Isabel, and after an adventuresome week, she was not sorry to retreat onto the firm ground of normality.

On Monday, after viewing the house in Bedford Square, she had paid calls to all the duennas of society who had offered her an invitation. Determined to win approval for her ward, she dragged along a Lucy who smiled politely and directed pointed remarks into Isabel's ears at all the wrong times. Thus, Isabel was able to contribute little to the gossip that flowed more freely than tea. However, all that was required of a good caller was an interested expression and the occasional "No!" and "You don't say!" By the time she returned to her house, Isabel was certain she had acquitted herself well enough to move upward on a few upper-crust invitation lists.

On Tuesday, she was at home to callers while Lucy pled a headache. Isabel suspected her of wanting to play with Brinley. But no matter: if friends could be won with delicious edibles, Isabel would be the most popular woman in London.

On Wednesday, there were more calls to pay, including one

to Lady Selina and the Duchess of Ardmore to congratulate Lady Selina on her engagement. At last, Lord Liverdale's heir had bent his knee and asked the lady to do him the honor. Privately, Isabel wondered if Butler's near arrest, which had forced the duke to admit that he still had his painting, had reassured the marquess's son that Ardmore would clear his debts.

Better yet, after paying these calls, Isabel visited a mantua-maker and a milliner. For the first time in a year and a half, she chose colorful garments. She ordered hats in cunning shades of gold and green and red, all of which she liked against her dark hair. A black hat, black clothing, simply made her look vanishing. But in color, she might regain a bit of her brightness.

She might develop some she'd never had before.

At the modiste's she flipped through pattern books, then decided on something entirely different. She'd no interest in the fat, puffy sleeves and fussy trimmings in fashion at the moment. After all, where had following the rules got her? It had got her a hidden room, a distant marriage, and a clinging, shameful feeling of ignorance.

No, she would dress in bright color and beautiful fabrics; perfect tailoring and simple lines. In fact, she had the modiste rip changes into a ready-made gown of green silk striped in gold, and once it was stripped of its flounces and tightened below the breasts, she wore it home. She liked the fit of it, spare and sleek. It was neither fashionable nor unfashionable; it was a gown apart from fashion, heedless of it.

And it made her bosom look *marvelous*, her hazel eyes dance. It flattered her lean form. Best to dress for the way she looked, not the way she ought to look according to a Parisian designer.

Did such color make a difference in her appearance? She hailed an acquaintance on the street, a Lady Riordan on whom she had called on Monday. This woman was a generation older, and while she was a bit gossipy, she wasn't unkind. She also had a son a few years older than Lucy, and he wouldn't be a bad matrimonial prospect at all.

"Lady Isabel!" Lady Riordan flicked back a plume leaning from her extravagant hat. "Goodness me, I hardly recognized you, dressed like that. How unconventional of you."

This was not exactly a compliment, but Isabel pretended it was one. "Thank you!" she said brightly. "Since it has been more than eighteen months since my dear Morrow died, I thought it was time to dress in color again. He loved color so, you know, with his eye for art. What could honor him better?"

Lady Riordan seemed not to know whether this made perfect sense or was utter rubbish. "Quite," she replied. "Well. I must be going, Lady Isabel—the horses are standing. Shall I see you at the Rushtons' musical evening tonight?"

A musical evening at the Rushtons'? Catherine Rushton was about the age Andrew had been, fifteen or twenty years Isabel's senior. She had been quite friendly to Isabel before Andrew's death, but she'd not called since. Isabel could not remember seeing an invitation in her recent correspondence.

"I cannot say," she excused. "My plans are unfixed just yet."

Lady Riordan nodded knowingly. "No invitation, eh? Don't let it get to you, my dear. She is matchmaking for her daughter, newly out in society, and will not want competition from you or your pretty ward. Riordan and I have been nothing of the sort for this thirty years at least! And we shall bring our son, the guest she truly wants." The older woman laughed, and with a friendly squeeze of the hand, she heaved herself into her carriage.

Isabel smiled her farewell, but her joy had been dimmed a bit.

By Thursday, the life of a proper widow had thoroughly lost its savor. She had kept busy, yet had done nothing of value. How many weeks had she carried out these same ceaseless inconsequentialities? And how many more weeks of the same loomed ahead?

She tried to make a game with Lucy out of their social obligations. They each took the stack of invitations in turn, pulling forth any they wished to attend. If they agreed on any, they would respond with an acceptance.

There were two problems, though. The first was that Lucy shrank from the sort of ball and ridotto and evening gathering at which one might have a significant chance to meet gentlemen. The second was that Isabel didn't receive nearly as many of those invitations as she had expected to.

During her marriage, each day of the Season had brought more correspondence than one could answer and more invitations than one could accept. During her year of mourning, a sparse acquaintance had been forced upon her out of respect for, if not a widow's grief, the conventions of a society that determined she needed to be shut away.

But Lady Riordan had seen more clearly than Isabel had: now that she had shaken off the remainders of mourning and reentered society with a pretty young ward at her side, fewer people seemed to want her at their parties. There were never enough gentlemen, and a rich widow was far less attractive to hostesses than a friendly wife had been.

Maybe she should arrange a dinner party after all. Though . . . to what end? Whose acquaintance was she attempting to cultivate? Once Lucy was wed, there was no one Isabel particularly needed to know. She wasn't hunting another husband, she didn't have a seat in Parliament that required her to exercise diplomacy, and she had an independent income.

She was sufficient unto herself. She answered to no one. There was nothing she need do.

Which also meant there was nothing to distinguish one day from the next. No one who needed her, particularly, or who relied upon her, save her servants—and theirs was an impersonal sort of need. Whether they worked for Lady Isabel or for someone else who paid them well and treated them courteously, it didn't matter.

She'd never been particularly well churched, but there was a quotation from the Gospel of Matthew that had often caught in her mind—especially since Morrow's death.

*Take therefore no thought for the morrow: for the
    morrow shall take thought for the things of itself.
Sufficient unto the day is the evil thereof.*

How apt the wording, for Andrew Morrow had taken thought for the things of himself. Even after his death, his evil remained. Not dramatic evil of the sort that caused death and destruction; evil of the quotidian sort. Selfishness and greed; mistrust and deception.

He was hardly alone in this. There was not a person alive innocent of these faults; Isabel herself certainly was not.

How did Callum Jenks walk to the Bow Street court every morning, knowing there would be sufficient evil—more than sufficient—to fill his every hour? Did anything he did or tried or said make a difference?

Yes. It did. It had made a difference to Isabel, when Andrew Morrow's body had lain on the floor of his own bedchamber, to be spoken to with sturdy calm. To be looked at with dark eyes that held questions, but no blame. Eyes that saw her as a person, and wondered about her.

Callum saw stories everywhere. Not only everyday crimes and trespasses, but the people committing them. Sometimes heedless, sometimes needing, hungry, desperate.

As she walked with him through London streets, he had shown her how to see that too. It had opened her eyes, and they had never quite closed on the same London since.

There was something she might do, then. Before she thought better of it, she scrawled a note to him. "Have this delivered to Officer Jenks," she told the footman, Douglas, and gave him the direction.

For the time until he returned, she paced. Wondered. Sat at the pianoforte and plunked out a few notes, but couldn't chain them into anything coherent.

Douglas returned with Callum's promise to call later. When he arrived, it was long past the dinner hour.

She had Selby show him into the morning room, remembering how tenderly Callum had kissed her last time amidst the litter of biscuits and nuts. The room was tidy this time, but she thought he hardly noticed his surroundings as he dropped into the chair she offered.

"Sorry I couldn't come earlier. I was working."

She leaned forward in her own chair, curious. "Another mock auction?"

"Something like that." He shut his eyes. Dark stubble stippled his jaw; dark shadows marked his lower lids. He looked unutterably tired, and she understood two things at once.

First, that his days were as full as hers were empty. He was accountable to many, and he would go without sleep or food before he would let them down.

Second: she was one of those people. He would never refuse to come when she asked him to.

"You didn't have to come," she excused. "I didn't mean to tire you further."

"You are not a frivolous person, Isabel. If you wanted to speak to me, I assumed you had something of import to say. You've got another scheme, haven't you? That's why you summoned me here."

She had, yes, but it wasn't the sort he imagined. "It's not more stolen paintings."

I want to become an investigator, she almost said. But now that she saw the hard slashes fatigue had made at the corners of his mouth, it didn't seem to matter after all.

"Maybe I just wanted to see you," she teased. Not that he would smile, because he hardly ever smiled, but maybe he'd get that lighter look on his face that was even better than a smile.

With an effort, he opened his eyes. "To what end?"

She blinked. "I . . . well, because . . ."

He rubbed his eyes. "Never mind. That was ungracious. Forgive me, please."

"Of course." Yet it was a fair question, and one he was far more willing to ask than she.

To what end?

To become friends? To pleasure each other? To concoct another scheme? What could a marquess's daughter and a Bow Street Runner be to each other?

She could put the question a different way, though. What could become of a gentleman's widow and a man who'd made arrests in the Royal Mint crime that had captivated all England?

What could become of a woman who wanted to learn everything and a man who wanted to help everyone?

Anything. Maybe something quite wonderful.

Maybe everything she'd never dared to dream of. Respect. Devotion. Trust. Love.

She wasn't quite sure, yet, which of these questions she wanted to ask. It depended on the answer he would give, she thought—and she wasn't at all sure what that answer would be.

So she said none of this. Instead, she said, "Come and have a rest."

"Nonsense."

"Not at all. I've a spare bedchamber. Are you due back

in court? Surely not, for it is . . ." She checked the clock on the mantel. "Eight o'clock in the evening."

"There's something I could be doing."

"But must you?"

He looked at her, then away. "I suppose not. I like your gown. You look lovely in green."

"I'm glad you like it. I do, too." She smiled. "Have you eaten?"

"Enough." Every syllable seemed wrenched from him.

Now she frowned. "Callum Jenks. You never run off at the mouth, but this is too much. Are you angry with me?"

"Not angry, no. Just tired. Too tired to keep from wondering things I'd rather not wonder."

"Such as?" Her breath caught.

A corner of his mouth lifted. "To what end, Isabel?"

She reached for him, catching his hand. "We don't have to ask that right now, do we? Can't we just . . . be?"

"Can we? I'm an Officer of the Police. Have you emptied out that hidden room yet?"

Stung, she dropped his hand and drew back. "You know I haven't. I don't know what to do with the paintings. I thought you would help me find a safe place for them."

"I will if I can. And I won't reveal your secret." He sighed. "The thing about secrets is you always have to keep those walls up. Every brick, every stone. Every word, every action. You're not Lady Isabel alone. You're Lady Isabel and Secret. A team."

"It's not even my secret!" she exclaimed. "That damned hidden room is part of my legacy from Morrow."

He looked at her. She looked back at him.

"If I am to choose a team"—she picked her words carefully—"I want it to be with you."

"We were a team for a bit." He paused. "I liked it."

Unmistakable opening. So she tried again. "I liked it too. Come and have a rest, won't you?"

He sighed. "You slay me, lady. I cannot fight you anymore."

"I wish you wouldn't." Taking his hand, she led him upstairs. Not to her bedchamber; not with all the servants knowing she had a caller. Instead, she showed him into a spare room, unused for . . . how long had it been? Yet there was a fine bed in here, with a mattress that was turned and re-stuffed as often as her own was.

"This is an elegant room," Callum observed.

True enough. The chamber was done in white and cream and crystal and glass, all colors of colorlessness. "Morrow picked it all out," she said. "This was his house. Never mine."

"You'll soon remedy that, though." He sat on the edge of the bed, then tugged off his boots with a groan of relief that made her grin.

"What about a bath?" she asked.

"No baths, temptress. But I wouldn't mind a moment off my feet."

Without even pulling back the counterpane, he flopped onto the bed. He fell hard to the pillow, like a brick being dropped, and rolled onto his front.

And he was out.

For a moment, Isabel hesitated. Should she move? Would she wake him?

Probably she wouldn't. Already his breathing was slow and regular. He must have been desperately tired.

Yet he had come to see her. An obligation alone, or had he wanted to see her as much as she him? Was she the part of his day without which there was no savor, no interest, as he was for her?

Probably, she admitted to herself, she was not. There was much more to his days than Lady Isabel Morrow. The knowledge made her ache, and she sank to the bed, balanced on the edge.

This was a small pleasure, giving him a place for the rest he needed. Getting him to accept it. She rested a hand on his back. Feeling the hard line of his spine, the thick muscles of his back. She had clutched it in passion. Just now, she felt something much different.

Fondness. Protectiveness. A desire entirely separate from lust.

He took care of others so often, it was a triumph to take care of him. And she wondered, what would she do for him, if he would only ask?

She eyed the boots tumbled to the floor, one of them sliced by a bullet he had taken because of her. And she had an idea.

After she crept from the room, she found Selby and asked him to bring her a tape-measure.

Callum had apologized for falling asleep on Isabel's bed—not once, not twice, but until she shoved him out the door with a laugh. A pity he hadn't made better use of her bed with her. There was really no excuse for that.

But he wasn't altogether sorry. They'd been together this evening without a murder or theft or flight or fraud to motivate them. If they had kept company in this way once, maybe they could do it again. And maybe the next time he wouldn't sleep through the whole encounter.

It really had been a long day, and despite his unintentional sleep, his footsteps were heavy and slow through the darkening streets. When he reached Drury Lane, almost home at last, he realized the day was to become longer still.

The street was lit by lanterns and gas, a comparative blaze of light when one turned from the neighboring darkness. In the center of the thoroughfare, a group of people— some of them familiar from the stage—were dancing. It was as if the stage show had spilled out of the theater and into the street. Certain members of the orchestra were out there, fiddling their elbows off, and the tipsy-looking dancers were swinging through what might have been a country dance if they had been steadier on their feet.

Statutes reeled through Callum's head. Public drunkenness. Dancing without a license.

Damnation.

They weren't hurting anyone, not like a murderer or rapist did—but he had already slept away several hours during which he ought to have been on duty. And being so close to the Bow Street court, the dancers were all but flaunting their lawbreaking in the face of the officers there.

The officer here. He was here, and a representative of the law, and if that meant anything to him at all, then he had to bring these people in.

Damn it all.

He went to the fiddler first, putting a staying hand on the man's bow arm and bringing the music to an instant end. "Sir. You can't play here." Raising his voice, he added, "Come with me, all. We're but a street away from the magistrate."

The violinist protested, belligerent. The dancers scattered—all but one. A man of about forty years began to cry, the sort of desperate weeping one heard only from a child or from a man deep in his cups. "I can't go to jail!"

Callum rolled his eyes. "You'll only be going to the watch house. You can see the magistrate in the morning."

"I can't wait until then! That's too long." The man fished in his pocket, held out a fistful of bills and coins evidently intended as a bribe. The coins rattled through his fingers, clinking on the street.

"Have a seat." Catching the man's elbow, Callum eased him to the curb. "For God's sake, man. Get off your feet before you injure yourself." With a few swift scoops, he gathered the fallen coins from the street and dribbled them back into their owner's hands. "Now. What is so bad about sobering up in the watch's house?"

"My wife will miss me."

"Nice for you," Callum said. "And nice for her to know you were doing something wrong."

"I wasn't, though. She's bound in a chair, and she knows I like to dance. She doesn't mind. But if I'm not home by midnight, she'll think I've left her." He covered his face, crying again. "I'd never leave her. I love her."

The violinist, a grim-looking older man, hesitated, uncertain. "Officer, is this necessary?" His expression softened as he looked down at the weeping inebriate. "He's too drunk to lie, and he's not hurting anyone. Can't he just go?"

Callum had been thinking the same before the elderly man spoke the words. Why should he take anyone in for dancing outside of a licensed room? Who the devil cared where people danced?

But what else could he do with himself? He was no tea seller, no grocer. He couldn't spend his life behind a counter catering to the whims of irritable servants and cits. He was an Officer of the Police, and either that meant everything or it meant nothing at all. And if it meant nothing, who was he, and what use had been the last years and years of his life?

"I'm sorry," he said, meaning it. "You've both got to come with me."

For the first time since joining the police force, Callum hated the sight of the court at Bow Street. He took the drunken man, the annoyed violinist, to the watch house and spoke to the man on duty there. They'd be transferred to court as soon as Fox was on duty the next day.

Callum patted his pockets, found a shilling. He handed it to the Watch. "Find a boy," he said, "and have him take a message to the man's wife that all is well, and he'll be home in the morning. Surely he's not too drunk to give you his own direction."

Exasperated, distracted, troubled, Callum turned his steps in the direction of his lodging again—only to be jerked from his thoughts by a crash and shatter and yelp of rage. He turned in the direction of the sound. In the illuminated circle of a gas lamp was a carriage; at its front, hardly visible in the dark, was an overturned table, and the smashed remains of plaster busts.

He recognized the scam at once: worthless broken pieces, arranged as if they were valuables destroyed by the careless driving of the innocent dupe in the carriage.

In grim admiration, Callum watched as the vendor pleaded and begged with the driver of the carriage. It was not a crested carriage—best not to aim too high—but a nice shining one. A merchant's carriage. A man who could see a bit of himself in the desperate vendor, maybe, and who would pay anything to banish that realization.

Callum wasn't of a mood to stop the transaction—and since he hadn't seen the table, he couldn't prove the busts had been smashed already. But he suspected the same plaster sculptures had been smashed again and again, all to the feigned shock of their supposed sculptor.

He let the scene play out, the carriage depart, then crossed to the vendor and gave him a word of warning. Helped him dispose of the broken pieces in such a way that they could not be retrieved, pretending he was doing the man a great favor and ignoring his sourness.

He could never so much as go home to his rented rooms without coming across some trespass against the law, could he? The more time he spent with Isabel, the less he worked.

The less he worked, the less good he did.

Or had he really done any good, just now? Who was better off today for having encountered Callum Jenks?

Maybe no one. But Callum Jenks was better off for having spent time with Lady Isabel Morrow. She was becoming indispensable not only to his happiness, but to his contentment. Without her . . . it didn't bear thinking of.

He forced himself to think of it anyway. He had been

more honest with Isabel than he intended: he was too tired
to keep his thoughts along their usual proper lines.

Then at last he reached his rented rooms, ate a cold
meat pie, and fell into bed feeling as if there was nowhere
he belonged.

Chapter Seventeen

Lady Isabel Morrow exists. To what end?

It was a good question. It was the *only* question. And
Isabel was not certain how to answer it—yet.

She had hoped Callum would help her. But he had
enough to be going on with, keeping London safe. And
Lucy was as mercurial as Brinley, leaping forward and
back: *I want to go out into society. I want to be silent. I want
to be courted. I want to be alone.*

If Isabel's questions were to be answered, she would have
to answer them herself.

So she did what she'd always done when she was uncertain: she tried to learn as much as she could. Dipped into the
books in the library, most of which were about history and
art. Not uninteresting, but she had had her fill of art for a
while.

Instead, then, she turned to novels for answers. The late
Jane Austen had put it beautifully in one of her final works:
a novel was literature, *in which the greatest powers of the
mind are displayed, in which the most thorough knowledge
of human nature, the happiest delineation of its varieties,*

*the liveliest effusions of wit and humor, are conveyed to the
world in the best-chosen language.*

Who would not benefit from a greater knowledge of
human nature? Especially a woman who sought to marry
off her ward, determine the course of her subsequent life,
and persuade a stubborn Bow Street Runner to fall in love
with her?

Just a few minor things to handle. Hardly a challenge
at all.

Ha.

Isabel had never been in love before. She had been fas-
cinated, attracted, dependent, befuddled. What she felt
for Callum Jenks was all of these, but not as she'd felt in
the past. All, and more, and—and surely she would *know* if
she loved him?

Oh, yes. She knew it. She didn't want to admit it, but she
knew it.

She didn't want to admit it, because she'd no idea what
he felt for her in return. He was so stubborn, so brusque, so
unflappable. Completely honest. If he loved her, wouldn't
his own internal code force him to admit it?

Fortunately, she had distraction aplenty. She now owned
two houses and was preparing to move her belongings from
one to the other. Then sell the first, furnish the second,
marry Lucy off, and after all of that, probably fall onto a
fainting couch with a cool cloth on her forehead.

Lady Teasdale's son had called upon Lucy. He had
brought flowers, which was good. He hadn't returned for a
second time, which was not good.

Although in *Northanger Abbey*, a single dance had
brought the heroine to the hero's attention. They ought to
attend more dances. Isabel made a note to sift carefully
through her invitations.

Into the midst of this quiet disquietude, Isabel received a
caller she had not expected in the slightest.

"A Mr. Gabriel to see you," Selby announced.

Isabel looked up from the writing desk in the morning room. It was early afternoon, but she had all but abandoned the drawing room of late. "Mr. Gabriel. I do not recognize the name. Have I made the gentleman's acquaintance?"

"He says you know him by name, but you have never met him in person." Selby paused. "I took the liberty of seating the visitor in the drawing room."

Curious. "I suppose that was for the best. I'll go in and speak to him. Please bring in tea as soon as a tray can be arranged." *And make certain he is behaving himself, whoever he is.*

When Isabel entered the drawing room, her caller stood. He was unfamiliar to her: a man of perhaps fifty years of age, with raven hair falling to his shoulders and streaked with silver. He carried an ebony cane with a great silver head, and his black waistcoat was shot with silver thread. The effect was harmonious and striking. Dimly, Isabel wondered what he'd have chosen to wear had he been born with ginger hair. A tartan waistcoat, perhaps. It would not have possessed the same dramatic appeal.

"Mr. Gabriel." Isabel crossed the room to face him, indicating that he might sit again. "I am told I know you?"

"Not by this name, which was a dodge."

He waited as Isabel seated herself, a small table between their chairs. "Much of London," he continued, "knows me as Angelus."

Isabel jerked. "Surely not."

Her caller looked wry, amused by his own nickname. "Melodramatic, isn't it? Yet who would obey a man named Stuart Smith?"

"*Is* your name Stuart Smith?"

"Not at all." His voice was low and carrying, with an accent she couldn't quite place. Northern England, maybe, with a crisp tonnish overlay. "It is Gabriel in this drawing room and Angelus elsewhere."

She was blinking too much. Or not enough. Something was odd about her eyes; they were having trouble communicating to her brain that The Actual Angelus was here in her drawing room.

But. "How do I know you are who you say?"

He leaned the cane against the table, steadying it with the barest flick of his fingertips. "Does it matter?"

"It matters very much, of course. How can I know how afraid of you I ought to be?"

"Dear lady, you need not be afraid of me at all."

She shivered at something cold and flat in his eyes. A coiled capacity for rage and revenge—and then he shut it off, like blowing out a candle, and smiled at her.

She said tentatively, "I thought you'd be . . ."

"Different, of course. More brutal, perhaps? Less polished? Tut, tut. If I were always so, who would do business with me? How I present myself is—"

"To do with money," Isabel realized. "Everything is about money." Callum had been right. How to win it, earn it, scare it forth: this was what the world wanted to know.

"Just so." Smith-Gabriel-Angelus folded his hands with satisfaction. "It is to do with money—or more rightly, the power that money can bring. And I am here, dear lady, because of that precise issue. You and I have an acquaintance and a business interest in common."

"Do we?" A business interest. She suspected she knew whom he meant.

At that moment, a servant entered with a tray. Teapot and cups, tarts and fruits and biscuits. As everything was arranged on the table between them, Isabel gritted her teeth, holding carefully onto her calm when she really wanted to scream *What did the duke say to you?*

When they were alone again, Angelus made a show of selecting an assortment of biscuits. "How hospitable. Black, please—and no, no lemon. Thank you. Let me see, what were we discussing?"

Isabel poured out, willing her hands to be steady. "I should be shocked, sir, if you ever forgot what you'd been discussing."

"Just so. Such pauses offer a man a chance to observe, so I make liberal use of them. I note, for example, that you are not as calm as you appear. The muscle of your jaw—it twitches."

"A toothache," Isabel lied.

"Of course." Angelus plainly didn't believe her at all. "The common acquaintance is, as you must know, the Duke of Ardmore. He has communicated to me that I cannot have my painting until he concludes a matter of business with you."

Isabel took a bracing sip of tea, thoughts racing. She would try to brazen it out, do a little observing of her own. "Me, he said? How odd. I'm an ordinary widow. The duke and I can have no business to conduct. And knowing you by reputation, Mr. Gabriel"—the caller nodded—"I am surprised that he is in a position to dictate terms to you."

"He isn't. But he piqued my curiosity, and I am not one to deny myself the chance to learn something I'm curious about."

"I behave the same way," she sighed.

"You sound as if the behavior has given you cause to regret it."

"It has. But not in this instance. I am sorry, sir, but I cannot imagine what the duke wants of me. My late husband sold him a painting years ago. A rather fine Botticelli study of the much larger *La Primavera.* I saw it in the duke's study not a week ago, but that does not mean I have business with the duke."

"It does not mean you don't." He drank from his own cup, eyes rather merry above its rim. She realized, with a hint of surprise, that she was more comfortable facing him than she had been talking with Lady Riordan during their recent chance meeting. What did that say about the sort of person Isabel was?

"You call yourself a proper widow," her companion observed, holding up the teacup to the afternoon light from the drawing-room windows. "How, then, do you account for my call upon you?"

"I thought myself a conventional widow too. Just as I'd been a conventional wife, bride, maiden, daughter. But I've been forced to face a few truths, Mr. Gabriel, and there's no going back from that. The world isn't the pretty place I once thought it."

The hidden room. The hungry boy who stole a pork pie. Butler, separated from his wife and harangued by those who ought to treat him as a kindred talent. Janey, stealing until her looks and health vanished.

Andrew Morrow, dead of a gunshot wound to the head.

Angelus set down his cup. "This is fine china. I once sold a cheaper sort outside Covent Garden for scandalous prices. In my much younger days, that was."

He narrowed his eyes slightly, an evaluating sort of look. "Such subjects you think on, my lady; you are becoming rather roguish. But do not let your joy disappear. The world is still a pretty place, just not the way you imagined it. But one wed to a notable dealer in art would know all about such beauty."

Isabel bit off a *ha* of scorn. "It is possible, sir, to love art too much. It can drive a wedge between man and wife, or—"

"Man and law?" Angelus selected an almond biscuit. "Tell me, Lady Isabel, do you know why your husband shot himself?"

"He . . . it was an accident."

Crunching a bite of biscuit, he pointed the remainder at her. "That's not what I hear."

Bewildered, she asked, "Why are you hearing anything about it at this distance in time?"

"Our mutual acquaintance has taken a particular interest in your affairs."

The duke. Damn the duke. She should have expected him to retaliate in some way, angry as he was over the painting they now all must pretend had always been real, never been switched. "What sort of interest? Since you and I have both agreed how proper I am."

"There was never any suspicion directed toward you? Any investigation of your behavior toward your husband, or your whereabouts at the time of his death?"

Angelus asked her all of this blandly, snapping his biscuit into pieces with each question.

Isabel gaped. "No! I wasn't near him when he shot himself—was shot? Accidentally—that was the ruling. I heard the gunshot from a floor away."

Angelus looked at her mildly. She realized, "You already know all of that."

He smiled. "Of course. But there's more to know. There always is."

"There is?" Yes, there must be. Callum thought there was too.

"Always. What's this, no biscuits for you?" Angelus asked. "Are you upset?"

"Yes, I'm upset," she said. "We're talking about death. It's all right to be upset by that. And I'll have three of the lemon ones, thank you." She bit into them, sweet after sweet, hardly tasting them. As she swallowed each one, she felt a little more at ease.

She finished with a sip of tea, then set down her cup with a proper near-silent *click*. "Do you know more than I do about my husband's death? Did the duke—does he—that is, is there anything more to what he says than innuendo?"

"I have my suspicions. However, I'm not a Bow Street Runner."

"Officer of the Police," she corrected without thinking.

"As you say. I conduct my own investigations. Your late husband concerns me only in that I do not yet have the painting. This is, I believe, the subject of the unfinished business the Duke of Ardmore has with you."

"It's not. I am almost certain."

He lifted a brow. "I am all ears."

She hesitated. Should she tell him the truth? Could she trust him? No, she couldn't trust him. But she couldn't think up a pack of lies that would serve, and she'd no desire to keep compounding the secrets and falsehoods she'd inherited from Andrew.

She settled on vagueness, leaving Butler and Callum out of the story entirely. Her husband, she explained, had hired an artist to copy selected works. When she learned that the Duke of Ardmore had such a copy and believed it to be original, she took it upon herself to replace it with the original art to which he was entitled.

"I did it to protect my ward," she explained. "I don't want her to be dragged into a scandal during her first Season, especially one that ought not to involve her at all."

Angelus listened in silence, his head tilted to one side. When Isabel finished talking, he said only, "Does the duke know you saw to the painting's replacement?"

"He does." This was perhaps overstating the duke's certainty. "That is, he knows a copy has been replaced with the original."

"And now he won't turn it over to me, when he was willing before. He wants to appear to pay his debts without truly doing so." His face contorted, all rage for a flicker, then resumed its steely calm. "Don't worry about the duke, or your ward. If he doesn't give me my painting, then I'll send

someone to get it, or I'll call in his debts. Either way, I won't
be subtle about the matter."

She had taken tea with Angelus. Isabel hardly believed
her own lips when she repeated these words.

It had gone cordially enough, for tea with a criminal
mastermind. His simmering anger hadn't seemed directed
at her, and when he'd left, he'd bowed over her hand with an
almost courtly air.

She was still bemused by the time she ordered the landaulet brought around for a bit of shopping. Since she'd be
able to take possession of the Bedford Square house within
the fortnight, she wanted to find art for it—for there was no
way, after all the trouble Andrew and his art had caused, that
she would bring along his chosen pieces.

When the carriage arrived before her favorite print shop,
she was all eagerness as she descended. Fine art, satirical
prints, fashion etchings: Bedwyn's had it all. There was
always something new in the window, something interesting
to look at. Perhaps she'd have to have it.

But when she stood before the plate-glass window, her
mouth dropped open.

Lady I— M—, A fashionable Widow, read the caption of
the print.

The color was lurid, the figures exaggerated. At center,
a black-haired, white-faced wraith lifted a gray skirt to reveal
mannish black trousers and boots, all the better to trample
a male figure beneath her feet. As his hair was dark, his head
oozing blood, the man was evidently meant to be Andrew.

A pox upon your House, said the trampling woman. In
the background, a fair approximation of the Lombard Street
house loomed, and a golden-haired maiden simpered out
the window. *Save me from scandal!*

Heedless of the other shoppers eddying around her,
jostling her, muttering curses or apologies, Isabel remained

transfixed by the print. *A fashionable Widow*, it said; she had never been featured in a satirical print before. A smile teased her lips. She looked quite good in trousers, even as a ghostly caricature.

And then she noticed that the widow in the print was holding a pistol, and the picture ceased to amuse her. Trampling Andrew was one thing; being held responsible for his death was quite another. She had killed him, the print implied, with her mannish independence. Never mind the fact that while he lived, she had been a proper little mouse. He might as well have been stomping on her until the day he'd taken up the pistol.

Why now, after so many months? Why was she the target of ridicule? For daring to order new gowns? For having money and no husband?

No. This, she realized, was the Duke of Ardmore's revenge upon her. He couldn't report a stolen painting. He would probably have to turn over the genuine Botticelli to Angelus. In matters related to his debt, his options were limited.

But socially, they were not. He could drag Isabel through the mud, and there was nothing she could do about it. He tugged at her reputation; her proper, mousy public self. The one she had assumed for Andrew and kept for Lucy.

Little did Ardmore know, she would not be sorry to see that reputation vanish. It was a cage. Andrew had left her in one after his death, as surely as when he'd been alive.

Now that she was fighting free of it, she would not go back in. There was one thing she could do to fight back, and she'd do it right now.

Adjusting her hat to a rakish angle, she barged into the print shop. "That print in the window," she told the proprietor. "You've not got my likeness quite right. Study it from life."

* * *

Indignation, determination, curiosity carried her back to the Lombard Street house—and as the carriage pulled up, she recalled Angelus's words. There's always more to know, he had said. About the ones we love, the ones we live with. About ourselves.

Before she sold this house, she ought to search it. What if there were other hidden rooms? Hidden drawers in the desk? Priest holes, even? No, that was silly. This was a newish London house, not a Tudor castle.

Andrew's study had been gone through, the correspondence and accounts dealt with long ago. He had no steward, for there was no land. Just this house, this great pile of a house.

But he hadn't kept his secrets in his study. He kept them in his bedchamber.

Entering it for the first time since retrieving the *Primavera* study, she wrinkled her nose against the stale smell. It was closed away, this poor room. It was not the room's fault it had been owned by someone who had kept so much hidden.

She searched it deliberately, pressing every seam in the wall-hangings. Shifting every cursed picture on the walls. Tossing back the carpet and treading each floorboard.

Nothing. Hours of nothing. Did that mean there *was* nothing, or that she simply didn't know how to find it? If she had to search every room in this house before knowing all of Andrew's secrets, she would never be able to leave it.

No, she would leave it no matter what. For all Angelus's knowledge, he was just a man. He was not omniscient. This was the end: of the Botticelli switch, of living in Andrew's house. It was an end she was happy to observe.

She rolled the carpet into place again, then sat down heavily on it, knees hitched up. Her skirts were powdered with dust. No matter; they would brush clean. The turkey-red print was still pretty.

On the subject of prettiness: she might take that writing desk with her when she moved to the new house. She didn't like much of the furniture in this house, but the desk in this bedchamber wasn't at all bad. It was lovely wood, and quite a useful little piece of furniture. Would it be odd to take something from the room in which Andrew had died?

No, she decided. The desk did not care that it had borne witness to the end of Andrew's life. She would let it instead bear witness to friendly correspondence. With whomever Isabel would write in her new house. Lady Teasdale, certainly. Lady Selina, most likely. The Duke of Ardmore, never.

She creaked to her feet and swiped at her skirts. Best to make sure it was cleared out. She thought she'd checked it after he died, to make certain there wasn't any correspondence she needed to answer.

One by one, she opened the drawers. Empty. Empty. Good. The last one wasn't, and she frowned at the dusty monogrammed writing paper still within. That could be pitched into the fire. No—that would be wasteful. It was fine paper. She'd cut off the monograms and give it to Lucy for sketching.

She dug her fingers into the edge of the stack, tugging it from the drawer in which it was stuffed. It was stuck, the paper the same size as the drawer, and she had to pull, ease her fingers deeper into the stack, and pull again.

With a wrench of her arm, she got the stack of paper free—and heard a rattle. From the drawer? She nudged it with her foot, and yes, there was the sound again. Yet it was empty.

It wasn't empty.

Setting the paper onto the desk's surface, she scrabbled for a penknife. Then she drew out the drawer and put it on the carpet. Crouching, she studied it all over. She poked every join with the penknife; eased the small blade into every crack. The dry wood of the drawer split and groaned, and at last it yielded its secrets with a *click*. A false bottom lifted away. The compartment below held a wooden box, flat and small, of the sort used for jewelry.

Isabel picked it up, weighed it in her hand. Holding her breath, she lifted the lid.

Within the box was a brooch.

A brooch? A piece of women's jewelry? She held it up, squinting at it. Surely she had never seen this before. A large and lovely pearl nestled at the center, surrounded by seed pearls set into gold.

Why did Andrew have such a piece? Why had he hidden it?

She stared at it, mystified. When she stood, she picked up the desk's drawer in her other hand. Should she put the brooch back? She looked from drawer to jewelry, jewelry to drawer. It was all very strange.

A voice sounded from the doorway. "Aunt Isabel, I've been wondering where you—oh!"

Isabel looked up to see Lucy, stricken and shocked. Her ward's eyes were fixed on the brooch in Isabel's palm.

"That's not possible," Lucy said. "It's not possible for that brooch to be here." Her face was drained of color; her slender form trembled.

Her parents were murdered during a robbery, Isabel had told Callum. *Only one piece of jewelry was taken. A pearl brooch that had been in the family for generations.*

And then Isabel realized what she held, and where it had come from, and she dropped the drawer on the floor so that it cracked into pieces.

Chapter Eighteen

"I'm sorry." Callum's voice was dim in Isabel's ears. "This is not the evidence I thought to find."

Of course she had summoned him, her writing frantic. Douglas, the footman, had picked up on her sense of urgency. He'd bolted off at her instruction, returning with Callum just as Isabel had managed to calm Lucy with quiet words and more than a little brandy.

She and Lucy were out in the corridor, because the room was again poisoned by its contents. Callum had looked at the desk. The broken drawer. The secret compartment.

The brooch.

When he finished, he rejoined them in the corridor. It was dark-paneled, the better to show off the art hung in gilded frames. Isabel wanted to smash it all, to get out of this house at once.

For Lucy's sake, she remained calm. Standing firm, she drew the younger woman into an embrace and patted her back. Over Lucy's shoulder, she said to Callum, "I never thought you'd find any evidence related to Andrew's death. It's just been too long. But this—this isn't related to Andrew at all, is it?"

"It was in his desk." Callum looked grave. "But that's not an answer in itself."

The brooch was related not to Andrew's death, but the death of Lucy's parents. Would Andrew have killed them? Had he known the criminal?

Isabel thought out loud, sorting through possibilities. "I don't understand it. I wish I could remember, was he here? He didn't keep a datebook. But surely he was never gone long enough to travel to Gloucestershire? No, never. It would have taken days, and he never departed for more than a single overnight."

Lucy pulled back, pale and shaky. "It couldn't have been him. It couldn't. It must be a coincidence." She dashed tears from her eyes. "Or he tracked down the killer, and he got the brooch back, and—and he was keeping it to surprise me."

This sounded entirely unlike Andrew, as impossible a suggestion as his journeying more than a hundred miles and back again within twenty-four hours. But the hope in Lucy's voice was pitiful and thin, and so Isabel kept her doubts to herself.

"I'm sorry," said Callum again. "I can make inquiries. But at this moment, all I can do is recommend a carpenter to fix the broken drawer."

"I don't think I'll bother," Isabel said. "But thank you."

They walked together down the corridor, Lucy turning off at her bedchamber with a promise to rest and relax. At the door of her own room, Isabel caught Callum's hand.

"I have something for you," she said. "Since you are here. Come in for a minute?"

He looked dubious. "The circumstances are not ideal."

"I know. But come in all the same." So he did, and she shut the door behind them. Crossing to her wardrobe, she opened the doors and drew out a large box. "These are for you."

He set the box on the bed and lifted the lid. "Boots," he said flatly.

They were not just any boots. They were Hoby's finest, sturdy and glossy and made to suit his feet exactly, thanks to the measurements she'd taken while he slept in her guest chamber.

But the expression on his face stilled her tongue, kept her from saying any of that. "Will you try them on?" was all she said.

He put the lid back onto the box. "Why did you get me boots?" His eyes searched her face.

"Because you need them, and you won't get them for yourself."

His lips tightened. "You don't have to look after me. You don't have to buy me gifts."

This was not the reaction she'd expected. She'd known he wouldn't be effusive, but she'd thought maybe she'd get a laughing thanks. A rueful look at the damage his own boots had incurred. The lack of emotion was strange.

"I know I don't have to," she said. "If I did, I wouldn't want to nearly so much. But it's my choice, and I want you to have these."

"That is thoughtful of you." He took up the box, turned to go. "Thank you. I'd best be going. I have to work for my bread."

"I know, and I thank you for coming by. Lucy was grateful too; I am sure she will tell you so when she's recovered from the shock."

He nodded.

She wanted to keep him there; she kept talking. "I hope you will come to the new house when we're settled in it. We do not see you enough." As he opened his mouth, she blurted, "And do not say to what end. Seeing you is an end in itself."

"Lady Isabel," he said softly. She winced at his use of her title. "I've always been aware of the end. Haven't we come to it?" He was so inscrutable, but his eyes were fathomless. She wanted to swim in them.

"What does that mean?" She clutched one of the bedposts, needing something solid to grasp. "You always thought of me as temporary?"

He answered her question with one of his own. "What would you do if you were not afraid?"

She blinked. "You remind me of my own wish to be braver."

His smile was small and wistful. "Even the bravest person in the world is afraid sometimes. Bravery has nothing to do with fear. But had you no fear, what would you do?"

The answer came to her lips in a second. "I would be with you."

"You see? You will not be with me." He adjusted the box in his arms. It was too large and heavy, coming between them, and she wanted to toss it away.

"You haven't asked me," she retorted.

"I cannot, Isabel. I haven't the right. You've the money and the connections. What would you give up for me? What would you lose?"

She slapped the bedpost with the flat of her hand. "Why must I lose anything? If you intend this conversation as some noble gesture, I find it lacking."

"And how did you intend the boots?"

"As an apology for having you shot. As a gift because I think of you often. As a sign of how much your comfort means to me."

"Ah." He looked at the box lid. "That is most kind. You've been cushioned, and it's not your fault. It's no shame. It's a good thing, to have a comfortable life. So good that I don't want to take it from you."

"Why, though, must I lose . . . what are you saying?" She struggled to understand. "I will still have money. A house. I would not change at all if we were together."

This was the wrong thing to say. She could tell at once.

"I don't mean that there would be no place in it for you," she added hurriedly. "I mean that there is. So much of my life has changed recently, that being with you would be a lovely continuation."

"In an affair? Would you keep me as your lover?" His mouth went tight at the corners, the look that was not quite a smile and not quite a grimace. "I would not be satisfied with that."

"So marry me, then," she flung at him, and now he was the one to hesitate.

"Best not," he finally said, as if she'd asked him whether he would take another biscuit with tea. "You're a marquess's daughter. I'm a grocer's son."

"And? So?" She had abandoned her pride; now a sense of injury swelled within her. "I never reminded you of that. You reminded yourself. And you're just as superior in your way as I am in mine, *Officer Jenks*."

He only lifted a brow, so she continued, pacing the width of the room from wardrobe to bed to wall and back. "Presuming I'm sheltered. That I cannot handle harsh truths. My body lives in ease, yes, but my heart has dealt with truths you've never imagined. You have parents who love you, Callum. A brother who cares enough to fight with you. An occupation that gives meaning to your every day."

He waited her out in silence, his mouth looking grimmer and grimmer. "It's not easy," he said, "to work for my bread."

She rounded on him, hands flying. "I didn't say it was easy! I said it had meaning. And by God, the choices you have just by being male." A harsh laugh. "Yes, I have money through no virtue of my own, but what can I do with it? Before I wed, nothing. Even as a widow, I haven't the freedoms you so often take for granted. To feel safe when you walk into an alley. To leave the house alone. To know that the law of the land and the unspoken laws of society regard you as competent to handle your own affairs, rather than regarding you as ignorant and inferior, then making sure such assumptions are true by placing insurmountable obstacles in your path."

He shook his head.

She felt empty, hollowed out by the escape of words she'd been waiting to say a long time. "I will leave no imprint on the world when I die, Callum. You leave one every day. It would be worth a lot of money to me to add meaning to my life."

"Easy to say when you've never been short of money."

She sighed. "Please! Don't you see? We both have privilege of different sorts. If we pulled together, what couldn't we do? In life, in investigations—all of it. I know that you are concerned for my welfare, or my reputation. But then who is it, really, who's separating us?"

His fingers tightened on the sharp edges of the box, denting and crumpling it. "Circumstance," he said. "The world. We met only by chance, connected by crime. First your husband's death, then my brother's."

"That's not all that connects us now," she said.

"It's not. But is there enough to draw us together, when you and I live in different worlds?"

She held up a hand. "Wait a moment. There are plenty of worlds that can belong to both of us. Vauxhall was one of them. And the theater—you live at the heart of the theater district. But who goes? Everyone."

"There's a bit of a difference," he said dryly, "between the boxes used by the rich and the seats on the floor where people buy oranges as a rare treat."

"What about the Duke of Ardmore's music room, then? We belonged there equally ill."

He cracked a smile.

"Or your parents' grocery. We had a fine visit. I got to meet your mother, which was nice since I never had any sort of a mother at all."

"To what end?" he said quietly. She had known the question was coming.

She didn't know. All she knew was she didn't want there to be an end, and she didn't see how there could be anything but.

"If you are asking the question," she said, "then you have already determined your own answer."

"You are the one with much more to lose than I if we are together."

"Ah, so you are being noble!" Her tone was bitter.

"That's the one thing, Lady Isabel, that I'll never manage to be."

She pressed at her temples. Why had she invited him in here? Had she thought the boots would make a terrible day better? They were not magical boots. This conversation would have had to happen eventually, without the play-acting of partnership to keep them together. "I don't want you to be anything but who you are."

"Yet you tried to make me into something I wasn't."

When he set the box down on the bed, her fingers went cold. "What was that?"

"Anything but an Officer of the Police. Upholding the law." He looked bleak. "That's all I should ever have been and done."

"I am sorry you think so." She turned away so he wouldn't see her eyes well up. So he wouldn't know how much it hurt that he would strike her from his life like an account dealt with, totted up, excised. "You realize now that you cannot forgive me for asking for your help switching the paintings?"

"No. I cannot forgive myself for giving it. And it's not only that there's no space for me in your life, Lady Isabel. There's no room for you in mine."

She heard him go, but did not turn around to watch. Her ears strained for his every footfall, though, until she could hear no more, and then the front door closed him out.

Darting to the window, she watched him depart. He walked away with a straight back, stubborn and proud and ethical and rigid and lawful and handsome and dear and unattainable.

There was no question in her mind now: she knew she loved him.

On the bed remained a pair of expensive new boots fitted just for him. They would never be worn, she supposed.

He had been clear about the matter: this was the end. They were done, and they would go their separate ways. Everything had to do with money; money and duty. Hearts had nothing to do with their situation at all.

Stubbornly, her heart ached like a wound within.

She knew she would never ask him to come back to her, and he would never offer.

Chapter Nineteen

He'd done what he thought was right, severing the connection with Isabel, but somehow it all felt wrong.

The inexplicable presence of the pearl brooch bothered him. The gift of the boots bothered him. The mysterious death of Andrew Morrow bothered him.

Yet those were distractions, all, from his work for Bow Street.

But the work was itself the greatest distraction of all, yet not distraction enough. Not for his heart, which ached for her summons. His eyes, which wanted to learn her every expression. His skin wanted her touch; his ears craved her voice.

He was in trouble. He'd thought he'd caught himself before the longing became irrevocable. Instead, every day without her was more flavorless than the one before. And as the son of grocers, he understood the importance of flavor. It was the difference between sustenance and pleasure. An existence, or a life.

But life with her would turn into existence, as he became nothing more than an appendage to a woman caught up in the whirl of the ton. No, this was best. Best to work, and work some more, and do what good he could even as his heart gave up and took leave of his body.

He had a long and grueling day, pounding the pavement for hours as seemingly every pickpocket in London tried his hand. When he arrived back at his James Street rooms at half six, feet throbbing in his damaged old boots, he wanted nothing but food and a long rest.

"You've a visitor," said Mrs. Sockett brightly. "A gentleman."

Callum's spirits heaved up, then dashed down all within the space of his landlady's greeting. *Isabel! Not Isabel.* "In the parlor?"

At her affirmation, he turned his steps toward that fussiest of rooms—then halted, found a few coins in his pocket. "Would you get me a plate, please? From the Boar's Head? Whatever they're serving tonight that's hot."

"'Course I will!" She patted his cheek, an odd motherly gesture, then set aside her broom and went on the errand.

No listening at the door for a little while. That was good. And a hot dinner would be good too.

He opened the parlor door, hardly caring who awaited him within. But the person who faced him—*no*. His head snapped up. His body recoiled. He slammed the parlor door closed, himself still on the outside.

Sir. Frederic. Chapple.

That utter snake. That complete bastard. Sir Frederic Chapple called on Callum in his rooms, as if . . . what? As if he deserved any more time from the Jenks family? As if he was owed an apology for his time in prison?

He wouldn't dare. Callum would kick him heels over arse and enjoy every moment of it.

Callum held fast to the door handle, keeping it closed. He tugged in a long breath. Another. All right. Sir Frederic Chapple was here, and either he would be reasonable or he would be kicked heels over arse.

Callum opened the door again, then entered the room as

calmly as if he had been expecting this caller all day. "Sir Frederic." He tossed his hat aside and took the spine-cracking chair, as Sir Frederic already had the comfortable one. "Why are you here?"

The baronet's round face had gone pouchy, his skin mottled, no doubt from too little sleep and too much drink. "I didn't feel right about going north without speaking to you again. Turned my carriage back, then thought better of it and headed on, then back again—more times than I can count."

"How nice for you." Callum folded his arms.

"I wanted to apologize. For your brother's death." Sir Frederic's eyes looked mournful. "No one was supposed to die."

At the words *brother* and *death*, a chill spike of anger stabbed through Callum. "So you've said, yet people did die. I don't want to hear your excuses. You seek to ease your conscience, but I can't remove the burden for you."

"You mean you won't."

Callum leaned forward, pinning the bloodshot old eyes with his gaze. "Do you need me to? Do you need me to tell you it was all worth it, Sir Frederic? That your clever scheme to rob the Royal Mint was worth a half-dozen lives?"

"No, I—"

"Yet you drove away from it. Turned your carriage toward Northumberland and headed off with your pockets full. Even if I could ease your conscience, I wouldn't do it. There's no justice here."

"There's not," said the older man. "And I'm selfish enough to be glad about that."

Callum jerked to his feet. Crossed to the door and held it open. "Time to go."

The baronet kept his seat. "You're a good man, Officer Jenks."

"I didn't ask for your approval."

"You have it all the same." Sir Frederic—Freddie, he

tried to get people to call him—twisted his fingers together. "You know, you could have claimed the Royal Mint's reward."

Callum tightened his fingers on the door handle. "I didn't want it."

This was a lie, especially now. Twenty-five hundred pounds, he'd have got. At the time, he hadn't cared about the money or the accolades. They'd all gone to Lord Hugo Starling. But now he couldn't help thinking of Isabel. The reward money would have put Callum on a footing closer to hers; maybe close enough that he wouldn't feel like such a fraud claiming a place at her side. All he had saved, scrimping on the job for years, didn't even come close to that amount.

It was a moot consideration now. They'd closed the door between each other and locked it.

"Have you said all you must, Sir Frederic? I've work to be doing."

"You've always work to be doing." The baronet gave a wan smile. "I'm here to offer my help, Officer."

And he explained: the same network of influence he held among London's petty criminals could be used for good, rather than for robbery and murder. "My informants," he said, "are now yours, if you'll have them. They see everything, know everything. They can help you solve cases you thought you'd never touch."

Callum dropped his hand from the door handle, staring. "Why?"

Sir Frederic sighed, looking like a popped balloon. "For justice. For atonement. I told you I was morally responsible. I can't bring back the lost lives. Maybe I can help you save others, though."

Callum fought the impulse of revulsion—*I don't want a damned thing from you*—and thought this over. He let the silence stretch, the baronet fidget.

Harry Jenks was nothing but silent bones, when he should have been a husband now. Maybe even a father. A brother, of course, and a son.

There was no good to be done there. But some good might be wrung from Sir Frederic anyway.

"All right," he said. "I'll think about it."

Sir Frederic's look of relief fell. But he nodded his agreement and rose to his feet, doubtless guessing this was all the reply Callum would grant him for now. "I'll write to you when I reach home again," he said. "And you can let me know how you want to proceed."

Callum already knew he would take Sir Frederic up on his offer, but he intended to let the man wait a while longer before telling him so. The baronet's conscience might be salved eventually, but Callum wanted it to sting and burn as he traveled back north.

When Sir Frederic passed through the doorway, Callum's hand popped out, surprising them both. Gingerly, the older man took his fingertips in a handshake, one quick up-and-down before they both recoiled.

"Thank you for listening," said the baronet.

"Thanks for coming back," Callum said grudgingly. "Truly. It was brave of you."

"It was the right thing to do." Sir Frederic ducked his head. Left the room. Exited the house.

It was too silent with him gone. Callum could hear every breath, every tick of Mrs. Sockett's beloved case clock. The house gave a creak, settling its old bones against an outside breeze.

Of a sudden, dinner and sleep were the last things Callum wanted. He clapped his hat back on his head and thundered down the stairs, turning his steps to the Bow Street court that had been his home for the past ten years.

Fox wasn't pleased to see Callum. Likely he'd hoped to clear his desk and head home without further interruption. But Callum was relieved, more than he could say, to see the lamp-lit office and his magistrate's familiar face behind the desk.

"I need to speak to you, sir."

"Come in, of course." Fox plucked off his pince-nez and tamed his disgruntled expression. "What's on your mind, Jenks?"

He indicated a seat, but Callum chose to stand. He tucked his hands behind his back, assuming the position he did when reporting on a case to his magistrate. "I have done something illegal, sir. But it was right."

Fox set the pince-nez down atop the paper he'd been reading. "So have we all, Jenks, but one never speaks of it. It can damage a case's standing in court."

"The law." Callum swallowed. Squared his shoulders. "The law failed to bring justice. Just as, in another case, it failed to give justice to my brother."

Harry was always on his mind, yet not every matter was of life and death. Sometimes a case turned on what sort of life one wanted. A fearful one or a secure one. A poor one or one enriched with ill-gotten gains. A scandal avoided, a wrong righted.

Fox rubbed at the bridge of his nose. "There are some crimes for which a man cannot be charged, but of which he is guilty nonetheless. The law is a tool for unlocking justice, though it is not a perfect one. But why do you come to me at this hour?"

"Because I just saw Sir Frederic Chapple again."

Fox cursed. "Why is he not up in Northumberland, instead of rubbing our faces in his escape from the gallows?"

"He was never headed to the gallows," said Callum. "Not one such as he. But we've arranged a way that he can make amends after all."

A hint of a smile touched the magistrate's mouth. "Do I want to know?"

Callum considered. "No, best not. But I wanted to tell you it had happened."

Fox shuffled his papers together into a single stack. "So I would reprimand you?"

"So you'd understand why I'm resigning."

Papers scattered. In the golden lamplight, Fox goggled at him; then his heavy black brows slammed down. "But this job is your life."

Like a gear clicking into place, a memory popped into his mind. Old Morrison, the tea seller, looking over the shop he'd owned for years. *I've loved the work*, he said.

If a man loved his work, then it was a good job. Anything from being a grocer to guarding the Royal Mint. Selling tea. Painting as beautifully as an Italian genius from centuries before.

And if a man didn't love his work, then it didn't hold any meaning. Not even if he removed a dangerous criminal from the streets. Not even if he wrung a confession from the man behind his brother's murder.

Maybe Callum had loved the work once. It had been a longtime infatuation, heady stuff: indulging in the power of his position, the knowledge of his own rightness.

But law and justice weren't always the same. There was always more work. The streets of London would never be clear of crime, and a man could grind himself to nothing trying. Callum wasn't a man of half-measures, but there was no life for someone who did nothing but work. When the streets of London crushed him and spit him out, no one would care.

He'd fallen out of love with the work as his life tipped out of balance—or maybe into it. As Lady Isabel Morrow filled up more and more space in his heart, his mind, his day, there was less time for work.

His mistake had been in thinking that was a bad thing.

"The job *has* been my life," Callum agreed. "And what does that mean for me? I've not had much of a life, have I?"

"I'd never have said that," Fox replied. "You've been a hell of an investigator."

"Maybe I still will be," Callum said. "Just not in the same way. I want the freedom to solve cases in my own way. I've a good bit of money saved up, and . . . I'll see, won't I?"

Finally, he knew for what he'd been saving his money all these years. Not for shiny boots or a high-crowned hat, no. His savings weren't enough to get him a place in high society, not that a person could buy a spot in the ton. But he had enough to be his own master. To take his own cases. To investigate as he saw fit.

To get a place of his own. Wherever he decided that might be.

"I wish you the best," said Fox. He extended a hand. Their clasp was firm, the sort of shake a proud father might give a son leaving home.

"I'll give it my all," Callum said.

And he would. There was just one more stop to make first.

The bell over the door of Jenks and Sons announced him with a cheerful jingle. "Hullo, Mum," Callum greeted his mother behind the counter.

"It's not your usual time!" said Davina. "I don't have my list ready." She fumbled for a pencil.

It was time for a conversation that had been too long in coming. "Do you only want to see me if you have a list ready?"

She shoved the pencil into her knot of hair. "Of course not. Only since you're here—"

"Mum. You have two shop assistants. Give *them* your lists."

She looked bewildered. "But, Callum! They can't get the deals on pork that you can."

"Then have them save the life of a butcher's daughter. Or simply pay tuppence more the pound."

Davina turned to bid a cheerful farewell to a man who, helped by Jamie, bought three of the long, braided ropes of onions. As soon as she turned back, the smile slid off her face. "Don't you want to help me?"

"Of course I do. But I'm not only your helper. I'm your son."

"What's going on?" Jamie sidled behind the counter, put his arm around their mother's shoulders.

Callum looked around the shop, familiar as the Bow Street courtroom. "We might as well gather everyone. What I wish to say affects you all."

From the back room, the upstairs, atop the flour barrel, the employees and family members collected. Davina noted a sale or two as they gathered, and when the shop was empty, she said, "What's all this about, Callum?"

"I'm leaving Bow Street."

Alun Jenks clapped his blocky hands together. "Yes! I've been waiting for this day. Welcome to Jenks and Sons. Running a grocery is the best job in the world! Let the greengrocer worry about fruits and vegetables that spoil quickly. Let the fishmonger deal with the stench of old shellfish, and the butcher have his blood and flies. A man who works in a grocery will never go hungry!"

Callum waited out his father's speech. "There are a lot of ways not to go hungry," he finally said. "I don't seek to be a greengrocer or a fishmonger. Or—what else did you say?"

"A butcher," chimed in Celia.

"Right. Not that either. I plan to become a private investigator. I've savings to tide me over until I make a go of it."

"But Jenks and Sons . . ." Alun's mouth closed. Opened. Closed again. "I hoped someday you'd want to join Jamie and work here."

Callum lifted a brow, regarding his brother. Jamie had turned as red as his beard. "You haven't told them yet?"

"Told us what?" Davina asked.

Jamie shook free of his mother. Glared at Callum. He muttered something below his breath.

"Told us what, Jamie?" asked Celia. Her eyes were wide and startled.

"Nothing, nothing. Nothing major. It's only . . ." Jamie

took a deep breath, then blurted in a rush, "I want to leave the grocery and buy the shop next door and become a tea-seller."

"Just . . . tea?" Davina looked blank.

Jamie stuck out his jaw. "Morrison made a go of it for years. I think I can do even better."

Young Edward, one of the shop assistants, waved a hand in the air. "I want to work for you!"

Jamie looked dubious. Mrs. Jenks looked even more dubious.

Alun rubbed at his grizzled chin. "He does love tea. Has a good eye for quality."

"Not for negotiating the price," muttered Jamie.

"So? You can do that," said Alun.

"Wait! You're not all right with this, are you?" said Davina. "What about Jenks and Sons? You already have only one son helping you, and we canna—"

"Never you mind about that," Alun cut in. "I was the only son helping my father, and the name went up on the shop window just the same. Callum and Harry, they never were cut out for keeping shop. S'pose I always knew that, though I wouldn't be bothered if ye changed your mind someday." He winked at Callum.

"But Jamie . . ." Davina said faintly.

Her husband patted her shoulder. "Jamie's old enough to know his own mind. Besides . . ." He eyed Lionel. "A man who marries a Jenks daughter becomes a Jenks son."

Lionel and Anna looked at each other. Blushed. Kept on looking at each other.

"Oh, for God's sake." Jamie rolled his eyes. "Lionel! Propose already!"

"You're one to talk," Anna retorted, with a meaningful glance at Celia.

Callum cleared his throat. This conversation was veering

away from the point. "You'll do well, Jamie. You'll love the work."

Helping people find tea, which was more than just a drink. It was comfort in a cup. The lubrication for every social interaction. The beginning and end of the day.

"You could come work for me," said his gruff brother. "If you ever got tired of chasing criminals and wanted a job with hours that ended sometimes."

Jamie cut a glance toward Celia. *A job that allowed a family*, he clearly meant but didn't say.

"That's not the job for me," said Callum. "But thanks."

"We'll make the best of these changes." Davina fished around in her knot of hair for the pencil, then drew a piece of paper across the counter toward herself. "Callum, now that you're away from Bow Street, you can stop by for a list more often."

"No."

Everyone went quiet. Stilled. Looked at him.

"I ran your errands once, when I lived here and worked for you," Callum said. "Now I don't. I'm not your errand boy."

As one, his parents protested.

"Why, we never—"

"But honestly, it's no skin off your back to—"

Callum held up his hands. "If you won't listen to me, I can't help you. If you do listen to me, I'll help you when I can. That's what family does. We don't use each other."

Person after person, he looked them in the eye. "We don't use each other," he repeated. "Now. I'm going to the Boar's Head for a pint. It's almost time to close the store, so if anyone wants to join me, I'd be glad for the company."

The jingle as he left the grocery seemed a mockery of cheer. But he wasn't unhappy. It felt right—thank God, something did—to say what he had.

Inside the Boar's Head, he took a chair at his favorite table. He ordered a pint of porter, nursed it alone, then thought about ordering another. He still hadn't had dinner, and the drink was going to his head. Best not.

He pushed back his chair, ready to leave—and then Jamie plumped into the chair opposite him. "Shame to have you drink alone," he said. "What are you having?"

And then came Anna. Lionel. Alun. Davina. Edward. Celia. All surrounding him. With each person seated, Callum's smile grew, until there was no more room at the table or on his face.

"Glad to see you all," he said. "Let's have dinner, shall we? And your first round's on me."

Chapter Twenty

At last, Isabel and Lucy were settled in the Bedford Square house, and the huge one on Lombard Street was for sale.

The shape of the new town house felt right around Isabel, as if everything too big and fussy were gone. Like the fashions she preferred, with furbelows stripped away, the house was designed to her tastes. Andrew's furniture, sold. The paintings on the walls, ditto. Isabel had kept a few pieces, items bought since their marriage.

She had brought nothing to it but money and manners, but Andrew had considered her taste when choosing a settee for her dressing room, and he had consulted her in the choice of a console table for the entrance hall. Oh, now!— to have the freedom to order one's walls painted in blues and greens, the plaster and wood whiter than ever snow was in London. No more silk paper on the walls, rich-looking for the sake of looking rich. No more gruesome figural paintings. The world was landscapes, blessed landscapes, blessedly free of fleshy, hairless nudes.

The garden outside was everything she'd hoped for, an elegant confusion of trees and a riotous arrangement of flowers. Blooms of all colors, her skirts trailing over them when she stepped from the path. And in the evening, when stars struggled through the smoke and fog, and the new gas lamps were lit, she always wandered from the path.

She wore color here, blues and greens the colors of sky and ocean and springtime leaves. She wore no rings, no jewelry save for a strand of pearls that had belonged to her mother.

Satisfying though it was to settle into the house, she was not *happy*. She had never held happiness as essential, growing up educated to become a lady of society. Better influence than happiness, better charm than education.

What was it all for, though? Making other people like her . . . why? For the sake of the liking itself? If that was the case, she'd failed to keep the liking of the one person whose esteem she truly coveted. Callum Jenks could not be charmed or tricked into thinking better of her than she deserved, or returning her love.

She'd seen him once, when her carriage happened—just happened—to be driving along James Street. She'd requested a different route when Jacoby drove her back home. Not because she didn't want to look upon him; because her eyes got spoiled for the sight of anything else.

After that, she'd gone to Kent for a short visit. It was long overdue; she had not visited her father's estate in more than a year.

Lord Greenfield, elderly and frail, hadn't known Isabel the last time she visited him. She hadn't expected he would this time either. But she had gone for herself: to see the home in which she'd grown up, the father who had approved her too-young marriage to a man who was no good.

Ultimately, marrying Andrew had been her own choice. And that choice had brought her here.

"It's good to see you, Papa." She had taken her father's thin fingers in one hand.

The old marquess had smiled, greeting Isabel by her mother's name. He'd scrabbled at his lap robe, growing agitated, and Isabel had helped him pull it back into place.

He'd sat often before the fire in the library, Martin had told her. Even as the earth warmed for summer, their father was always cold.

Martin had peered in every so often—making sure Isabel wasn't being disruptive, she'd assumed. She hadn't been. Plucking a book from the library shelves, she'd pulled an ottoman over beside her father's chair. She'd sat on it and read to him while he gazed off, contentment taking the place of agitation.

When he began to doze, she'd closed the book and sneaked out. Eager for a bit of country air, she'd stepped outside. At the base of the stone steps, Martin had been surrounded by a swirling, yapping mass of beagles and foxhounds.

"I should have kept Brinley," Martin had called over the noise. "He'd have grown up to fit right in."

She'd clipped down the steps, laughing. "That's why you should have kept him? Not the fact that he was a mischievous little ball of fur that was completely full of devotion?" And urine, she had not added. And endless noise.

Martin had looked sheepish. "He's happy with you, though, isn't he?"

"He would be happy anywhere. It's a gift of his. But yes, he's been happy with us." Isabel and Lucy. They made a fine household of two.

After spoiling her nieces and nephews, praising her sister-in-law's latest changes to the estate, and throwing more sticks for Martin's dogs than she could calculate, she'd returned to London. Again, James Street called to her.

To distract herself, she kept her Tuesday afternoon at-homes. She always enjoyed the company of Lady Teasdale. Happily betrothed, Lady Selina Godwin was a cheerful visitor. Even anxious young Mrs. Gadolin, eager to ascend the ranks of society, called a few times. When she did, she confided to Isabel that her dear Gadolin was *very* interested in the Lombard Street house, because their current home was *too* small and the neighbors were *not* the right sort.

Neither was the former master of the house, Isabel thought, but she only smiled and told Mrs. Gadolin she hoped they would be happy in the house if they chose to buy it. All the servants who stayed behind to maintain the place, she provided her highest recommendation.

Finally, she cleared out the hidden room. She took the paintings from it by night, with Butler's help, and stowed them in a bedchamber of the new house. Inside a locked wardrobe, within the mattress, beneath a sofa. All covered, preserved, hidden. And then all the furniture went under Holland covers, and she locked the room and did not give the key to the housekeeper.

It was not as secure as having a hidden room, but it would have to do. She and Butler had not done badly, considering that they hadn't the help of someone with a deep understanding of stealth and criminality.

Although maybe Isabel had learned more from Callum than she realized.

In the past few years, her life had become a puzzle, and it was almost solved. It did not look quite like anything she'd ever imagined when the pieces were all scattered and the solution was in the future. But it was a fine picture, one she'd put together herself. There was only one piece missing: love.

She had tried for it. The less said about that, the better. Now she would try to find it for Lucy.

But the coveted invitation to Lady Selina's engagement ball—which, rumor had it, would be the greatest, grandest crush of the Season—did not arrive by the morning post on the expected day. Nor did it come in the afternoon, or the evening. A widow with money and a maiden without: neither was an attractive guest for a matron seeking all the attention for her daughter.

Lucy kept peeping into the entry hall, looking for new post on the silver tray Selby kept for the purpose on the console table. Isabel hated to see her look away disappointed, time after time.

"I am sorry I failed you," she said after the last post of the day was delivered.

"Not at all!" Lucy pasted a bright smile onto her face. "There are lots of balls, every week. And if I don't marry, I'll live with you and teach art lessons, and it'll be fine."

Ever since they had found the pearl brooch, unspoken worries were like a wall between them. How had it come to be in Morrow's desk? Isabel didn't know. She didn't know if she ever *would* know, or if she wanted to. Lucy said she did not; she didn't want to think about it anymore. She had taken the brooch, put it in her jewel box, but she never wore it.

The following morning, the invitation arrived, just late enough to make clear that they hadn't been on the first list. Or the second. But there it was.

Naturally, they would attend, and they both had new gowns for the occasion. Lucy was a copy of a fashion plate from Ackermann's Repository, wearing white muslin trimmed in pale pink, and with a complicated truss of plaits and fillets atop her head.

Isabel wore a gown of gold satin overlaid in gauze, the waist right beneath her bust so the skirt draped in a long, sleek column. The sleeves were short and full, but the dress was otherwise unornamented by the epaulettes, the rouleaux and braids and trims and loops favored by other women. She was apart from fashion. She wore the gown rather than the reverse, and she loved it.

If only Callum Jenks could have seen her in it. The gold really was most becoming.

When they arrived at the rooms rented for the ball, a crush of carriages blocked the road, so they descended and walked the rest of the way. As they drew near the steps, a hubbub spilled forth from the rooms. Inside, where guests were announced, the enormous space was suffocatingly hot.

They could hardly squeeze into the crowd, could hardly look around the room. What Isabel could see of it was decorated with frescoes of classical scenes. Any woman who was scantily draped was hairless, docile-looking, dazed.

Andrew would have loved them.

Lucy paled, looking over the crowd. "There are so many people."

"I know, dearest. But we can only speak to one person at a time, and so it doesn't matter if there is one person here, or five hundred. Whom shall we speak to first?"

"Um . . ." Lucy looked dazzled.

"Our hostess, then," Isabel decided. Finding their way to the Duchess of Ardmore was a feat requiring fifteen minutes of struggle through the crowd. Along the way, Isabel made introductions to Lucy when she saw a familiar face. Mrs. Gadolin flicked her fan in greeting, thanked Isabel for agreeing to her dear Gadolin's price on the Lombard Street house, then looked about to see whether anyone had noticed and whether it was quite the thing.

When they finally reached the Duchess of Ardmore, she seemed pleased by their congratulations, distant and vaguely friendly as ever. She held a small flask from which she sipped occasionally, no doubt dosing herself with the medicine that left her in a perpetual cloud.

And then they encountered the Dowager Lady Mortimer, whose younger son Isabel had thought might be a match for Lucy. The dowager had responded to this assay with a disapproval that she seemed still to hold tightly.

"Lady Isabel! And Miss Wallace. I'm so glad you could attend. I didn't know if it was your sort of affair anymore. You seem to have different tastes these days. I saw the most startling print recently!"

Life was too short for veiled innuendo. "Do you mean that caricature of me wearing trousers? It wasn't a bad likeness, but it wasn't accurate either. I've never worn an outfit such as that."

The dowager pursed her lips. Had she powdered her hair? It was gray as a ghost, and her face held the same chalky color. "I did wonder, though, about the other part."

"My hair?" Isabel tutted. "It was in terrible disarray. I had a word with the printmaker." She patted her own neatly dressed locks.

"No! The . . ." Lady Mortimer leaned forward, confiding behind her fan. "The pistol."

Honestly. If the woman wanted to gossip with her, she might as well be straightforward. "You were curious about my husband's death? You're not the only one, my lady. I've wondered about it since the day it happened. I wouldn't be so gauche as to speak about it, though. Would you?"

The older woman's mouth opened and closed.

"I didn't think you would." Isabel smiled. "I've always known you as a woman of impeccable manners. Thank you for your concern, of course. Look, Lucy—there is George. Shall we say hello?"

Isabel pushed through the crowd. The room was huge and warm, lit by hundreds of candles and stuffed with hundreds of elegantly-dressed bodies. The air was all perspiration and perfume and the hot burnt scent of melted wax.

George was an elegant fixture at the ball in honor of his sister. He looked still better than the last time she'd seen him, without the puffiness of dissipation. The leanness she remembered from their late youth was coming back into his features, his form. It suited him. She watched narrowly as he took a proffered glass of champagne, then handed it off to someone else.

"Abstaining?" Isabel asked.

"Only from champagne." He winked. "If it's not fun anymore, then what's the point of it? And I've never thought a bubbly wine much fun. A good brandy, now . . ."

Isabel laughed with him. "I prefer port, myself."

Attending the ball was like slipping on an old garment. It still fit, and there was something nice about seeing it again. But it didn't suit her like it used to. She felt more comfortable at the edges of the party. Because she was a widow, and she didn't want to look for a husband as the Isabel of ten years ago had? Because she liked looking at people now, noticing what they were doing? Who was angry, who was flirting, who was hoping to retreat unseen. Everyone had a story, and if one thought only of oneself, one's slippers, one's next dance, then all these other stories were lost.

She wondered what the person slipping away around the edges of the room was up to. He was too far away for Isabel to recognize him, though he had the sleek confidence of a scion of the ton. A bit of the look of Andrew. Oh! Maybe that was Lady Selina's betrothed. What was he up to?

Probably he was looking for the necessary. Isabel thought it was in that direction. Lucy had murmured something about finding it, and she and Isabel had been separated in the crowd before they reached George. No matter. Somehow they would find each other again.

She was pleased to come upon Lady Selina, quite the belle in a gown of silver and blue. "I'm glad you could come!" said the duke's daughter, sounding perfectly sincere. "I remember our discussion about marriage, and—well, you see that I took it to heart."

"Our discussion?" Isabel cast her mind back. Yes, she did recall a few sentences tossed back and forth idly. She'd been distracted at the time, wondering how to find the Botticelli within Ardmore House. It seemed ages ago. "You are wedding for love, then, as well as the more common reasons."

"Not as well as, but instead of!" Selina beamed. "I've no need to marry for money or security."

Yes, because you've had them in abundance since the day you were born. But: "Fortunate you," was all Isabel said. "I am glad you are so well pleased."

"I wanted to tell you." Selina put a confiding hand on

Isabel's arm. "Just because you *needn't* marry for those reasons doesn't mean you *shouldn't*. A woman can never be too secure."

With this, Isabel could not disagree. "It is certainly easy for us to lose what we have."

"Especially reputation, which cannot be bought back once lost."

Isabel's brows knit. "I agree, but I do not take your meaning as it applies to me."

Selina laughed. "Why, Isabel, you are becoming such a rogue! Taking your own household, throwing off fashion."

"I rather thought I was setting it," Isabel sniffed.

"Taking a lover . . ." Selina whispered. "Have you? Haven't you?"

"As if no widow has ever done such a thing before?" Isabel gave Selina's hand a reassuring pat. "Thank you for your confidences, my dear. You may be assured, I will be careful to hold tight to the things that are important to me."

"Good, good." Selina looked uncertain—then pulled her into an impulsive embrace. "You've always been such a good friend to George and me. I do want you to be happy, you know."

"I'm sure I shall be. It just might not be in the way I expected."

For one could be happy alone, couldn't one? It was better than being wed to someone who never thought much of her, and far better than being paired with someone unkind.

The only option compared to which everything else paled was the one she yearned for: being with someone wonderful, and damn however suitable or unsuitable he might be.

"Excuse me," said Isabel. "I'm going to see about getting a dance for Lucy."

"Of course!" Selina smiled, reassured that all was well as long as there was dancing.

But she didn't see Lucy in the ballroom. Not at the edges,

either, where the wallflowers and matrons sat. She wasn't at the punch table, or in the supper room, or playing cards.

Isabel fought down a tide of worry. There was no need for concern. Yes, this was the first great crush Lucy had been to, but it was perfectly safe. Isabel might have missed seeing her. Or Lucy might still be waiting for a turn in the ladies' retiring room. Yes, that was probably it. Isabel would slip out of the ballroom and find her.

No. Lucy was not in the retiring room.

Had she got lost? Impossible, with the clamorous noise from the huge ballroom to orient one. Even here, she could hardly hear her own footsteps over it.

There was another corridor, heading farther away. Plain-papered and narrow, it was clearly meant for servants. It probably led to the kitchens, where food for hundreds was prepared and plated. Isabel peered down its length.

And everything fell apart.

Because the corridor wasn't empty. And it didn't only hold Lucy.

Callum Jenks was there, with those redheaded twins she'd met at Bow Street. The woman was holding fast to a struggling Lucy while the man bound her wrists with rope.

On the floor lay a body. Dead? Unconscious? Callum was crouching over it, hunting for a pulse. The prone figure was the man Isabel had seen leaving before—a man she now recognized for certain as Lady Selina's fiancé. His scalp was bloody, and there was a bullet hole in the wall.

Chapter Twenty-One

Callum had wanted nothing more than to see Isabel again—but he would not have chosen a moment like this for their reunion. Never like this, with her ward in makeshift cuffs and a marquess's heir lying in his own blood.

She laid a hand against the wall, bracing herself. "What is this? What is happening? You—what are you doing to Lucy?"

"The Duke of Ardmore asked the Bow Street magistrate, Fox, to recommend some people to keep peace at his daughter's engagement ball. Guess His Grace was wiser than I realized." Callum picked up the pistol from the floor beside the prone lord. "Lady Isabel, this belongs to you." He offered it to her grip first.

She extended a hand, looking full of questions.

"It was your husband's," Callum explained.

At once, she recoiled. "I don't want it. I don't even want to touch it. But—why is it here?"

Callum looked at Lucy. Isabel's gaze followed.

"Lucy!" She took the girl's shoulders, shaking her gently, even as Charles Benton put another knot into the cord about her wrists. "Lucy? Is—did he—what has happened?"

"He made me pose," she whimpered. "He made me pose for him."

"What is she talking about?" Isabel's wild gaze swung between the Bentons and Callum. "Tell me right now. What did this man do to her?"

"Why . . . nothing." Cass spoke haltingly. "He didn't even touch her, not that we saw."

Isabel crouched beside the man. Lord Wexley, Callum thought his name was. She swallowed heavily as she looked at the injured man, but she did not flinch. "She shot him, didn't she? The bullet grazed his scalp and was buried in the wall."

Callum held out a hand to help her upright. "Exactly right. I believe he'll come to at any moment."

"But . . . she *shot* him." Isabel's brows were knit. "Why? I don't think she's ever even *met* him."

"He made me pose for him," Lucy cried. "I've been carrying his gun in case he made me do it again."

"His gun . . ." Isabel's eyes widened. "Dearest. Lucy. Who is it that you shot at? Who made you pose?"

"Uncle Andrew. Up in the hidden room. I had to pose like his paintings while he looked at them and he . . ." She was crying now, great blubbery tears. "I had to agree. You always said how nice it was that I was an agreeable girl, and I knew I had nowhere else to go."

Cass looked away, her eyes wet. Callum found it difficult to watch the girl too. For she was just a girl—terribly young, and more fragile than he could have imagined. He understood now, and he guessed that Isabel did too: in her distress, Lucy had mistaken Lady Selina's fiancé for Andrew Morrow. Dark hair, going silver at the temples. In his early forties. There was a marked resemblance.

Lord Wexley moaned, coming to. "What happened to me? Am I shot?"

Charles left Lucy's wrists and helped the man to his feet. "Not mortally. But that head of yours could use stitches."

When Wexley took a step forward, Lucy screamed. "No! Not again! Not again!"

"Who—why is she shouting?" He put a hand to his head, then flinched when it came away wet with blood.

"What sort of posing?" Isabel had gone pale. "What sort of posing, dearest?"

Lucy cringed, hiding behind Isabel as if she were a wall.

"Oh, God." Isabel looked stricken. "Morrow did—and I made you believe that—oh, Lucy, oh no. No, no."

Gently, Callum put an index finger under Lucy's chin. "Lucy. Miss Wallace." He waited until her gaze flicked upward to meet his. "Did he touch you?"

"I don't even know her!" Wexley yelled.

"Not you," Callum all but snarled. "Andrew Morrow. Cass, will you go find Lady Selina? And Charles, a physician for his lordship. Or even a seamstress."

When he returned his attention to Lucy, his voice was gentle. "Did Andrew Morrow touch you?"

"He never put a hand on me. But on himself, he did. He touched . . ." She turned her head away. Isabel stroked her hair, a mass of plaited gold. "I was so afraid. It kept happening. It happened again and again, even before I came to live with you."

"Even before . . . ?" Isabel shook her head. "He didn't—I don't understand."

Callum thought he did. He wished he didn't. "I shouldn't be surprised if her parents treated her much as Morrow did."

She took his meaning at once. "Oh, my poor girl. My poor girl, so trespassed against, and so violent. And I thought to marry her off, never suspecting how unhappy she was."

"She might not have been unhappy with you."

Lucy Wallace was a shrinking figure, a pitiable one. She had not committed a crime for gain. She had not done it for money. No, Callum had been incomplete when he'd once told Isabel that everything went back to money. Some things were even deeper. Sex. Power.

The need to save oneself.

What privilege he had grown up in, to be protected and kept safe by his parents. Compared to that, Lucy Wallace's silks were nothing.

As Wexley leaned against the wall, dabbing at his scalp with a handkerchief, Isabel and Callum teased out the missing pieces of Lucy's story.

Her parents had abused her, and in desperation, she one day shot them. She escaped with the pearl brooch—but after she came to live at Lombard Street, Andrew found it among her things. He made her pose nude, barely more than a girl, with the bare, false portraits in the hidden room.

Mutual blackmail. Mutually assured silence. These circles were dangerous and fragile. Lucy had shattered it at last, warning Andrew Morrow that she would tell Isabel about the posing and the pictures and the hidden room. Everything.

He couldn't stop himself. And he couldn't bear for his fraud and exploitation to be revealed. So he ended himself.

Isabel stroked Lucy's back, just as Callum had seen Lucy pet Brinley. "Shhh, shh. I know now. It's over. It will never happen again."

Lucy was calm now, quiet. She had retreated within herself, like a turtle pulled into its shell. All they saw now was the shell. Callum did not know when she might come out again.

By this time, Lady Selina had returned with Cass and a grim-faced housemaid was plying a needle in Wexley's torn scalp. There ensued a clamor of explanations, reassurances, re-reassurances, and many complaints from the stitched-up lord.

"We're all witnesses, Mr. Jenks," Cass said solemnly. "To how you saved Lord Wexley from the poor mad girl."

Isabel shut her eyes. "But what you all heard about Morrow—"

"I don't know what you mean," said Cass. "I heard nothing except Lady Selina's thanks for ensuring the safety of her betrothed. Miss Wallace was out of her wits, poor lamb. Raving. It was impossible to make sense of what she said."

The lanky redhead's certainty was like a dash of cold water to the nerveless paleness of the duke's daughter. "Of course," said Lady Selina. "I cannot think what would be gained by looking for evidence of further crimes the girl had committed. I certainly observed none."

Isabel looked mulish. "Now that I know that Andrew—"

"Lady Isabel." Charles looked solemn for once. "In the eyes of the law, his trespass against her was nothing that is not excused every day. But hers against her parents or Wexley could see her hanged. You could best protect her with your silence."

Isabel pressed her fingers to her eyes. "It's unfair, all of it."

Callum knew what she meant. Andrew Morrow had escaped the consequences of his actions again and again, finally choosing death as a blanket over the truth. Who he truly was would never be known to the world.

"Isabel," he said gently. "We know. That's the most important thing. We know." He touched her arm lightly. "Remember, you've always acted for Lucy's benefit, ever since the first time you summoned me."

To steal a painting and save a reputation. For Lucy, it had begun; for Lucy it would end here, and these few people would hold the truth in their hearts.

Isabel held Lucy tightly, the girl's head cradled under

her chin. Callum had seen artwork like that before. It was always called *La Pieta*.

"Do not let her be taken to a madhouse, please," Isabel said. She exchanged some private words with Lady Selina, during which the young woman's eyes grew round with shock, then soft with pity.

"I shall not lay evidence against her," said the duke's daughter. "Nor will I protest whatever arrangement you think best for her."

Wexley grumbled a bit, but he too agreed. His adoration for his young betrothed was clear. And he would get to play a heroic, embattled figure when this scene was described for eager ears and scandal rags in the days to come.

"You are very generous," said Isabel. "I cannot thank you enough."

Cass took one of Lucy's arms, Charles the other. They guided her down the corridor as one would walk a puppet. She was still but a shell, compliant and silent. Lady Selina and Lord Wexley followed them from the corridor, prepared to rejoin the ball.

Isabel followed them all with her gaze.

"You are blaming yourself," Callum said. "I see it in the slump of your shoulders."

With an effort, she drew herself up straight and turned to face him. "How can I not blame myself? She was mine to protect."

"And before you, she was her parents' to protect, and then Andrew's. You alone took proper care of her. You gave her a year and a half of peace."

"But the anger and sadness were only waiting to come out again."

"How were you to stop that, if you didn't know it existed?"

"I don't know." She seemed transfixed by the bullet hole in the wall.

"Did you do your best by her?" Callum pressed. "Would you have protected her if you knew what Morrow was doing?"

"I hope so. I cannot be sure." She folded her arms across her chest. "I did not always know how to protect myself."

He nodded, accepting. "With every case, there are what-ifs. Too many of them can break a person's heart."

"I do not know which crime I ought to regret the most," Isabel said. "She did wicked things, terrible things. But wicked things were done to her first."

"If there's one thing I've learned well since knowing you, Isabel, it is that the law and justice part ways more often than the police realize. She protected herself; she counted on nothing else."

Isabel swayed on her feet, then took a step forward. Another, blessedly, until she stood right before Callum. He took her in his arms, wrapping up all that gold silk in his plain black-coated embrace.

"She will be safe," Callum assured her. "And others will be safe from her."

"Yes," said Isabel. "I will see to it." She pushed back, dashing a hand against her eyes. "Sorry. Thank you. You prevented a disaster, Callum. I can't think what would have happened without you."

"Oh. Well." He scuffed one of his boots against the floor. The warmth in her eyes was everything he wanted but never dared ask for.

"Come, let's get away from this grim place," she said. He agreed, slipping the unwanted pistol into his pocket after making sure it was unloaded. They retraced the steps to the ballroom, the sound and heat multiplying like fireworks as they drew closer to the grand space.

At the edge of the ballroom, they halted. "Do you need to make a report to your magistrate?" Isabel asked him, low under the noise of music and conversation.

"I do." Callum tilted his head, speaking near her ear.

"Though he's not my magistrate anymore. I've resigned my position with Bow Street. The Bentons and I were here as private security, as I said. Ardmore hired me. I hired them."

"But you resigned? You love that job!" She pulled back, sounding genuinely shocked.

"No," he said. "I love many things, but that job is not one of them. I love justice more than the law. I love seeing right done. And I love the woman who helped me realize all of that."

"You . . . love . . ." Isabel tipped her head. "You love her. You love her?" A smile spread across her features. "She must be marvelous."

"She is," he said. "I was a fool to think I could do without her. But I don't know how she's doing without me. I've never wanted to impose on her good will or her wealth. There is so much that I cannot give her."

Isabel shone like gold guineas: her eyes, her gown, her smile. "No one but you, Callum Jenks, can give me your heart. I have all else that I want and need. Will you make me utterly spoiled and utterly happy?"

"Spoiled, you could never be. Happy, I would that you'd be always."

"No more of that nonsense about us not suiting each other?"

"I'm greedy," he said. "You suit me, and if you say I suit you, I'll never give you up."

She leaned against the wall, putting her hands behind her back. It was an enticing pose, pushing out her breasts. Her smile was flirtatious. "I have an idea about how we shall make our way in society. It will be rather like being an investigator."

"Oh? Do tell."

"We play the game, Callum. We follow the rules." She grinned. "These people have manners, but they're afraid.

They don't want to do anything wrong lest they topple. So we only have to show them that it's not wrong to accept us. It's quite right."

He considered. "Being accepted by the ton could be good for business. As a personal investigator, one could charge more."

She gave a determined nod. "There, an economic argument for tonnishness."

"A personal investigator wouldn't work well alone, though," he said. "I would need a partner."

"I'd be wonderful," she said. "You ought to hire me."

"Done. And I already have a consulting office large enough for two. I took a lease using my savings." He coughed. "It's not far from Bedford Square."

She laughed. "You really do love me! I love you too, you know. I was trying to tell you that when I gave you the boots."

He looked down at his battered pair, rueful. "I wish I'd known. I wish I'd taken them, too."

"You can have them," she said, "as a wedding gift. If you ever end up asking me to marry you. And in whatever we take on together, we shall succeed."

Was he wearing boots? No, he was flying. "I like a lady with ambition." He sank to one knee, took her hand in his. "Lady Isabel, will you have me? I'm not a sentimental man, but I love you deeply. Dearly." He smiled. "Irrevocably."

"Of course I will. And I love it when you smile."

"That's good, because I can't stop just now. Oh, you ought to have a ring. Let me see." Releasing her hand, he stood and patted his pockets. "Ah, this will work."

"My thimble?" She held up her thumb, mystified, as he slipped the silver cap onto it. "You kept it all this time?"

His face heated. "I might be a little bit of a sentimental man."

"You are an utter rogue, Callum Jenks."

"Then we are perfect for each other," he said, and he kissed her soundly. So soundly that heads turned, whispers eddied, and the orchestra even missed a beat.

It was one more scandal to add to the total at Lady Selina's engagement ball, making it the pinnacle of the elite's Season.

Epilogue

Lucy Wallace was sent to the country, to a farm run by a placid, sturdy widow. There Lucy sketched occasionally, but mainly cared for animals. These included Brinley, who loved no one so much as Lucy—with the possible exception of Callum's old boots, which he got to have as toys in his new home.

The farm was in Kent, on land owned by Isabel's father. Martin knew that Lucy had been abused and was to be treated with care—and not approached. He saw to her security. If Lucy was not threatened, she would be a threat to no one.

For saving the life of Lord Wexley, Callum Jenks became a hero. It was the most natural thing in the world that he should become fashionable. It was not even a surprise, not really, when Lady Isabel Morrow wed him.

For Lady Isabel had become a bit of an eccentric. She'd always seemed so proper! But how roguish she was now. And yet it suited her.

She and her new husband lived on the edges of society, not quite of it, not shunned by it. Just separate, in a category of their own. Like those dresses Lady Isabel wore. No one knew quite what to compare them to except themselves.

The Jenkses lived in a house bought by the lady, but they set up a consulting practice in a set of rooms fitted out by the husband. And by the following year, life had taken on an intriguing new pattern.

Despite running a busy investigative consulting practice, Isabel and Callum still occasionally had leisure enough to slip away during the day. The Summer Exhibition, set up for all London to admire in the great rooms of Somerset House, featured a number of paintings they were eager to see.

More than one of them was by a talented artist named Ignatius Butler, who was making a name for himself in portraiture. As he stood proudly beside his work, dressed in his Sunday finest, he was applauded by a beautiful dark-skinned woman in blue, and by two rangy girls he was proud to introduce as his daughters Elizabeth and Margaret.

Judging by the interest of the crowds, and the plum spot the pastel portrait of Angelica Butler received by being hung at eye level, Isabel suspected Butler would finish the exhibition with as many commissions as he could handle.

"I'm glad we hired him before he became tonnish," she told Callum as they joined the applause. The last bit of the money Butler needed to bring over his family had come from a portrait Isabel had ordered from him: the newly wed Mr. and Lady Isabel Jenks. It hung now in their consulting rooms.

The butler, Selby, shuttled between the Bedford Square house and the consulting rooms. He was constantly offended by Callum's informality—but unable to deny how happy her ladyship was in her second marriage.

There was room enough to spare in the Bedford Square house, now that Lucy was no longer living with Isabel. Isabel had also opened up the previously locked bed-chamber in which all of the paintings from the hidden room were stored. She had found a ready taker in a certain Mr. Gabriel, who accepted them all.

"I should be glad to get rid of them," said Isabel. "But you could never display them. Not without causing a scandal among society's elite. Those who did business with Andrew Morrow think they own the original and only versions of their precious artwork."

Gabriel-Angelus laughed. "If any of society's elite find their way into my private quarters, they will have more to worry about than what I have hanging on the walls."

So it was over at last, the whole affair that had drawn Callum and Isabel together. But they were knit tightly now by law and love, not by circumstance.

Upon returning from Somerset House, Isabel asked, "Do you think your friend Cass would like to come work for us?"

Callum sifted through correspondence atop their desk. "We've got business enough. Do you want the help?"

"I just wondered. We might need it if our family begins to grow."

His head snapped up. "Why, Lady Isabel Jenks, are you trying to give me some news?"

"It's too early to be sure yet. I'm merely preparing you for the possibility."

He strode around the desk and caught her up in his arms. "Preparing me?" he teased. "To what end?"

"Why, to happily ever after, my love," she said, and pulled his face down for a kiss.

In the game of seduction, everyone wins . . .

FORTUNE FAVORS
THE WICKED

"Richly rewarding."
—*Booklist*, starred review

INDECENTLY LUCKY

As a lieutenant in the Royal Navy, Benedict Frost
had the respect of every man on board—
and the adoration of the women in every port.
When injury ends his naval career, the silver-tongued
libertine can hardly stomach the boredom.
Not after everything—and everyone—he's experienced.
Good thing a new adventure has just fallen into his lap . . .

When courtesan Charlotte Perry learns the Royal Mint is
offering a reward for finding a cache of stolen gold coins,
she seizes the chance to build a new life for herself.
As the treasure hunt begins, she realizes her tenacity is
matched only by Benedict's—and that sometimes
adversaries can make the best allies. But when the search
for treasure becomes a discovery of pleasure, they'll be
forced to decide if they can sacrifice the lives they've
always dreamed of for a love they've never known . . .